Desired by a Highlander

By

Donna Fletcher

Donna Fletcher

No part of this publication may be used or reproduced in any manner whatsoever, including but not limited to being stored in a retrieval system or transmitted in any form or by any means, electronic, mechanical, photocopying, recording or otherwise without permission of the author.

This is a book of fiction. Names, characters, places, and incidents are either the product of the author's imagination or are used fictitiously, and any resemblance to actual persons, living or dead, business establishments, events or locales is entirely coincidental.

Desired by a Highlander
All rights reserved.
Copyright July 2019 by Donna Fletcher

Cover art
Kim Killion Group

Visit Donna's Web site
www.donnafletcher.com
http://www.facebook.com/donna.fletcher.author

Chapter One

Willow hid in the bushes, the thorny leaves pricking at her skin through her wool garments and tugging at her dark red hair. She kept her hand clamped over her mouth fearful of gasping in fright and her eyes were spread so wide since the attack had begun that she feared she'd never get them closed again. Her heart pounded mercilessly in her chest and fear trembled her body. She wanted to turn away, not watch the brutal battle, but she couldn't. It wasn't wise. She had to watch, had to see what happened... had to run if needed.

Lord Ruddock of the Clan Northwick, her sister Sorrell's husband, had sent a troop of twenty of his warriors to escort her home. They were only a day away from arriving at the Clan Macardle. It had been difficult bidding her sister Sorrell farewell until they got to visit again, but she was happy with her husband and her new home and that had made Willow's leave-taking a bit easier. Besides, her sister Snow needed her, an accident having blinded her some time ago. She could see shadows now, but no more, and Willow wondered if it was even more frightening to constantly have shadows surrounding you and not know who they were than living in complete darkness. Though, she had left her sister in good and capable hands, her step-brother, James. was to look after her as well as a new servant, Eleanor. Still, she was eager to return home to Snow and tend to her needs.

She cringed as the clash of metal grew louder and men fell to the ground wounded. Fright prickled her skin as badly as the thorny leaves of the bushes that concealed her. Her breath caught in her throat as she watched William, the warrior who had insisted she run and hide and stay hidden until he came for her, fall to the ground, blood running from his head down along the side of his face.

He wouldn't be coming for her.

Ruddock's warriors fought bravely, but they were outnumbered. It hadn't appeared that way at first, less than a dozen men had been spied heading their way, but William had been cautious and she was glad he had been. More than two dozen men had descended on the troop after the fighting had begun.

It was obvious the men who attacked them were mercenaries, men for hire. There was no color plaid that united them as a clan and they were ferocious warriors. Their battle roars alone could shiver the devil himself.

Willow couldn't help but wonder why they had attacked. Mercenaries never did anything without some type of reward being involved. Ruddock had had problems when he and Sorrell had first returned to his home, but they had been settled. So it didn't seem reasonable to think this attack could have to do with Ruddock? She and the warriors carried no coin, nothing of value. What then could they possibly want?

Willow eased her hand off her mouth and watched as the last of Ruddock's warriors were disarmed and made to kneel on the ground. She was relieved to see that most of the warriors while wounded were alive, though William had yet to move.

A man, of good height and size, with bright red eyebrows as bushy as his bright red beard and wearing a dark shirt and dark plaid stepped in front of the kneeling warriors.

"Where is she?" the man demanded.

Willow's brow shot up. Was he asking about her?

Not one of the warriors responded.

"More afraid of what Lord Ruddock would do to you than anyone of us if you surrender her," the man said and burst out in a hardy laugh, the other mercenaries joining him. "Can't say I blame you. The man is a barbarian." He let loose with another burst of laughter.

The red-haired man turned to his cohorts. "We'll get nothing from them." He looked back at the warriors, then scanned the area beyond them. "She couldn't have gone far." He scratched at his beard. "I'm too tired to give chase." He turned to look at his men again and they all agreed with nods and ayes, calling him by name.

"Aye, Beck!"

Willow gave thought to running, but that wouldn't be wise. Besides, she doubted she could untangle herself from the thorny bush. She stayed put and listened, fearing this would not end well for her.

Beck raised his voice as he called out, "Hear me well, lassie, show yourself or I'll kill these warriors one by one until you do."

Willow didn't doubt he would do as he said and what choice was left to her anyway? She would never let another die if she was able to save them.

Beck gave a nod to one of his men and he raised his sword and approached the first warrior in line.

"I'm here. Don't hurt him. I'm stuck in the bushes," Willow called out.

Beck roared with laughter and pointed to two men. "Get her."

Willow did her best to free herself before the two men reached her, but it was difficult. Every time she moved, a thorny leaf would prick at her, tearing at her clothes and skin.

The two men gave no heed to her situation. They reached in and yanked her out and she winced at the pain of her skin being torn. The two all but dragged her to Beck, giving her a shove when they neared him.

Willow stumbled but managed to remain on her feet. "What do you want of me?"

"You'll find out," Beck said and nodded to one of the men. "Tie her wrists."

Willow glanced at William and saw a slight movement. "Please, let me see to the fallen warrior first, then I'll go with you and give you no trouble."

"I care not about him and as for you giving me trouble, a good beating will have you obeying."

"If you beat me, how will I tend your wounded men?" she asked calmly, though she shivered inwardly.

"They can see to themselves like always," Beck grumbled and turned away.

"And what of you?"

Beck turned and glared at her.

"That old wound on the back of your hand isn't healing. If it's not tended to properly it will turn putrid, fever will set in, and you'll die."

A small spark of fear ignited in his eyes. "You'll tend me." He nodded toward William. "You'll not waste your time on him. He'll not last the night."

"Let me at least offer him some comfort and prayer," she pleaded.

Beck looked about to deny her, then ordered, "Be quick about it,"

Willow hurried to William and when he tried to speak, she pressed her fingers to his lips. "Quiet and let him think I pray over you." William remained silent and she quickly tore a piece of cloth off the hem of her shift beneath her tunic. She wrapped it around his head and kept her voice low and her head bent as if in prayer. "You're not going to die, William, though he will leave you here thinking you will. It is nothing more than a gash. Remain still, as if near death, and once we leave and you regain your strength go to the Macardle keep for help. It's the closest." She placed her hand on the top of his head when he looked about to nod. "Do not move."

"Enough," Beck bellowed.

"My fate is in your hands," she whispered and he blinked his eyes rapidly at her.

Willow stood and went to Beck. "You're right. He will not last."

She was going to inquire into the fate of the other warriors, but she saw for herself what that would be. Beck's men were tying each of them to a tree and those that had suffered no wound were sliced on the arm or leg. They were being left for the forest animals to feast on.

It made her realize the severity of her situation even more. Beck was a man without morals and honor and that was dangerous, for there was no telling what he would do. She reminded herself that William was young and strong. He would be on his feet not long after their departure. He would free the others and they would get help, and she would be rescued. It was a reasonable and plausible thought. All she had to do was survive until then.

"We go. You can tend my hand at camp," Beck said and shouted to his men to hurry and finish.

Willow was made to walk along with a few of the men while others rode. It was a quick pace Beck set for them, berating any who couldn't keep up. Willow's legs burned with pain by the time they reached camp hours later. She dropped to the ground, thinking she would never be able to stand again.

"Don't get yourself comfortable, lass," Beck said, walking over to her. "We'll be leaving as soon as you're done tending to my hand."

Willow wanted to weep. She didn't know how she would take another step today.

"Tend my hand well and I'll let you ride the rest of the way," Beck offered with a grin.

Willow would have jumped up and hugged the man if her aching legs would have allowed her to, though it wouldn't have been the wisest thing to do.

"Let's get this done, lass," Beck demanded. "I want to get home tonight."

While she didn't want to budge, she needed water not only to tend his hand but to quench the dryness in her mouth that no doubt would grow worse with every slow, agonizing step she would take. The small stream they had camped by would serve her well. She just had to get to it.

Beck laughed, realizing her dilemma, yanked her up by the arm, and propelled her toward the stream, depositing her on the bank to sit.

"Quench that thirst of yours, then get to my hand," he ordered.

He didn't have to tell her twice. She didn't even bother to cup the water in her hands. She grabbed her braid that had fallen in disarray and held it back while she bent over and drank until she could drink no more.

Afterwards she got busy on his hand, a hundred questions rushing to her tongue, but keeping silent. She would learn more by watching and listening and, though it was difficult, she did just that.

She worked as gently as she could, the area that was red causing her the most worry. It didn't look like it had turned putrid yet, but one could not always tell. When she finished cleaning it, she applied some honey from the small pouch, Sage, Ruddock's new healer, had given her in case it would be needed on her journey home. She had never thought she would be using it on a man who had taken her captive.

"You hold your tongue. That is a good quality in a woman," Beck said.

"What is there for me to say? You will tell me nothing until you're ready to."

"You have good qualities. You will fetch a good price," Beck said with a grin.

"You intend to sell me?" she asked, the thought filling her with fear. *Please. Please, William, hurry and get help.*

He chuckled. "We'll see. Maybe. Maybe not."

He was teasing her or he was telling the truth and didn't want her to know yet. "Since I have little say over it, what does it matter?"

"You never know. It might matter," he said.

They spoke no more. She tore off another piece of her shift, though this time from her sleeve. It was cleaner than her hem after having walked so many hours. She wrapped his hand.

"Good, we can be on our way," he said.

She looked around, her brow wrinkling. Two campfires had been started and two men entered camp with four rabbits, skinned and ready to cook. How could they be leaving when the men were settling in.?

Willow found out soon enough. She and Beck were the only ones taking their leave. Her wrists were tied and she was placed in front of Beck on his horse.

"Hold on, we ride fast," Beck warned.

The air was cold, more so with it slapping against her face as they rode across the land. Her wool cloak kept the chill at bay, though it might have been the heat from Beck's body that did that. The ride seemed endless and her thoughts drifted to how difficult life had been for the last few years. Her father's mind had betrayed him and he had made unwise decisions in regards to the clan. If her mum hadn't sent for James, their father's bastard son, she didn't know what would have happened. Her mum had encouraged her and her sisters to trust James, that he was a good man. She'd been right. Willow just wished her mum was there to see it. She died from problems sustained from a fire in the keep, the one that had blinded Snow.

All seemed like it would do well with Sorrell's marriage to Ruddock, the Clan Northwick being a powerful clan. It meant the Clan Macardle no longer had to worry about protection or food for the winter or trouble that had been brewing with the neighboring Clan MacLoon, or be beholding to Tarass of the Clan MacFiere, also known as the Lord of Fire, an intimidating warrior.

She and Snow also did not have to worry any longer about an arranged marriage. Ruddock had freed them to make a choice of their own. That had pleased her and Snow. Now, though, none of that mattered, not unless William managed to get help. Otherwise her life that had recently taken a change for the better, had been pitched back into the darkness.

It was near dusk by the time they rode into what appeared a small village. A longhouse sat in the middle of several hut-like structures, and smiling faces shouted out greetings to Beck.

About six men approached them as Beck brought his horse to a stop.

"You got her," one said in surprise.

"You doubted I would, Rob?" Beck shot back.

"No, it's the consequences we talked about that worries me."

"As it should all of us," another man said.

A third man joined in. "Lord Ruddock is not one you want as a foe."

"Worry not, it will go as planned. Take her, Geary," Beck said.

Geary reached up and grabbed her at the waist to pull her off the horse and settle her on the ground. "Where do you want her?"

"In the hole with the other one," Beck ordered.

"You're going to put her in there with *him*?" Rob asked startled.

"Isn't that what I just ordered you to do?' Beck said, sending Rob a nasty glare.

Willow listened, her fear growing with each word.

"Help him, Geary," Beck ordered. "Coyle, you come with me. We have things to discuss."

Willow was taken to a spot on the side of the longhouse. Night was falling rapidly, but she could make out three wooden grates laying on the ground a few feet from each other.

Seeing them, she knew what Beck intended. She would be placed in one of the holes and from what they had said, she wouldn't be alone. She'd be with a man. Fear gripped her stomach, roiling it, the thought frightening her senseless.

She was familiar with such punishments or keeping a prisoner confined like that, having seen it once when she had gone with her father to a neighboring clan. A hole was dug only deep and wide enough for a person to stand in.

One person.

How she would fit with another person in there, she didn't know, and she would rather not find out.

Rob moved the wooden grate aside. "You got a guest," he yelled down into the dark hole.

No response was heard.

"It's a woman," Rob said and waved to Geary to bring Willow to the hole.

"Best grab her legs as she comes down or she might make it uncomfortable for the both of you," Geary warned.

Willow wanted to scream out and beg them not to put her in the dark hole with a strange man. But if she did that, she would show her fear and weakness to the man in the hole. The man she would be stuck with for who knew how long. She had to swallow her fear, tamp it down, let no one know she was frightened more than she had ever been in her life. And for the first time in her life, she couldn't make sense, see reason, for what was about to happen. Reason had always helped her deal with things, but when reason was lost what did one do?

Rob grabbed her under one arm and Geary the other, then they held her over the hole and began to lower her down into the dark pit.

Chapter Two

Willow shut her eyes. She didn't know why, instinct probably. She tensed when hands caught at her ankles and thought she would scream when they slid slowly up under her garments along her bare legs almost as if the hand was caressing them. She squeezed her eyes shut tighter when his hands went to her bare bottom, roaming over her cheeks to settle a squeeze on them before holding her there in place.

"Let her go," the strong voice called to the two men.

They did and he held her firm as she slowly slid the rest of the way down into his arms, her shift and tunic bunching up at her waist as he eased her to her feet to rest against him.

It was when she felt his manhood press against her that she realized he was naked. She hurried her arms down to adjust her garments, but they landed on his bare shoulders and her worst fears were confirmed. He was completely naked.

"There is no room to turn or do anything but to stay as we are," he said, a bit of an angry bite to his tone. "If you remain still, I'll adjust your garments for you."

Willow didn't know where his anger came from, but then she had stolen what little space he had. She dropped her arms to her sides. "I can do it." She gasped when she felt him squeeze her backside.

"No, you can't."

She went to step away from him and he yanked her up against him.

"There is little room to move. Back up too fast and you will dislodge the earth wall, and possibly cause it to come crashing down around us."

Instinct had her pressing herself against him as if she couldn't get close enough. Good Lord, could things get any worse?

She felt something stir between her legs, and it took her a moment to realize what it was.

"I'm not a eunuch and I've been too long without a woman. I have no doubt Beck did this on purpose. What that purpose is, I'm sure we'll find out. So, lass, let's get you covered and I will do my best to ignore your inviting scent and how nicely you fit in my arms."

He eased her a bit away from him and struggled to get her garments down around her, mumbling a few oaths as he did.

She almost sighed with relief when her shift brushed her shins and fell to her ankles. When his hands fell away from her, she went to stand straight, if only to keep a hair's breath away from him, but her legs were so limp from walking, riding, and fear, that they gave way on her.

His arm hooked around her waist in an instant. "Damn. You're weak."

"I am not weak. I'm fatigued from walking and riding at a ridiculous pace, and fearful of being trapped in a dark hole with a crazed man who has gone too long without poking a woman," she argued, tired of all she had suffered and in only one day. "And if you think I won't fight you if you dare try to poke me, you're wrong."

"So you rather the walls crash in around us than me poke you? A shame since I do give a woman a good poke."

Sound reason fled her, she responded without thinking. "I have no way to judge how good a poke you give since I've never been poked."

"Good God, woman, that's not something you should be telling me," he scolded.

Willow held her tongue, having no good response. Whatever was the matter with her? She knew better than to offer such personal information that left her even more vulnerable. While there was no excuse for it, she blamed it on her day being more difficult than usual. Her strength had waned. She could barely keep herself upright. The day had caught up with her and so had the cold night. She shivered and wobbled in his arms.

"Damn, you're exhausted. Rest against me," he ordered.

"And chance getting poked, I think not," she said with as much courage as she could muster, which wasn't much at all.

"I give you my word, I won't touch you," he said. "Rest against me and sleep."

"How do I know your word is any good?"

"You'll need to trust me on that," he said and eased her against him.

She had no choice. She was too tired to fight and didn't have a lick of strength to do so. She let herself drop against him, laying her head on his shoulder, while she let her arms rest at her sides. His chest was muscled, but comfortable or else she was just too fatigued to think otherwise. In no time, she was sound asleep.

***

He kept her tucked snug against him, her clothed body giving him warmth he hadn't had in a couple of days. The heat felt good as did she, though she shouldn't be here. Beck shouldn't have sent her down here with him. He did it to toy with him and once free, he intended to see the man suffered a similar fate.

First, however, he needed to survive his time in the hole with her and that wasn't going to be easy. Her hair tickled at his nose, the pine scent not only enticing, but it let him know that she had been in the woods for at least a few days. Then there were her slim legs, smooth and silky to the touch and their length letting him know she was of fair height, the fact that her head reached just past his shoulder confirming it. Her bottom was round and firm and he could feel her full breasts pressed against his chest through her garments. But it was her womanly scent that really made things difficult for him. He probably wouldn't have detected it if the source of it hadn't passed so close to his face when she was lowered down. He couldn't get the enticing fragrance out of his nostrils.

Damn, Beck. He knew how much he loved a good romp with a woman and it was something that had been denied him for months. He had had more important matters to handle and just when he thought he had solved his problem... all had gone to hell.

The woman gave a soft moan and moved her face up higher on his chest, tucking her head in the crook of his neck, her soft breath fanning along his skin.

This definitely was not going to be easy.

He looked up, through the wooden grate at the night sky and stars. They were bright, no clouds concealing them, a relief since rain or snow was not one's friend when stuck in a hole in the ground.

The woman moved again and he tightened his hold on her. He couldn't chance her moving and disturbing any of the earth. He had gotten so mad when he had been tossed down here naked that he had punched the earth wall and cursed himself when he watched it begin to fall in on him. He had quickly repacked it and had been careful ever since.

He hoped Beck came to his senses and removed the woman, but the man could be an ignorant fool at times, actually most times. He wondered who the woman was and what Beck was doing with her and his intentions. One thing was for sure, she couldn't go around letting anyone know she was a virgin. Beck could get a small fortune for her if he found out, unless he already knew.

He'd find out more tomorrow and finally get a look at her, and he'd do what he could to protect her. He couldn't wait for this to be over. He'd had enough of this hole and he'd had enough of Beck causing more problems than he was worth.

He closed his eyes, thinking sleep would elude him like it had been doing. It didn't. The heat from the woman's body, the way she rested comfortably in his arms, and the pleasant scent of her hair lolled him to sleep.

***

Willow stirred and moaned, aches assaulting her entire body and reminding her of her dire circumstances. She kept her eyes closed... almost. Her eyelids fluttered lightly and she got a glimpse of the chest her head rested on. A stranger she shared this god-awful hole with, though after their brief conversation last night he wasn't a complete stranger. Not that she needed to know he'd been too long without a woman. However, she had been grateful and relieved that he had kept his hands off her. But for how long?

At least with it being morning, she'd get a look at him. A face could tell a lot about a person. She would be able to measure his character better by being able to see him when they spoke.

She shifted slightly, needing to ease some of the stiff aches out of her body, but stilled when she felt him grow aroused against her.

"My apologies, he often stirs, sometimes even before I wake in the morning, and even more so when enticed."

"I didn't mean to—"

"I know it wasn't intentional, but let's stay aware of the close quarters we share."

"Of course," Willow said and decided it was best she introduce herself so he could do the same. She raised her head slowly. "I'm—"

"Willow?"

"Slatter?"

They both stared at each other.

Willow couldn't believe her eyes. It was Slatter the man who had set fire to a couple of sheds the same night her father had accidentally set a fire in the keep that led to her mum's death and had been responsible for her sister going blind. James had returned home with him after going to see Lord Cree of the Clan Carrick. Lord Cree had captured Slatter and had handed him over to James to face punishment for his crime. With no cell to hold him, James had turned him over to Tarass, the Lord of Fire to be imprisoned there and his fate determined.

She had treated a wound he had received when he had tried to escape unsuccessfully. She had been warned about him before she had been allowed to enter the cell to tend him.

"He mesmerizes the women with his devilish tongue and his exceptionally fine features, then they do his bidding without question. So watch yourself, lass, or he'll have you under his wicked spell in no time," the guard had warned her. "It was how he almost escaped. A woman helped him."

Willow had been skeptical, but she realized the truth of the guard's words at first sight of Slatter. He had the most stunning features for a man that it was difficult if not impossible not to stare at him or get lost in his good looks. Though, it was his dark eyes that actually captivated the attention. There was a passion in them that seemed to reach out and stroke you without even laying a hand on you. It was one time she had been grateful for her practical nature. And with being in such close quarters with him, she reminded herself that she needed to keep hold of sound reason or like others, she would surrender to the devil.

They both questioned at the same time. "What are you doing here?"

"You first, *leannan*," Slatter offered.

And there it was, his charming tongue, calling her sweetheart. Willow promptly ignored it. "I was returning from visiting my sister Sorrell and her new husband when the troop escorting me home was attacked. Beck's men outnumbered Northwick warriors, though they fought bravely."

"Beck attacked a Northwick troop?" Slatter shook his head. "He's beyond a fool. Ruddock will see him suffer and die for this."

Willow had caught a flash of shock in his dark eyes at the news. "You know Ruddock?"

"I know how powerful a man he is," Slatter said and shook his head. "He wed your sister Sorrell of his own free will?"

"Why wouldn't he?" Willow snapped, catching a humorous glint in his eyes.

"Ruddock is a big man, Sorrell not so much. He's also a man of few words, Sorrell definitely not so much."

His chuckle sounded loud in the confined space and she felt the rumble of his body resonate against her own. "How do you know this?"

"Tongues wag even in a dungeon."

"Or perhaps your charming tongue gets them wagging," Willow suggested.

"Jealous?" he asked, a wicked smile surfacing.

His accusation annoyed her, but his smile sent her stomach fluttering madly. Even with dirt marring his features, he was far too handsome.

"Why would I be jealous?" she asked calmly while the flutters continued to torment her.

"You're a practical, dependable woman, Willow. People turn to you out of need and for guidance, but when else? And when was the last time anyone told you that you were beautiful, *leannan*?"

Mum.

The thought was like a punch to her stomach, chasing the flutters away. Her mum had been the only one who ever told her that.

He mesmerizes women with his devilish tongue.

The guard's warning echoed in her head.

"You met me one time and only for a short while. You don't know me at all," she said, annoyed that he assumed to.

"One time was all I needed. Your focus had been on my wound, nothing else. The few questions you asked concerned only my wound. Not only did the guard at the door inquire about something that had been ailing him, but several other guards stopped to ask you about their ailments as well, yet not one offered a pleasant greeting or inquired about you. And you paid no heed when I asked any question pertaining to you. It was as if you didn't even hear me."

"Did you not think that could have been on purpose?"

"I considered it briefly, but with how easily I charm women I quickly dismissed it. The conclusion was obvious. You think on others needs and wants and never your own… not ever. You're so accustomed to it that you ignore even the friendliest phrase, *leannan*," he said, his dark eyes holding a hint of a challenge.

"Do you actually think it appropriate that you refer to me as sweetheart while in this situation?"

"I should wait until we get out of here to be sweet and kind to you?"

Once again she felt his small rumble of laughter, their bodies just too close not to.

"I expect you to be practical and honorable," she warned.

"Practical isn't in my nature. Honorable?" His smile faded. "That would depend on what you consider honorable."

"An honorable man wouldn't set fire to two of my clan's structures."

Before he could respond a laughing voice called out, "Up and out!"

Slatter hated to dash her hopes that she was being released, but better she knew. "I've been let out in the morning to eat and to see to my needs, then again before nightfall."

Willow couldn't hide her disappointment. Yesterday she'd only had to spend the night down here and most of it was spent sleeping from exhaustion. How would she be able to last an entire day?

The wooden grate was moved off the top and Geary called down, "Send her up, Slatter."

"Don't let her fall, Geary," Slatter called out.

"You just hold her good and tight until we get a grip on her," Rob yelled back.

"I need to get a good hold of your legs and bottom to get you up to them."

She was afraid to ask, but she hurried the words out. "Which means?"

"I need to get my hands under your garments again."

"Why under them?" she asked, though knew well why and he said what she had thought herself.

"If I try to lift you with my hands on top of your garments, you could more easily slip from my grasp and that could prove disastrous for us both."

"Come on, Slatter, or you both can stay down there until later," Rob yelled down.

"Hurry and let's get this done," Willow said eager to get out of the hole if only for a while.

Slatter didn't wait a minute longer. He wanted it done as quickly as she did. He bunched her garments up and rested his hands to her bare backside. He was reminded how round and firm she was to the touch and he pushed the thought from his mind. At least he tried to.

"Put your hands on my shoulders and as I lift you, give yourself a push up, then stretch your arms up," he instructed.

Willow nodded, trying desperately to ignore the strength of his hands on her bare backside.

"Now," he said.

She pushed as he lifted and she stretched her arms up as if reaching for the sky. His hands slipped down to her thighs and continued pushing her up and up. Hands grabbed at her arms, yanking and pulling, and she winced and was never so relieved when she found herself deposited on the ground. She took great gulps of the chilled air and sat, her legs aching from standing for so long.

When she watched a ladder being lowered down to Slatter, she got annoyed. Then she realized that there hadn't been enough room for a ladder with them both in there, and she certainly wouldn't have been able to lift Slatter up. She had to have been the one to go first.

It felt good to sit, get off her feet, and she intended to do so until she was forced to stand. She watched as Slatter rose out of the hole and hurried to turn her head just before his entire nakedness was exposed. Then she heard clapping and hooting and she turned back to see Slatter bowing gallantly to a group of women a few feet away.

"You look lovely as always, my dear ladies," Slatter said and threw a kiss to them.

Old and young alike smiled, some blushed, others expressed their opinion about what a fine, well-endowed man he was.

"Enough with you now, be gone, and shame on the lot of you," Rob yelled.

"Strip the woman bare and you'd be doing the same," one woman yelled and the others agreed with shouts.

Willow pulled her cloak more tightly around her and prayed the two men wouldn't oblige them.

"Now, lassies, what good would that do when she is not near as fine a woman to look at as the lot of you gorgeous women?" Slatter said, a lilt to his voice that cajoled.

Willow wondered if he said that to help save her from such indignity, or if he meant it. She was aware that she was nowhere near as beautiful as her two sisters, her features far too plain and her hair dark red with stubborn waves running through it. But what did her features matter now? She had more pressing matters to worry about.

"Be gone with you, I say," Rob ordered again, then turned to Slatter, handing him a swath of plaid. "And you cover yourself up and stop showing yourself off."

"How can I not brighten the lovely lassies day?" Slatter asked with a chuckle as he fitted the plaid around him.

Willow almost laughed at his audacious behavior and she had to admit, from what she saw—the back of him—he did have a fine body. Broad shoulders, defined muscles, narrow waist, tight buttocks, and muscled legs though not overly so. He really was nicely proportioned.

Enough, Willow, you don't need to be thinking of him that way," she chastised herself silently.

"You'll both see to your needs, eat something, then it's back in the hole until later," Rob instructed.

It didn't take long to see things done and when a bowl of gruel that looked days old was handed to her, she wanted to cry. She was so hungry.

"Eat." Slatter encouraged. "The other meal may be worse."

She grimaced with the first taste, but knew he was right. If she wanted to survive, until she was rescued, she had to eat.

There was a heavy chill to the air and grey clouds floated along gray skies and she tried not to think of what might happen if it rained.

"Where did you get those scratches on your face and the rips to your garments?" Slatter asked.

"I hid in thorny bushes during the battle and got stuck there. Beck's men weren't gentle when they pulled me out."

"Some on your face need cleaning, they swell red."

Willow looked toward Rob and Geary talking between themselves a few feet away. They didn't care about her wounds. She'd have to do the best she could herself. She tore off a small piece of her shift and soaked it with the stale ale she had been given to drink, to clean the scratches.

"Let me," Slatter offered, taking the scrap of cloth from her hand before she could protest.

He dabbed at the scratches with a gentle hand. She was a brave one. He had thought for sure she would have panicked when she was lowered into the hole with, at the time, she thought a complete stranger and to find him naked. She could have started screaming like a banshee, but then she had been exhausted, not much strength left in her. Still, she had handled herself well, had remained calm, had not lost her mind, an easy thing to do when stuck in such a confined place and in the ground.

He finished dabbing at her scratches and thought of something she had said earlier and never got to respond to. "I didn't set fire to your sheds."

"I am to take your word for it? The word of a man whose lies slip more easily from his lips than the truth?

Sorrell told me how a lie you helped spread caused Ruddock's family great pain and sorrow."

Slatter's hand stilled. "When was this?"

"A few days ago when I was visiting her."

He gave his head a slight shake. "No, not when she told you. When did I spread this lie and where?"

"You lie so much that you don't remember?" she asked and would have found it amusing if it wasn't so telling of his disreputable nature.

An angry spark lit in his eyes, but stopped before fully igniting by a smile that suddenly appeared.

"Lies and truths often get confused," he said.

"An easy solution to that would be not to lie," Willow suggested, to her the more sensible thing to do.

"How do you like my gift to you?" a voice boomed.

They both turned to see Beck headed their way.

Willow hurried to her feet with the help of Slatter, his hand going out to take hold of her arm.

"So she's mine then?" Slatter asked, keeping a tight grasp on her after they were both on their feet.

Beck threw back his head and laughed. "I'm not that generous."

"I didn't think so. What do you plan to do with her?"

Beck laughed again. "You think I'm going to tell you that? Give her a good poke while you can." He laughed harder. "If you can. Those are mighty tight quarters you two share." His body shook with more laughter.

"You underestimate my skill, Beck," Slatter said with a chuckle of his own.

Beck's laughter stopped. "There's no room down in that hole to poke her."

"There is if you're skilled at poking a woman."

Willow wished she had Sorrell's talent with words and her fearlessness to say whatever she pleased. She'd have threatened both men by now and ranted at them so badly that neither of them would probably want anything to do with her. But that wasn't Willow's way, though being sensible certainly didn't help her in this senseless situation.

Beck rubbed at his bushy, red beard. "I tell you what. You poke her down there in that hole and she yours. You can have her once you're ransomed."

"Your word on that?" Slatter asked.

"My word. You poke her and she belongs to you," Beck said with a firm nod.

Willow couldn't hold her tongue any longer. "What if I don't want to be poked?"

Slatter turned his head and smiled at her, though his eyes seemed to send her a warning. "Trust me, *leannan*, you do."

Beck laughed again. "Fight him if you want. Then he looked to Geary and Rob. "Get them down in the hole and let's see how talented he is."

Chapter Three

Once in the hole, Slatter held her close and whispered in her ear. "I'm not going to poke you. I would never force a poke on a woman."

How did she trust a liar?

"Get it done," Beck yelled down, staring down in the hole along with Geary and Rob.

Slatter looked up. "That's why you don't please women, Beck. You don't take your time with them, make them want you, make them crave you, make them moan and scream out your name in pleasure."

"I've heard you grunting and groaning with plenty of women, but I've never heard a woman moan or scream out your name," Geary said to Beck and got a punch in the face for it.

Slatter returned his attention to Willow. He placed his hand at the back of her neck and brought his mouth close to hers. The men looking down would assume he was kissing her.

"I'm going to make it look like I'm poking you. I'll let you know how to respond. You'll be freed with me and I'll see you get home safely to your family."

"I hope you aren't lying," she whispered near his lips.

"Trust me," he said again and began yanking up her garments.

What choice did she have? At least, if she was freed with him, she'd have a chance to escape should it prove necessary. Whereas, she had no idea what her fate would be with Beck, though she feared it wouldn't be very pleasant.

He was naked again and when he pressed her to him, she felt his flaccid manhood rest against her, then he began to move against her. His mouth went to her neck near her ear and while it appeared he was kissing her, he spoke in whispers, his warm breath tickling her skin.

"Don't move yet," he murmured and continued rubbing against her.

She felt him grow aroused, but then she supposed it couldn't be helped. He had told her he'd been too long without a woman. And she was not ignorant of the act of coupling, her mum having explained it in detail to all three of her daughters. She simply needed to keep reminding herself that this was only pretend. It was also the cost of freedom and safe passage home.

"Moan softly," he whispered.

She had no problem doing that, since his breath sent pleasurable tingles along her neck.

"Good, now move against me, slowly," he murmured, and she did.

Willow shut her eyes and ignored the stirrings that began to build and spread in her. It was a natural reaction and one she could control since she had no desire to couple with Slatter. Though, she had wondered how it would feel to know a man.

He pressed harder against her and when his manhood rubbed in a particular spot, she was so caught off guard that she moaned loudly without being told. And, Lord, help her when he continued to rub against her, hastening his movements. It felt heavenly and she found herself matching his movements and moaning without thought.

"Scream when I tell you," he whispered.

Everything seemed to fade around her as a powerful sensation took hold of her and began to build, growing stronger, reaching for something, stretching, needing it, wanting it...

"Slatter!" she screamed out as the powerful sensation rocked her body and exploded with such intensity that it buckled her legs, and she was glad Slatter's arm tightened around her waist as he let out a roar.

"Damn, he did it," Rob yelled out and got a slap from Beck.

"She's yours for good now," Beck yelled down and the grate was moved over the hole.

Willow's head rested on Slatter's shoulder as she tried to gather her senses. An impossible task since tiny shivers of delightful pleasure continued to trickle through her.

When she found herself able to speak, she said, "You did that on purpose."

"It was the only way," he said. "They had to believe we were coupling and you never would have been able to fake a good climax, since you've never had one... until now."

She was going to ask him about his roar, had he faked it? But being she felt him still hard against her, she got her answer.

She felt a bit ashamed that she had allowed herself to lose control while pretending and in front of others and kept her head on his shoulder, not wanting to look at him.

"Willow," he said softly. When she didn't respond or lift her head to look at him, he continued, "Believe me when I tell how truly sorry I am, but I don't regret what I did. You don't want to be stuck with Beck. When I saw a chance to help you, I took it. I'm only sorry it had to be this way. I will make certain you get home safely to your family."

"My garments," she said and Slatter quickly eased them down, covering her.

She didn't want to speak of it any longer. She wanted to forget it happened, forget how she responded to him so easily. Forget that the three watched from above, though she was glad they were in the hole and the men couldn't see them too clearly, especially with the darkening skies.

She had reminded herself it was a natural reaction she had, but she should have been able to contain it, not let it go as far as it did, not have responded so easily to him.

"You are being held for ransom?" she asked to get away from her disturbing thoughts.

"Aye, I am."

"How important are you that Beck holds you for ransom?"

"I'm of no importance at all. We have an ongoing feud."

"He wins this time since he ransoms you?" Willow asked.

"Actually, ransom or not, I win since he lost you to me."

She quieted again and while Slatter felt none too proud of what he had done to her, it had been necessary. Willow could have met a far, far worse fate if she were left with Beck.

Slatter had no doubt that whatever Beck's intentions with Willow had been, it involved getting the highest coin he could for her, whether through ransom or more likely through sale to the highest bidder. He couldn't let that happen to her. She didn't deserve such a terrible fate.

She raised her head to look at him and she caught a soft concern there in his dark eyes that she hadn't seen before.

"Do you think you'll be ransomed soon?" she asked.

"One can only hope."

She wanted to try and keep a sliver of a distance between them if she could, but it was cold and leaning against him kept her warm. She imagined it did the same for him. So did she deprive not only herself of warmth, but him as well?

She was too practical to ignore the obvious answer and when she felt him shiver, she did what was best for them both. She leaned against him.

"For warmth we both need," she said, not wanting him to misconstrue her intentions.

Slatter slipped his arms around her, tucking her flat against him. "Your warmth and thoughtfulness is much appreciated."

There were times he sounded kind rather than charming and it was those times she felt more inclined to believe him. She only hoped she wasn't wrong.

"The last time I saw you, you were a prisoner in the Lord of Fire's dungeon. How is it that you're here a prisoner in this godawful hole?" she asked.

"Pure luck," he said with a chuckle. "The Lord of Fire decided that an appropriate punishment for me was to hand me over to a tribe of barbarians he was familiar with for an undetermined amount of time. What neither the Lord of Fire or the barbarians knew was that I'm exceptionally skilled at escaping from almost anywhere or from any one. I escaped the barbarians on my second night with them, only to find myself captured by Beck. Naturally, he wasn't about to just hand me over without being compensated for his fortunate luck in coming across me. So here I sit and wait, a hole in the ground not easy to escape."

"How long were you here before I arrived?"

"Two days," he said, his glance going to the one scratch on her face. "That scratch looks to have worsened."

"The ale did that, but it will also help heal it," she said, seeing concern with the way his brow narrowed as he stared at the wound. Even a scrunched brow couldn't mar or hide his fine features. It seemed no matter what expression the man wore; his good looks didn't suffer for it.

"You're not only beautiful. You're a fine healer."

"That tongue of yours lies easily," she accused.

"My tongue is talented and does a lot of things with ease, but it doesn't lie... this time."

"It doesn't?" she asked with a tilt of her head. "Then why did you say that I wasn't as beautiful as the women who watched you and called out greetings when you exited the hole this morning?"

"You're too intelligent not to know that I was telling the women what they wanted to hear, since they no doubt don't hear it from their husbands. Besides, being nice to them has earned me extra food. They drop it down to me every now and then. And all women are beautiful in their own way."

"I can't be sure if you're being sincere or not."

"I suppose you'll have to get to know me better to find out," he said, and raised his hand to gently probe the area around the reddened scratch.

She winced and he cringed, which made her smile. "You suffer along with me?"

"Of course, you belong to me now. It's my duty to see you safe and cared for."

"I don't truly belong to you," she disagreed, though part of her thought it would be nice to finally belong to a man and he belong to her. But this was nothing like that. "I don't belong to anyone."

"Until you wed, then you belong to your husband."

"And he belongs to me," she said.

"And, of course, you'll make sure there'll be rules to follow," he teased with a smile.

"There will be love to be shared," she corrected.

His dark eyes took on a soft sadness. "Love isn't easy to find."

"It's worth the search." She smiled gently. "And I'm patient."

"Won't a marriage be arranged for you?"

"Luckily, no. James has pledged fealty to Ruddock and he sees that the Clan Macardle is protected and has no fear of starving, leaving no reason for an arranged marriage. Ruddock has claimed that Snow and I are free to wed of our own choosing."

"And you?" she asked out of curiosity, not that it mattered to her.

"Marriage is not for me," he said and turned a wickedly disarming smile on her. "Though I do have a lot to offer a woman. I'm charming, I have far better features than most men, a fine body, and once I poke a woman, no other man satisfies her."

Willow had to laugh. "I'm sure there are many women who would find what you have to offer them, irresistible."

"And you? Do you find me irresistible?"

He sounded like he half-joked and was half-serious and that gave Willow pause to answer.

"You hesitate," he said with a look of surprise.

She spoke bluntly. "I'm not sure what to make of you, Slatter."

"I'm a mystery. Does that at least not intrigue you?"

"What intrigues me is how you will evade capture once the Lord of Fire finds that you're not where he sent you."

The Lord of Fire could be a relentless man when he wanted something. She had seen how he had been with James when he had insisted that Sorrell agree to an arranged marriage with a man from a nearby clan to help unite the clans in the area and have them pledge their fealty to him. If it hadn't been for Ruddock, the Clan Macardle would be beholding to the Lord of Fire.

"I won't be caught again," Slatter said with confidence.

It struck Willow then. "You will be caught if you see me safely home."

Would he deserve that after helping her? But then would he truly see her safely home?

"Worry not, you'll get home and I won't get caught."

She quickly asked, "Will you trust me to another to take me home?"

"I would have to have great trust in him to do that and there are few people who I trust that much. Besides, what belongs to me I take great care of and protect."

She was getting used to seeing that wickedly teasing smile of his and smiling along with him. "And you take great care in reminding me that I belong to you."

"Let me enjoy having a beautiful woman belong to me, if only for a while." He didn't like that her smile faltered. "It saddens you that you belong to me, since it certainly can't be that you doubt your beauty."

"You don't have to lie to me. I am well aware that I have plain features."

"Who told you such nonsense?" he demanded as if her words offended him.

"No one told me. I have eyes to see for myself. My two sisters got the beauty in the family, especially Snow," Willow said with a soft smile.

Slatter rested his brow to hers. "You are beautiful whether you believe it or not. You have the most gorgeous green eyes I have ever seen. The color reminds me of the spring when the dormant grass bursts into a luscious green color. And your cheeks blush a rosy pink more often than not, highlighting your pale skin. Then there are your lips, rosy and plump and begging to be kissed.

He brushed his lips over hers and Willow didn't move. His words alone had sent a rush of flutters in her stomach and flared a passion that was far too new to her to fully understand.

His lips brushed hers again, then whispered, "To me, Willow, you are the most beautiful woman I have ever seen."

This time he didn't brush his lips across hers, he pressed them against hers, kissing her with an intensity she instinctively responded to. His hand went to the back of her head to rest their as he tempted and teased her into parting her lips and when his tongue slipped into her mouth, the flutters in her stomach went wild and her passion sparked to a flame.

"Good, he's at it again. Now watch and learn, because I'm tired of your fumbling pokes."

The woman's voice ended their kiss, Slatter and Willow both looking up surprised to see that the grate had been removed. And even more surprised to see a woman and man looking down.

"A pleasant day to you, Maddie," Slatter said, a smile spreading wide across his face as his arms hugged Willow protectively.

The short, thin, pretty woman with long dark hair grinned. "A pleasant day to you, Slatter, and I see that it is a very pleasant day for you." She held up a stuffed sack. "I have some fine food for you, but only if you'll let my husband here watch you poke the woman. I'm tired of his unsatisfying pokes and fumbling hands."

"I give a good poke," a man of fair-sized height and fine girth argued.

"Half the time when you got me on my hands and knees, you can't even find the right place to put that useless rod of yours," she complained.

Her husband hurried to clarify. "That happens only when I drink too much."

"Aye, you keep making that excuse," Maddie shot back.

Slatter called up to the arguing couple. "I'd be glad to speak with your husband when I'm let out of here later today, Maddie, but I won't have anyone watching me couple with *my* woman."

"You did it for Beck," she argued.

"Only to have Willow for myself."

Maddie grinned. "So you like her."

"I do and I'll not disrespect her again by having someone watch us make love," Slatter said.

Maddie punched her husband in the arm. "You hear that. He doesn't poke his woman, he makes love to her. You'll be talking to him later, Kevin, or you'll not be poking me, not ever again."

Her husband rubbed his arm. "I love you, Maddie. I have since we were bairns. If this will make you happy I'll talk to him, but you can't go telling people I don't give you a good poke."

"I won't have to after you talk with him and I love you too, Kevin." Maddie looked down the hole. "Kevin will be waiting for you when you get out of there later.

Now watch out, I'm going to drop the sack down to you. You and your woman need some decent food."

"Keep your head tucked against my chest," he ordered Willow and once she did, he called up to Maddie. "Bless you, Maddie. You're a beautiful and kind woman."

"See. See how he tells me I'm beautiful," Maddie said and punched her husband in the arm again. "I want you telling me that like you once did. Unless you don't think I'm beautiful anymore."

"You will always be beautiful to me, Maddie," Kevin said, rubbing his muscled arm again.

"Then tell me more often," she all but ordered him, then held the sack over the hole. "Here it comes, Slatter and *mòran taing*."

"You're welcome, Maddie," Slatter said and caught the sack in his hand.

"Be gone with you, Maddie, and what are you doing there, Kevin?" Rob called out.

"Stopping my wife from giving the prisoners food," Kevin said. "Now come on home, woman."

"Good, man," Rob said.

"And I'll have a talk with Slatter when you get him out later and let him know to leave my wife be," Kevin said.

"About time a man makes his wife obey," Rob said, coming to a stop by the hole.

Slatter lowered his arm to his side so Rob didn't see the sack of food.

"Got some news for you, Slatter," Rob called down, peering over the hole. "Your ransom arrives tomorrow and you'll be freed."

"Thank God," Willow whispered, raising her head off Slatter's chest.

"Good to hear," Slatter called out.

Rob chuckled. "Beck has a gift for you before you leave."

"I suppose you're not going to tell me what it is," Slatter said.

"It's a surprise," Rob said and slid the wooden grate back over the hole and walked away laughing.

Chapter Four

It was late and Willow was not only feeling the cold, she was also feeling anxious about far too many things. She remained still as best she could, not wanting to wake Slatter. He had tried to assure her that whatever gift Beck had for him, it most likely didn't have anything to do with her. She was safe and soon-to-be going home.

Willow wasn't so sure about that. When they had been taken out of the hole for supper, she had watched Rob and Geary cast chuckles and whispers their way. Slatter had been too busy speaking with Kevin, as he had promised Maddie he would, to notice. Something was brewing and she didn't have a good feeling about it.

Her worries had her stir a bit in his arms. Yesterday their combined body heat had helped keep them warm, but it had turned colder tonight and it felt as if the cold had settled down into the hole, wrapping around them like a chilling blanket. Or perhaps she was so concerned with tomorrow that she couldn't get warm.

How did she trust him to take her home? She wanted to believe that he would, but since he lied with ease and little to no regret, how did she trust him? And if that wasn't enough to cause her concern, there was the kiss.

Why had he kissed her? There was no reason for him to. No one was watching them. Had it been because it had been too long since he tasted a woman's lips? Was she simply convenient? Or should she be asking herself why she enjoyed it? And what would have happened if Maddie and her husband hadn't come along? Would it have gone farther than a kiss?

Don't be foolish, Willow. You would have stopped him," she scolded herself silently. *You would not have let him take advantage of the situation. He is a liar and do-no-good and you would not get yourself involved with such a disreputable man.*

"What troubles you, Willow?"

She jumped, startled that he was awake and his voice was filled with such sincerity.

Slatter quickly hugged her tight, stilling her. "Careful, we don't want to disturbed the walls of our lovely abode."

"You startled me. I thought you were asleep," she said, settling in his arms.

"I felt your unease."

"I woke you? I'm sorry," she apologized, meaning it. It was better he slept, less chance he would kiss her again.

"It's all right, Willow. Any bit of noise or stirrings wake me. I sleep light. Now tell me what bothers you."

"The cold," she said quickly, comfortable that there was some truth to her words. "It is much colder tonight than last night and I feel it in us both.

As if to prove her words, snow started to fall on them.

"Damn," Slatter mumbled.

Willow had to agree with him, though she didn't swear. An early snow always proved troublesome. It could leave a light coating on the ground or dump a sizeable amount. Her concern and the cold shivered her.

Slatter ran his hands up and down her back, trying to rub some warmth into her, but he felt the cold himself. It and her gentle stirrings had been what woke him.

Willow rested as close as she could against him. "Can you spread my cloak over your shoulders?"

Slatter did as she suggested and, with her pressed tight against him, he was able to get her cloak to rest partially over his shoulders. Still, it would not be enough to keep him or her warm if the snow worsened.

And it did.

The snow turned heavy and Slatter knew if it continued throughout the night they could be in trouble.

"Cover your ears, *leannan*," he said.

She didn't think to ask why. She did as he said and a shudder ran through her when he let out a ferocious roar. It sounded like the ones the warriors used when going into battle. He didn't wait long afterwards to let loose another one.

Pounding feet could be heard after his roar settled and light sparked near the top of the hole.

The grate was removed and Rob peered down. "What are you doing?"

"Letting you know that no ransom will be given if you find me and my woman dead in the morning, you idiot."

Rob's eyes burst wide as if just realizing something, then turned wider when Beck's bellowing shout pierced the night.

"Get them out of that hole! And who was the fool on watch tonight? I'll have his head for not alerting me to the snow. I'll get no coin for a dead man."

Willow shivered in relief.

Slatter's arms remained firm around her. "You'll be warm soon enough."

At that moment, she couldn't be more grateful to him, though a little voice whispered in her head, *I'll miss your arms around me.* She quickly chased it away. She would miss his arms for warmth and that was all, nothing else.

Willow didn't mind this time when his hands touched her bare, icy bottom as he pushed her up and out of the hole. They were actually warm and sent a brief shot of heat through her.

Once out of the hole, Slatter wasted no time slipping his arm around her and tucking her against him.

"Geary, get them in the hut Maddie made ready and have two men stand watch outside the door," Beck ordered, then turned to Rob. "You have some explaining to do."

Willow remained in the crook of Slatter's arm, having grown accustomed to being attached to him, though it could be because she felt protected in his arms.

Geary opened the door to the small hut. "Don't try and escape. We have men posted."

"Why would I be so foolish to do that when I'm to be ransomed tomorrow?" Slatter asked, shaking his head and hurried into the hut, his arm still firm around Willow.

Slatter went straight to the fire pit in the middle of the small room and stood there with Willow to let the flames' heat wash over them.

Never had heat felt so welcoming to Willow. She let herself sink against Slatter's side, her arms going around his waist, her head on his chest, as they both stood there getting warm.

After a few minutes, Slatter peered around the room, spotting what served as a mattress, a straw-stuffed mat and a blanket. He reluctantly moved his arms off Willow. "Wait here a moment."

She didn't let go of him. She didn't want to. She felt safe at his side.

Slatter slipped his fingers underneath her chin and raised her head so he could look in her eyes. He didn't like that he saw worry there.

"You're safe. I'm just going to get that stuffed mat and blanket over there," he said with a nod toward it. "We'll finally be able to lie down."

Willow nodded, eager to get off her feet, her legs aching from standing so long.

Slatter felt a pang of emptiness when her arms fell away from him and he turned away from her and scowled. He had never felt that way leaving a woman's side, but then he had never been so protective of a woman as he was toward Willow.

He hurried and got the mat and blanket close to the fire and when he spied a crock and two tankards near the fire pit, he silently thanked Maddie. He filled both quickly and handed one to Willow.

She sighed after taking a sip. "Hot cider. How wonderful."

Slatter felt the same way, sipping the hot liquid slowly.

"We must get you beneath the blanket," Willow said, giving him a little push.

"That eager to cuddle with me?" he teased, his wicked grin surfacing.

"Aye, I am," she said seriously. "We need warming down to our bones if we are to survive and more so for you since you are naked."

Slatter leaned down, bringing his face close to hers and whispered, "Your beauty keeps me warm."

Willow stared at him a moment, then said, "Does that smooth tongue of yours ever stop sweet-talking?"

"Shall we find out, *leannan*?" he murmured and brought his lips to hers.

Willow felt a spark about to ignite and stepped away from him.

Slatter chuckled. "Afraid of what you feel when I kiss you?"

"It's not proper for you to do so and I don't feel anything when you kiss me," she chastised. "And I'll have your word that you will not take any more liberties with me."

"Are you sure that's what you want, *leannan*?"

"I'm sure, and you will stop calling me sweetheart," she ordered and was surprised when she felt a tinge of regret.

"I give you my word that I will take no liberties with you this night." He held his hand out to her. "But I will not stop calling you *leannan*, since you truly have a sweet heart."

Willow shook her head. "You never stop trying to charm."

"And you forever refuse compliments," he said and his hand shot out to snatch hers. "Now let's do something that has been denied us... sleeping on what serves as a mattress."

Willow couldn't stop herself from smiling. She slipped her hand out of Slatter's, placed her tankard near the fire pit, and hurried off her cloak and placed it on top of the blanket that was folded partial down along the mat.

Slatter placed his tankard beside Willow's and helped her to sink down on the mat, then he joined her. They slipped under the blanket together and Slatter turned on his side and eased Willow on her side so he could wrap himself around her.

She didn't protest when his arm fell across her chest just beneath her breasts and he tucked her back against him tightly. Or when he draped his leg over hers, locking it firmly around her. She wanted him there wrapped snug against her, sharing his warmth, feeling his strength, feeling safe.

Neither spoke as the heat settled around and through them and as Willow drifted off, Slatter whispered near her ear, "Liar. My kiss stirred your passion and you enjoyed it."

***

Willow woke wrapped comfortably and toasty warm in Slatter's arms the next morning. She didn't want to move; she was far too comfortable.

"You slept well?"

Willow turned her head up to look at him. He was a feast for the eyes. A woman would never grow tired of looking at him. And those dark eyes of his, Lord, could they seduce with just one glance, pulling a woman in, stroking her, stirring her to passion-filled madness. She inwardly shook her head at her crazy thoughts.

"Aye, I slept well," she said, trying not to look in his eyes.

"Why do you ignore the obvious?" he asked, taking hold of her chin and forcing her eyes to meet his.

"What do you mean?" she asked with feigned innocence.

Slatter smiled. "You are far from an ignorant woman. You know exactly what I mean, but I'll say it for you. Why do you ignore and refuse to admit even to yourself that you're attracted to me?"

Willow sighed and did the reasonable thing, spoke the truth. "You're right, I am attracted to you, but what woman isn't? You have the finest features I have ever seen on a man and your tongue charms a woman senseless. You were also right when you called me a liar last night. I did enjoy your kiss. And you are right that I am far from an ignorant woman. You have many things a woman desires, but there is one thing I want in a man you can't give me."

Slatter grinned that wickedly sensual smile. "I doubt that."

"Really?" she asked with a wicked smile of her own. "What of love? Can you pledge your undying love to me and promise me you will love me and only me forever?"

Slatter was struck silent.

"That's what I thought," Willow said and couldn't understand why it disturbed her.

Slatter went to speak, but a voice called out from outside the door.

"Coming in."

Maddie entered the hut smiling and with a bundle in her hand. "Morning to you both. I cleaned your garments, Slatter, and had them waiting for you." Her smile grew. "Kevin and I owe you, Slatter. We had the best night we ever had last night and I look forward to many more."

"Kevin is a good man and he loves you. I'm glad for you both," Slatter said.

"Your ransom is not far off. I will bring a bucket of water so that you may freshen yourself and some food so you will not leave here hungry," Maddie said and gave a nod before leaving.

Things got busy after that, leaving little time for Willow and Slatter to talk. They both freshened themselves with the water Maddie had supplied and Willow was grateful for the comb she lent her.

Willow undid her braid and ran the comb through her long, dark red hair. It fell in its usual stubborn waves around her face and down over her shoulders.

"You should leave your hair loose like that, it becomes you," Slatter said.

"I often wear it loose," she said, not wanting him to think she did so now because he had commented on it.

They ate far tastier food than the gruel they had been given yesterday and Willow was grateful for the hot cider, it warming her insides good.

She couldn't help but cast an appreciative glance at Slatter once he had donned his garments. He wore a plaid well, though the dark colors were faded some and his tan shirt a bit frayed at the cuffs. He had scrubbed his face clean and had run some water through his hair, waves settling just above his shoulders as it dried. He pulled his boots on and lastly, he draped his wool, hooded-cloak over his shoulders.

He snatched her cloak up that had gotten entangled in the blanket and draped it over her shoulders, then held his arm out to her.

"Shall we go meet our fate?" he asked with a smile.

A slight shiver ran through and she nodded, worried what fate had in store for them.

They stepped outside to see that snow covered the ground, enough to leave a deep imprint.

Rob was outside the door, his one eye swollen shut and a bruise to his jaw, a punishment from Beck for not tending to his chore last night.

"They're not far off," Rob said.

"And that gift Beck has for me still awaits?" Slatter asked.

Rob grinned and winced. "Aye, it does."

Slatter made sure he kept his arm tucked around Willow's. He didn't know what Beck had planned, but there was no way he was letting him take Willow.

It wasn't long before a group of six riders and a horse without a rider entered the area. They varied in size and dress. Some wore plaids while others wore leather leg wrappings with tunics that fell to their knees. They all wore cloaks and carried weapons and not a one of them smiled.

Rob escorted Slatter and Willow to stand behind Beck, who waited in front of the longhouse.

Two dismounted while the others remained atop their horses.

The shorter, though broader, of the two men approached Beck.

"We've got your coin, but I'll hear from Slatter that he is unharmed," the man said.

Slatter spoke up. "I am unharmed, Walcott."

"Your coin," Walcott said, holding up a small sack. He tossed it to Beck.

Beck caught it, opened it, and smiled. "He's all yours."

Slatter stepped around Beck, keeping a tight hold of Willow's arm, though it mattered little since her grip was strong on him. He wondered if she worried that he would leave her there or if Beck would demand she stay.

Slatter barely reached Walcott when Beck called out.

"You can't leave without my gift to you."

Willow turned with Slatter.

"I feel responsible for throwing you two together, so it wouldn't be proper for me to send you off in an improper manner." Beck grinned, though his eyes narrowed. "I told you she belonged to you, but she has to belong to you properly if you intend to leave here with her."

Willow moved closer to Slatter and his arm tightened possessively around her.

"What game do you play now, Beck?" Slatter demanded.

"A woman only belongs to a man if she's wed to him. So if you want to leave here with her, you'll wed her," Beck commanded, leaving no doubt he meant what he said.

Slatter thought quickly, whispering to Willow. "It's a handfasting he wants and we can see that easily absolved once we leave here."

He was right. Handfasting was common among the Highlanders unless, of course, a cleric married a couple. It was more permanent in the eyes of the church. The handfasting could be done without difficulty.

She nodded.

"We'll wed," Slatter called out.

"They wed," Beck called out and the people who had gathered to watch cheered.

Walcott cast a doubtful eye at Slatter.

"It will be done and undone quickly," Slatter whispered to him.

"I would not trust Beck if I were you," Walcott warned.

Willow's stomach roiled, thinking the same.

"My gift," Beck shouted out and a cleric stepped out of the longhouse. "Now you can wed properly."

Chapter Five

"Are you hesitating, Slatter? If you are, I'll gladly take the woman off your hands. I know how averse you are to having a wife. I can't say I blame you with the way the lassies so eagerly chase after you. Why settle for one woman, when you can have many? So what say you? Will you wed the woman?" Beck challenged.

Willow felt fear race through her clear down to her toes. What did she do now? Wed and be stuck with a man who wants nothing to do with a wife? Or did she take her chances with Beck and hope that Ruddock's warriors had managed to make it to her home and James had gathered enough men to come to her rescue? Or would word have been sent to Ruddock and his warriors were on the way to find her now. That meant time though and anything could happen before they reached her.

"Of course, you could refuse to wed him," Beck said, giving Willow a choice.

"Not an option," Slatter said. "You gave your word."

"And I'm keeping my word. Like I told you, the only way a woman truly belongs to a man is if he weds her. You shouldn't have poked her if you didn't want to wed her." Beck laughed hardily. "Thought you had me, didn't you, but I got you on this one, Slatter." He snapped his hand. "Now give her over to me and be on your way."

"Like I said, not an option. We wed," Slatter said.

Beck turned to Willow. "What say you? Do you want to wed this rogue and be stuck with him forever?"

Willow wanted to ask what other options were available, but Beck wouldn't be honest with her.

"No need to ask her," Slatter said. "She's mine now and I'll make the decision for us both."

"That's it, take charge from the start, so she knows her place," Beck said, keeping his eyes on Willow.

Willow greatly disliked the situation she was in, but that didn't help her any. If she wanted to get home, then she had to be practical about this. She would wed him and see what could be done to absolve their marriage.

"My place will be beside my husband and I will be a good wife to him," Willow said. She had no worry that Slatter would take what she said literally, since he had considered her an intelligent woman and would do the sensible thing.

Beck laughed again, though not a belly shaking laugh. "And what about you, Slatter? You'll be a faithful and loving husband?"

Slatter didn't hesitate. "Every day of our lives together."

Willow smiled, his words clearly letting her know that he too intended to find a way to absolve the marriage. It made exchanging vows with him that much easier.

"Bless you both," Beck said.

Willow didn't care for Beck's sly grin. The man always seemed to be one step ahead, as if making sure no one could best him. What else did his devious mind have planned since no doubt he had expected his gift to be rejected?

"Let's be done with this. I want to be on my way," Slatter said.

"I never thought you'd be so eager to wed." Beck chuckled. "But I suppose miracles do happen." He turned to the cleric. "Come, Cleric, and wed the loving couple, so they may start the rest of their lives together."

The ceremony was brief and not a single word of congratulations was offered to them from anyone.

"I'm sure we'll cross paths again," Beck said after Slatter mounted his horse behind Willow.

"No doubt, Beck, though circumstances will be much different," Slatter said.

"A warning?" Beck asked, looking not all disturbed by it.

Slatter looked directly at the man. "A promise."

Willow wished she felt relieved, but she didn't. And the further they got into the woods, the more she feared that at any moment Beck's men would jump out and drag her away and leave the men to die.

"We'll get this marriage thing settled as soon as possible," Slatter said as the horses ambled along a worn trail.

Willow was glad to think on something else, not that it was that much less upsetting. "I have heard that annulments have been granted to some, though the circumstance must be exceptional."

"I would say our circumstances weren't only exceptional but forced as well. Neither of us wished to wed the other."

"Isn't that the way of most arranged marriages. Neither wish to wed the other, but they do anyway?" Willow asked, the thought casting doubt on how easily and quickly their marriage could be absolved, if ever.

"We will see what can be done," Slatter said.

"My brother James may be able to help. We can speak to him as soon as we arrive at my home. How long do you think before we reach it?"

"I'm not taking you directly home." His hand shot up when she hurried to object. "I have a matter that cannot wait. As soon as I finish with it, I will see you get home."

"You don't need to take me home, simply send some of your men along with me," she offered, anxious to get home to her family and put this whole terrible ordeal behind her.

How did she do that, though, when Slatter was now legally her husband?

"I won't chance you going with anyone but me," he said as if it was settled.

Worry had Willow rejecting his plan. "I expect you to honor your word, Slatter, and take me home."

"And I will, but not immediately and I will hear no more about it for now," he warned.

"The charming Slatter, turns into a tyrannical husband," Willow accused.

"My *leannan* turns into a demanding wife?" Slatter countered.

They both turned silent.

"*Leannan*," Slatter said gently after a while, "I gave you my word that I would get you home and I will keep my word. I will send a message to your brother that you are well and unharmed, and will be returned home safely in due time. You may include your own message so they don't worry needlessly about you."

"For that I thank you," she said, realizing arguing with him would do no good and she was grateful that he would at least notify her family that she was safe. "You will not let them know we are wed. It is better I tell them when I return home."

"As you wish."

They turned quiet again and Willow's thoughts drifted to how natural it felt to be in his arms. Had the time spent with him in such a confined space, under dire circumstances, and how she had no choice but to rely on him, made her trust him more than she would otherwise? He had proven he could be trusted, but was it a trust that would last or had it been born of forced circumstance?

"This matter that needs your immediate attention, perhaps I can help you with it," she suggested, thinking it would help get her home faster.

"It's a puzzling matter, not easily solvable."

Her green eyes brightened. "I'm good in handling puzzling matters."

When her eyes sparked like that and she smiled with delight, her hidden beauty was revealed. Some might think she had plain features, but she had a rare beauty that most would never recognize until it struck them in the face. Then they would find it difficult to keep their eyes off her, just as he did now.

"I search for someone who has wronged me," he said, finding himself confiding in her, though warning himself to be careful of revealing too much.

"How did he wrong you?" she asked, shifting in his arms so she didn't have to keep craning her neck to look at him, and settled more comfortably in the crook of his arm.

"He stole a great deal from me and I want to see him punished for it," he explained, keeping watch on his words.

"What did he take?"

"That doesn't matter now. What matters is that I find him."

Willow continued to question, curious now. "What is his name?"

"He uses mine."

"So you don't know his true name," she said.

"No, I don't."

"And why you can't take me home right away has something to do with him?"

"I've just missed catching him the last couple of times and Walcott found out where he may be and I don't want to chance losing him again."

"He's a slippery one then."

"And once he slips away, it is difficult to locate him again. He has a way of manipulating, cajoling, and convincing. Lies fall easily from his lips. And before you compare him to me know I mean harm to none... unlike him."

"Lies can hurt whether meant harmfully or not," Willow argued.

He grinned. "You mean like you hurt me when you lied about enjoying my kiss?"

"I don't believe for one minute I hurt you."

"You most certainly did hurt me, wife," he said with humor. "You were the first woman to ever deny that my kisses affected you, and that simply could not be." His humor faded and he turned serious. "I am far too skilled a lover to disappoint a woman."

Willow was at a loss at how to respond until her practical nature surfaced. "I'll have to take your word for it, since I'll never know if you speak the truth."

"We're wed. It is proper for us to couple and I could make your first time memorable."

"Coupling would seal our vows for good. We'd have no chance at an annulment," she reminded.

"No one need know. It would be between you and me."

She gave a slight tilt of her head as she said, "And perhaps the bairn that might come of our coupling?"

Slatter shuddered. "Bairns. I don't need any of those."

"I do," she said. "I look forward to having a large family and there to be much smiles and laughter shared." She thought a moment and there was sadness to her words when she said. "We do not want the same things. It is good we seek an annulment or we would be unhappy with one another."

"Then at least let me teach you the pleasures of a good kiss, so you don't suffer bad ones." Why his own words irritated him, he couldn't say? Or did the thought of someone else kissing her after he had been her first disturb him more than he cared to admit? Something else that irritated him.

"That won't be necessary. I intend to wed for love and however my husband's kisses, to me they will be... magical."

"An odd choice with you being so sensible." Again irritation jabbed at him. She would forgive the clumsy kissing fool anything because of love... foolish.

"And where do you plan on finding this man you intend to love and whose kisses will be magical?" he asked his voice ripe with annoyance.

"Fate will deliver him to me," she said with a smile and with confidence.

Silence trailed along with them once again and she was glad when they finally camped for the night. The men had brought food with them. A light fare of bread and cheese, but enough to keep the stomach feeling full.

She stretched out on the blanket Slatter had spread close to the fire and was surprised when he joined her, wrapping himself around her as he had done last night in the hut, only this time he wasn't naked.

"You don't have to—"

He didn't let her finish. "A husband sees to his wife's care. I am your husband and I will be your husband until I am no more."

She was too tired to disagree with him. She relaxed against him and abruptly fell asleep.

Sleep was more difficult to come by for Slatter, conflicting thoughts messing around in his head. Only knowing Willow a short time, he couldn't understand what it was that had her settling so deeply in his thoughts. She was there all the time and he couldn't chase her away. He'd never spent so much time thinking on one woman. It made no sense to him. As did the thought that had rushed into his head and almost out of his mouth when she talked about marrying another for love.

You're my wife and you'll stay my wife.

He didn't want a wife and he didn't want bairns. At least that's what he told himself. It made it easier than facing the truth.

Willow turned in her sleep, snuggling tight against him and slipping her one leg between his before resting her head on his chest. He wrapped her in his embrace and knew then and there that he didn't want to let her go. But where that crazy thought came from, he had no idea.

***

They entered the village on foot, mid-morning the next day. It was market day and the area was bustling with activity. People had traveled from other villages to sell their wares and to buy what they needed.

One of the men remained with the horses in the nearby woods. Slatter left her to walk with Walcott while he went on ahead alone to see if he could locate the man he was searching for. She helped Walcott with his purchases; ground wheat, a small crock of honey, and some cheese. She had taken over negotiating prices when he was about to pay too much for a crock of honey after grumbling in displeasure at the cost.

"Is your honey made of gold?" Willow had questioned the seller. "That price will not do."

They had bartered back and forth until she had been pleased with the price, and Walcott had smiled at her.

"I'll leave the haggling up to you," he had said after that.

With the coins they had saved, Walcott bought her a honey cake and cider and left her to sit on a small, barrel to enjoy the treats.

"I need to get these things to Millard for him to get packed on the horses before it's time to leave," he explained, his arms full. "Don't move off this barrel. I don't want to have to go in search of you. I'll be back right soon."

"I'll be waiting," Willow said, taking great pleasure in eating the honey cake.

She just finished the last of the cider when she spotted Slatter. She was about to call out to him when a woman sauntered over to him. She reached out to stroke his face, and his arm snagged around her waist and rushed her between two sellers' stalls and out of sight.

Willow didn't think, instinct had her getting up and hurrying to see what her husband was up to. Did this woman have information about the man he was searching for? Or was her husband's need for a woman about to be satisfied?

She stopped at the entrance to the narrow passage between two small buildings and peered down. Willow couldn't tell if Slatter was whispering in the woman's ear or nibbling at her neck. She had to contain her urge to confront him, since she didn't know if his behavior was necessary in his search for this mysterious man who had wronged him.

Willow decided to turn away and ask him later about it, when he his head turned toward her.

He stared at her, in shock or annoyance, she didn't know. Then a wicked smile spread slowly across his face, not his usual teasing smile, but a strange one, and it caused her to shiver.

"Willow?"

She jumped at her name being called out and turned shocked to see two of the Lord of Fire's warriors, Owen and Thad, the ones who had guarded Slatter when he was held prisoner, standing a few feet away. She was about to hurry toward them, not wanting them to see Slatter when someone shouted her husband's name.

"Slatter! You good for nothing whoremonger."

Owen and Thad turned and so did Willow.

Her husband stood on the opposite side from where she stood. She wondered how he had gotten there so fast, but she supposed he was as quick on his feet as he was with his mouth, since he had bragged to her about being able to escape most situations easily.

Slatter didn't hesitate. He landed a solid punch to the man's jaw who had called him a whoremonger, dropping him to the ground. He gave a sharp snap of his head to the left, warning Willow to go as Owen and Thad rushed at him.

She gave a brief thought that this could work in her favor. Once home, things could be sorted out, then she recalled Tarass, the Lord of Fire, and how stubborn and unmovable a man he was, and she knew it would never work. Tarass would return Slatter to his dungeon, and there was a good possibility he'd make her a widow.

Her choice was easy.

She ran forward to help her husband and just as she did, an arm snagged her around the waste and yanked her away.

Chapter Six

Willow struggled to break free only to be spun around to face the man who had snagged her. She silently admonished herself for not realizing that Tarass wouldn't only send two warriors to find Slatter. She was familiar with this warrior as well, Rhodes. He had come to her complaining of a rash when she had tended Slatter. However, she was not familiar with the three other warriors who rushed past them to join in the hunt for Slatter.

"You'll stay with me until this gets sorted out," Rhodes commanded.

She had little choice, since his hand moved to keep a good grip on her arm.

Chaos reigned with the warriors rushing through the market and it didn't take long to realize it was as if they were chasing a ghost. There was no sight of Slatter. He had disappeared.

"Find him!" Rhodes shouted when the warriors stopped and looked around confused, one scratching his head.

They scurried at Rhodes' command, spreading out throughout the market.

Willow hurried her steps to keep up with Rhodes as he rushed her past the market stalls to the front of the village, away from curious eyes and whispering tongues.

"What are you doing here?" Rhodes asked. "I thought you were visiting Sorrell."

She turned the question on him. "What brought you here?"

He responded as she expected he would, since most people respond to a question without thinking about it.

"Slatter escaped the group he had been handed over to and we've been sent to find him."

Willow noticed that Rhodes didn't mention that the group consisted of barbarians, but then the Lord of Fire often seemed a man of mystery to her, keeping things to himself.

"And you? Where is your escort?" Rhodes asked.

Willow turned her head casually from side to side. "They're somewhere around here."

"They leave you alone, unprotected?" Rhodes shook his head. "That is unacceptable. I will have a word with them."

He obviously didn't know that she had been abducted. Either William had never made it to the Macardle Clan or Rhodes and his men had left before the news of her abduction arrived. The problem now was what did she do?

Rhodes would soon discover she was not with Ruddock's warriors and would question what had happened to her. Did she speak the truth? Did she return home with Tarass's warriors? Did she have a choice?

She wouldn't tell Rhodes about Slatter. As odd as it seemed, she felt that if she mentioned anything about him, she would be betraying her husband. Besides, he had helped her escape Beck and she was grateful to him for that. She could return home and say nothing about her marriage to Slatter. No one would ever need know.

But *she* knew, and her sensible side warned that secrets don't stay secrets forever. The more people who knew your secret the better chance you had of it being revealed.

It wasn't long before all the warriors returned, and without Slatter.

"I don't know how he got away from us," Owen explained. "One minute he was there and the next minute he was gone. It was like chasing a ghost."

The other warriors nodded in agreement.

"Did you see any of Lord Ruddock's warriors?" Rhodes asked the men.

They all shook their heads while Owen said, "Not a one of them."

Rhodes looked to Willow. "As I said, you will stay with us until this gets sorted out."

Willow didn't expect to feel disappointed. She supposed it was because she expected a different ending to her situation with Slatter, one that was satisfying to them both. If she was her usual sensible self she would have realized from the beginning that would never be possible.

But nothing had seemed sensible since she'd been lowered in that hole with Slatter.

"We'll return you home to speak with your family and Lord Tarass," Rhodes said.

Willow stood her ground. "You need not do that. Lord Ruddock's warriors are probably chasing Slatter as we speak. I will wait their return."

"Then we will wait with you for their return," Rhodes said.

Willow didn't have to see his face to know that he didn't believe her, she heard it in his voice, and it annoyed her.

She folded her arms across her chest and spoke with firm authority. "As I said, you need not do that. You are not responsible for my safety. Take your leave. I have no need of your help."

"I cannot do that," Rhodes said, letting her know it wasn't negotiable. "We will wait and see you turned safely over to Northwick warriors."

Frustrated, Willow didn't know what to do. She looked to the woods where Walcott and the other men waited. Or had they left at the first sign of trouble? Had Slatter left with them? Had he left her behind?

Why does that matter? She scolded herself silently. Maybe Slatter felt she would be better off returned to her family. And didn't she want to go home? Funny, she should question that. With all that had gone on while visiting her sister, then the attack on the way home, and spending time with Slatter in that godawful hole, she felt more alive than she had in some time.

"We're camped over there," Rhodes said with a nod to the left.

Willow almost groaned when she saw the campsite. There had to be twelve or more of Tarass's warriors there. She was going home, whether she was ready to or not.

"We have drink and food," Rhodes said and stretched his arm out for her to precede him.

Willow walked as if she was being escorted to the gallows and admonished herself for thinking so dramatically. If it was Sorrell who faced this dilemma, she would already have fashioned an escape plan.

She picked up her pace as the other warriors walked past her, determined to find a way out of this and see to settling things with her husband before returning home.

One of the men in camp began waving frantically to Rhodes and pointing to a man, standing beside a horse.

Willow's stomach soured. She dreaded her thought, but it seemed the most logical. News had been received about her abduction.

She hastened her step again so that Rhodes would, and he did, rushing past her. With all the warriors congregated in one place, Willow took a chance, turned the other way, and took off running.

She prayed they wouldn't notice, at least long enough to give her a good start. She had only gained a short distance when Rhodes yelled out, ordering her to stop.

"Willow, stop!"

She paid him no heed. If she could get to the woods, she might have a chance, or so she tried to convince herself. As soon as she heard the thunderous beat of horses' hooves pounding the ground, she knew she didn't stand a chance.

"Willow!"

She turned recognizing the voice. It was Slatter and his horse was bearing down on her. She stopped and stood where she was and watched with amazement and shock as he leaned over the side of the horse, his arm extended out as he drew near to her.

She raised her arms, realizing what he intended, and in the next moment she was scooped up and deposited on her stomach to hang over the horse face down in front of him.

"Stay still," he said, his hand pressed against her back, and headed for the woods.

Once there he hurried her off the horse, depositing her on her feet, and pulling her into a tight hug that she welcomed. It was a relief to feel his arms snug around her, holding her like he never wanted to let her go and to feel how their bodies melded together as if fearing they'd be parted again.

"I thought I lost you," he whispered and brushed her lips with his before he eased her away from him when he wanted nothing more than to hold her close.

Her lips tingled and wanted more, but all she could do was stand there speechless. Had she heard him correctly? Had that been fear in his voice? Had he truly been worried that she had been lost to him? Had that also been her biggest worry all along… that she would never see him again?

"We have little time," he warned. "You will go with Walcott."

He didn't wait for her to respond. His hands went to her waist and with one quick lift, she was deposited behind Walcott already mounted on a horse.

"Hold on tight and I will see you soon," he said to her and gave her leg a squeeze, then looked to Walcott. "I'll lose them. You know where to take her."

Walcott nodded and took off before Willow could speak.

She held on tight to Walcott as he raced the horse through the woods while she sent silent prayers to the heavens to keep her husband safe.

It was dusk when they finally stopped and he sheltered the horse behind high bushes and hurried her into a small cave-like dwelling.

"No fire," he said, keeping his voice low. "We can't chance being found. We'll leave at first light and be home by dusk tomorrow."

"The others?" she asked.

"They left as soon as the chaos started."

Afraid to ask, but needing to know, she said, "Slatter?"

"Worry not about him. He'll lose the warriors and meet us, though he shouldn't have taken such a chance," Walcott grumbled, while sounding confident that Slatter wouldn't be caught. "Now rest. We have a long ride tomorrow."

***

Walcott had been right about the long ride. It had taken all day with a few brief stops until near dusk they had finally entered a village, if it could be called that. There were maybe two, habitable cottages and some hut-like structures worn from age and weather. There was no main structure, no longhouse, no place of leadership, and it struck Willow then that this was no clan. It was a group of people brought together by circumstance.

People hurried around Walcott as soon as he brought the horse to a stop.

"Where is Slatter?"

"Is he all right?"

"He wasn't caught was he?"

"Who is she?"

"Does she bring trouble?"

"Willow, here, is Slatter's wife," Walcott announced and everyone turned silent.

He dismounted and assisted Willow off the horse. She kept a pleasant smile on her face, but it wasn't returned. All they did was stare at her.

"Where is Slatter?" someone asked, breaking the silence.

"He will be here soon," Walcott assured them

"Does she bring harm?" another called out.

"She is his wife, and Slatter would expect you to welcome her and treat her well," Walcott said. "Now get some food and drink and bring it to his cottage. She is tired and hungry as am I."

The people began drifting off and mumbling among themselves.

"We don't have much, but we share what we do have," Walcott said and handed the reins of his horse to a young lad. "Follow me and you can settle yourself in Slatter's cottage."

Willow had been concerned for her clan with the approaching winter, but seeing this small group with few sturdy abodes and, what looked to be only one shed to store food and small at that, she couldn't help but think that they'd never survive.

It also made her wonder about Slatter and the small group of people. Were they people of misfortune or liars and thieves who had banded together? If so, where had they gotten the coin to ransom him?

"Here you are," Walcott said, stepping into the small cottage. "It's probably not what you're used to, but it'll keep you warm."

Willow glanced around, but stopped when she heard the door shut behind her. She didn't think Walcott liked her, or perhaps he was annoyed that circumstances had forced Slatter to wed her. Whatever the reason, it seemed the people here might agree with him. She continued to look around the room. A bed, the size two people would have to squeeze together to fit in, was pushed against one wall. A small table, with a jug and two tankards atop in the center and two chairs tucked beneath, sat close to the fireplace. A good-sized chest sat against the wall next to the door and higher up were a few pegs, though no garments hung from them.

She slipped off her cloak and hung it on one of the pegs, then went to the hearth to warm her hands. Now that she was here, her thoughts turned sensible. What did she hope to accomplish by staying with Slatter? She had seen him with another woman and all he had done was smile at her. And she had heard him called a whoremonger. Did that not warn her about what type of man he was? Had his fine features and charming tongue made her lose all rationale thought?

Yet he had sounded so sincere when he had told her that he had feared he'd lost her. Or was it a lie to benefit the situation? Did he have other plans for her, rather than helping her. Could he intend to benefit from her as Beck had planned to do?

The door opened without warning and Willow turned with a start.

A young woman entered and placed a bowl with half a loaf of bread and some cheese and a pitcher on the table. She blatantly glanced over Willow, shook her head, and walked out the door. Evidently, she was letting Willow know she didn't approve of Slatter's choice for a wife.

She pulled a chair out from the table and sat. The only thing she could do was talk with Slatter when he returned and see what he had to say, but would he speak the truth to her?

What if he had been caught by Tarass's men? What then? Would he tell them where she had been taken? Or would he fear what might happen to the people here?

She let out a sigh and shook her head. This was what happened when sound reason was ignored and for what... caring about a man she barely knew?

Caring about what happened to the man, not caring for the man himself, she quickly corrected herself. Or did she care for Slatter? Had she been as foolish as all the other women he had sweet talked and surrendered to his charming tongue and good looks?

What a mess she had gotten herself into. Her two sisters, if informed that she had lied to Tarass's men and had gone off with Slatter instead of returning home with them, would never believe it. She was far too practical of a woman to do something so foolish, and yet, she had.

She nibbled on the bread and cheese and after a few sips of cider drank no more, it being too sour for her taste. Several yawns and aching limbs reminded her how tired she was and she had always believed that a good night's sleep would bring brighter perspectives on any problems one had.

She stood with a stretch, slipped her tunic off to drape over the back of the chair, and rested her boots by the hearth so they would be warm when she wore them next. She climbed into bed, the mattress lumpy, though it was far more comfortable than standing in a hole in the ground all night, and pulled the wool blanket up around her.

Whispered prayers fell from her lips as they did every night and before she finished, she was fast asleep.

***

Slatter stood over the bed, looking at his sleeping wife. It was late, only a few hours from morning. He had ridden all day and night to get home, to make sure his wife was safe. He had lost Tarass's men easily, but he had wanted to make certain they couldn't follow his tracks before he headed home.

His heart had slammed in his chest when he had seen his wife with Tarass's warriors. Worse, he wasn't sure what she would do. Would she go with them? Would she turn him over to them? Or would she foolishly think that they could return with the warriors and he would be safe because she was his wife?

He had just been about to close in on the man he was searching for when he spotted Willow with the warrior, Rhodes. He had been one of the warriors who had turned him over to the barbarians. Then the man called him a whoremonger and all hell had broken loose.

His greatest fear had been for his wife. All he could think about was that he had to get to her. He had to keep her safe. He had to make sure no one took her from him.

When he had seen the warriors leave her side, he'd seen his chance and taken it and was relieved when he had seen Willow run for the woods, trying to escape them.

He was also relieved she was there safely tucked in his bed and he wasted no time in shedding his garments and joining her. The bed wasn't a good fit for two people, but that was an easy adjustment to make. He went to ease his wife on her side to wrap himself around her when she turned and snuggled against him.

"Slatter," she whispered, a warm breath fanning his neck as her head rested on his shoulder.

"Aye, *leannan*," he murmured and wrapped her in his arms, wondering if he had lost his mind caring for this woman, thinking she belonged to him, when he had no choice but to eventually let her go.

Chapter Seven

Slatter left the bed as soon as he woke the next morning, not trusting himself to remain there until his wife woke. He'd been with his fair share of women, had fun with them, cared about them for the brief time he'd spent with them, but never did one of them linger in his mind the way Willow did.

The strange part about it was that he had found her appealing when he had first met her. He had asked himself why ever since. She hadn't shown any interest in him at all. Her only focus had been his wound. He had tried to work his wiles on her, thinking perhaps he could get her to help him make another escape, a successful one this time. He had realized soon enough she was far too sensible a woman and would inform the guards of his action, which made him wonder why she had chosen to escape Tarass's warriors and stay with him?

She had wanted to go home, would have to return home eventually, so why delay it? Why not take the opportunity that had presented itself?

She'll have a rationale reason.

He smiled at the thought and closed the door quietly behind him as he stepped outside.

A light snow had fallen, dusting the land, and the gray skies hinted that more might follow. It would be a cold winter and he feared for the small group that had taken refuge together. It annoyed him that he had yet to settle his problem, but then it hadn't been as easy to solve as he had first thought it would be.

Walcott approached him and he could see by his sour expression that something was wrong. Though, if truth be told Walcott wore a sour expression more often than not.

"Tell me and be done with it," Slatter said when Walcott stopped in front of him.

"They think your wife brings harm."

"The men or the women?"

"Mostly the women," Walcott confessed.

"And what of you, Walcott, do you think she brings harm?"

Walcott stepped closer and kept his voice low. "Of course she does, how can you think otherwise after what happened at the market? Lord Ruddock will hunt us down when he finds out about this and now the Lord of Fire—God help us—will be after us. You should have let his warriors take her and be done with it."

"She's my wife, and don't tell me I shouldn't have wed her. You know as well as I do what fate she would have met if I had left her with Beck," Slatter said.

"I won't argue that, but you should have let her go with the Lord of Fire's warriors."

"And you think that would have stopped them from coming after me? Rhodes would have had her escorted home while he continued to hunt me."

"So you give him more of an excuse to hunt you? And need I remind you of Lord Ruddock again, and what about her clan? Don't you think they'll be hunting you as well? And I can see she steals your thoughts.

She brings trouble down on us. Let her go before it's too late."

"Or work whatever the trouble is to your advantage," the gruff voice said.

Slatter grinned and shook his head when he turned to see his longtime friend, Devin, approach. They'd been friends forever and if he trusted anyone the most it was Devin. He was a big, burly Scot with features so plain that they would never catch and steal a woman's heart, which was why everyone wondered how Devin snagged the sweet, tiny May as his wife.

Devin pulled Slatter into a hug and gave him a slap on the back, then looked to Walcott with a grin that spread from ear to ear. "I see you're still your usual smiling self."

Walcott shook his head. "When you're done taunting me, please talk some sense into him." He pointed to Slatter.

"First, what are you doing here?' Slatter asked.

"A visit to see how things go," Devin said.

"Not as I'd like," Slatter admitted.

"He has a wife," Walcott announced.

Devin's eyes almost popped out of his head. "Did you say wife?"

Walcott nodded. "I did. He wed one of the Macardle sisters."

Devin looked to Slatter. "With Sorrell wed to Lord Ruddock that leaves either Willow or Snow. Don't tell me you wed the blind one."

Walcott answered with a shake of his head.

"Willow then." Devin shrugged. "I heard she has become a good healer, following her mum's path, sensible too. But you know it can't work. Why ever did you wed her in the first place?"

"It was either that or let Beck keep her," Walcott said and went on to explain the whole ordeal to him.

"Naked, you say, in a hole in the ground with her?" Devin asked with a laugh. "However, do you get yourself into these things?"

"Fate hates me," Slatter said and Devin laughed harder. Walcott didn't crack a smile.

"Then my original advice holds. Use this unforeseen union to your advantage," Devin said.

"She is an innocent in this, I won't use her," Slatter said adamantly, leaving no room for negotiation.

"Then if she is no use to you, be rid of her, unless…" Devin let his unfinished remark hang in the air.

"What are you implying, Devin?" Slatter asked with a touch of annoyance.

Not averse to sharing his opinion, Devin said, "Maybe your wife means more to you than you want to admit."

"I barely know her," Slatter snapped.

"You were naked in a hole in the ground with her. I'd say you got to know her well enough," Devin said with a chuckle.

"I've had enough," Slatter said. "I will not discuss Willow with either of you."

"That's not an option, my friend, and you know it," Devin said. "This has to be resolved and quickly. You need to concentrate on finding him. This mess has gone on far too long."

"I almost had him," Slatter said and looked away, shaking his head, annoyed he had failed.

"Let's discuss it and see what might be done," Devin suggested.

"We've done everything and still he eludes me," Slatter argued.

The cottage door opened. "Have you tried setting a trap?"

The three men looked at Willow.

"You should have whispered—though I don't think any of you know how to do that—if you didn't want me to hear," she said.

A slight smile broke at the corners of Slatter's mouth at his wife's blunt remark and his eyes remained fixed on her. She looked refreshed after a good night's sleep, her cheeks a rosy color, her green eyes bright, and her dark red hair loosely plaited with a few wavy strands falling around her face. She was beautiful and she was his... for now.

Willow walked over to her husband relieved to see that he had made it here safely. When she woke and found herself alone, she feared something may have happened to him. It was when she caught a whiff of his scent on her that she realized he had been wrapped around her last night. She had hurried and dressed, eager to see him. That was when she had heard the men talking, and she had listened.

She smiled when Slatter stretched his hand out to her before she reached him. She took it and was immediately planted snug against him and tucked in the crook of his arm.

"Willow, this is Devin, a longtime friend," Slatter said.

"It is a pleasure to meet you," Devin said and gave a nod toward her.

"We must talk so I can learn more about my husband," Willow said and it wasn't lost on any of the men that she made it clear she was Slatter's wife, her intention.

"Devin is sworn to secrecy," Slatter said and chuckled, "unless you give him a pint or two."

Willow smiled and seeing the look the two men exchanged, she had no doubt Devin would keep Slatter's secrets. That Slatter had such a loyal friend was a good thing to know, since it told her that Slatter was just as loyal to Devin. Not something you would expect from a man known for his charming tongue and lies.

"Have you tried setting a trap?" Willow repeated, refusing to have her question ignored.

"It's difficult to set a trap for one so slippery," Walcott said.

"Then one must be as slippery as he is," Willow said.

"So how does one set a slippery trap?" Devin asked with curiosity.

"My wife doesn't need to be involved in this," Slatter said.

"Why not?" Willow turned her head to look at him. "It seems that this problem, for some reason, takes precedent over the problem of our unconventional marriage. Once it is settled, we can take the necessary steps to see our marriage absolved and to see you rewarded for saving me."

Slatter understood what she was saying. Once this was done, they could end their marriage and his reward would be freedom from punishment for his previous deeds. Had that been her thought when she attempted to escape Tarass's warriors?

"Tell us then, how do you trap a slippery good-for-nothing?" Devin asked.

"Be as slippery as he is," Willow said.

Walcott scratched his head. "What do you mean?"

"Enough," Slatter said. "Another word will not be discussed until I can talk with my wife privately."

"As long as we have a plan before I leave in two days," Devin said. "My wife, May, expects me home by then and I can't disappoint her or she'll come looking for me."

"I thought this was your home," Willow said, looking puzzled. "Where is your home?"

Devin appeared a bit flustered as he looked from Slatter to her, his mouth opened to speak but nothing coming out.

A piercing screech had them all turning to see a young lass, no more than eight years, crying and clutching her arm as several other children gathered around her. One ran ahead to pound on one of the cottage doors.

"Erna's hurt!" the young lad called out frantically.

The door swung open and the woman who had brought Willow food last night rushed to the lass, her face turning pure white when she looked at the wound.

Willow didn't hesitate, she rushed to the lass's aid.

Slatter followed along with Devin and Walcott.

"I'm sorry, Mum, I'm sorry," Erna cried. "I shouldn't have climbed the tree."

"Hush now, it's all right," her mum soothed, but the deep worry that wrinkled her brow showed otherwise.

"May I help?" Willow asked when she reached them.

"You'll stay away from my daughter," the woman ordered, stepping in front of Erna.

"I would rethink that decision, Roanna," Slatter said, coming to a stop behind his wife. "Willow is a wise healer and can help Erna."

"There is talk she will bring us harm," Roanna challenged.

"Do you truly believe I would wed a woman and bring her among us if I thought she would bring us harm?" he asked.

"If you loved her, aye, but you wed this one," — she nodded toward Willow— "to save her. That is no marriage. So how then do we trust her?"

"I trust her, Roanna. Isn't that enough?" Slatter asked.

"Mum, it hurts," Erna cried and had her mum turning to her. "I'm going to die just like Da." Tears rolled down the young lass's cheek while fear filled her wet, brown eyes.

"No. No, Erna," Roanna said, her own tears falling.

"But the same happened to Da's leg and he died," Erna cried, the hurtful memories running a tremble through her small body.

"Let me have a look and let's see what can be done," Willow said, stepping over to Erna.

This time Roanna didn't stop her.

A cracked bone was protruding slightly from her forearm. Willow had seen her mum mend such a wound, though it hadn't been easy, especially when fever had set in, but in the end the man had healed and still praised her mum's healing skills to this day. Willow only hoped she could do the same for the lass.

"I believe it can be mended," Willow said and she caught the doubtful looks on all those who stood around watching, Devin and Walcott included. She didn't know what her husband thought, since he stood behind her.

"I'd be most grateful for any help you can give my daughter," Roanna said, her tears still falling, which meant she didn't believe Willow either.

Willow turned her focus on Erna. "It's going to be painful since I must push the bone back into place, then I'll wrap your arm and you won't be able to move it for at least a full moon cycle or more, but I'll fashion a sling for you to help with that."

"What about fever?" Roanna asked.

"Time enough to worry about that if it happens. Right now I need to get that bone together and the wound covered, then Erna needs to rest," Willow said.

"Our cottage," Roanna said, slipping her arm around her daughter gently and leading the way.

"Anything I can do?" Slatter asked as his wife went to follow.

"No, but if I should need you, I will let you know," she said and hurried after Roanna.

"I could use a drink and we should talk," Devin said. "I brought ale and food with me. They're in the cart."

"Walcott, take some men and see to it," Slatter ordered and Walcott hurried off.

Slatter wanted to stay near in case Willow needed him, but the air was cold, nipping sharply at the face, and he expected more snow would fall before the day's end. His cottage wasn't far from Roanna's. He'd be able to reach Willow soon enough if she needed him, yet he was still reluctant to be away from her.

"You care for Willow," Devin said.

"Don't be foolish," Slatter snapped and headed to his cottage annoyed that Devin saw in him what others couldn't.

"I've never known you to care for any woman. Why her?" Devin asked, hanging his cloak on a peg and going to take a seat at the table. "And don't bother to deny it. I've never seen you reluctant to leave a woman's side. And there have been plenty who would have gladly have you remain with them. So, again, why Willow?"

"I don't know," Slatter said annoyed and joined his friend at the table. "I feel protective toward her and worry over her when she's not close to me." He shook his head. "I can't explain it or make sense of it."

"Damn, you're falling in love," Devin said with a grin so wide it looked like it would split his face in two.

"Don't be absurd. I barely know her."

"That means nothing, that you married her means something."

"I married her to save her," Slatter reminded.

Devin laughed. "You keep telling yourself that."

The door opened and Slatter hurried to stand, then sat when he saw it was Walcott.

"I figured you'd want this," Walcott said and placed a jug on the table.

"Good man, Walcott," Devin said and had two tankards filled with ale before Walcott closed the door behind him.

Slatter took a hefty swig as soon as he took the tankard from Devin. "Even if I did care for her, there's no point to it. Our marriage must end, she to return to her life and me to mine."

"Are you going to confide everything to her?"

"That's a good question and one I don't have the answer to yet."

***

"I can't thank you enough," Roanna said, looking from Willow to her daughter sleeping peacefully, her arm in a sling.

"She's a brave one. She suffered through the pain with courage and not a complaint," Willow said, having been impressed with the young lass's strength.

"She's like her da. He was a strong and brave one," Roanna said, a tear slipping from her eye. "She won't die, will she?"

Willow did her best to calm the woman's fear. "Fever is always a cause for concern, but we'll keep a watch and make sure she heals well."

"I'll do whatever you say," Roanna said. "As soon as I saw it, I thought death stalked her just like her da when he broke his leg. I couldn't bear losing my daughter like I did my husband. After he died, I couldn't keep up the farm on my own. My husband's brother came to help and not long after he found a woman for himself and kicked me and Erna out, saying the place was his. If Slatter hadn't found us half-starved and brought us here, I don't know what we would have done. It's been so difficult. I think that's why I got upset when hearing you were Slatter's wife. I think we all fear that you'll take him from us and we'll once again have nothing, no protection, no help, no family. And while we may not have much here, at least it's something."

"Mum," Erna called out softly and Roanna hurried to her.

She felt the lass' head and her sigh of relief let Willow know she'd felt no warmth.

"Thirsty," Erna said.

Willow went and got the chamomile brew she had made for Roanna to give her daughter and handed the tankard to the woman.

"Fetch me if needed," she said and left mum and daughter alone.

Snow was falling when Willow stepped out of the cottage. It had to have been falling for a while, since a fresh blanket of snow covered nearly everything. She looked around as she stepped away from the door. She saw a man missing the lower half of his left leg and using a sturdy branch limb to get around. A woman whose neck showed signs of what was left of a severe burn ran after two small bairns who laughed with glee. And an old woman who could barely shuffle along on her feet, held tight to a young lad of about twelve years who held her arm and helped her along with a smile.

Had Slatter provided a home for those who found themselves unable to provide for themselves? Had he no home as well? But what of Devin? He was a longtime friend of Slatter's, which meant they had to have reached maturity together, yet he didn't make his home here.

"You shouldn't be out in the cold and snow."

Willow jumped and when she turned, she found herself in her husband's arms, a place she found herself enjoying more and more.

"I was just headed to your cottage," she said. "All is well with Erna so far and I pray it stays that way."

"Let's get you inside, I have a question to ask of you." With his arm firm around her, he headed to his cottage."

"I have one myself," she said, though didn't wait until they reached the cottage. "What were you doing sneaking off with a woman at the market and kissing her?"

Chapter Eight

"You saw me kissing someone?" Slatter asked once they entered the cottage.

Willow almost missed the peg she went to hang her cloak on. "Don't tell me you don't remember the woman. She certainly looked no stranger to you. And you looked straight at me and smiled. I almost got the feeling you wouldn't mind if I joined you both." She wrinkled her nose at the thought. "It was shortly after that that a man called you a whoremonger and I couldn't believe how fast you got to the other side of the market." Her brow knitted as she tilted her head in question. "How did you get to the other side so fast?"

Slatter didn't answer, instead he turned a question on her. "Why didn't you go with Tarass's warriors? They would have taken you where you want to go... home."

"Why did you return for me? Why not let me go and be done with me?" she shot back.

"I suppose I'm not done with you." Slatter looked as startled as she did by his response and hurried to explain. "I can't just have you return home without finding out how we can absolve our vows and be husband and wife no more."

His explanation made perfect sense, or so he told himself. He'd never questioned or needed to convince himself of his decisions until he'd met Willow, and the thought rankled him.

"What of you? What brought you back to me?" he asked and saw her shiver. He turned a chair toward the hearth and took hold of her arm and hurried her to sit. "You need to get warm."

Your arms would keep me warm. She kept her lips tightly sealed afraid her thought would voice itself. Instead, she hugged herself, rubbing her arms and thinking on what an impact Slatter had made on her life in only a few days. It was sheer foolishness for her to be having such intimate thoughts about him.

When he brought the other chair to place beside her and sat, she knew he would pursue an answer from her.

She didn't delay her response. "Like you, I believed there were things that needed to be settled between us before I could safely return home."

"Of course, it would be difficult to return home with the likes of me as your husband."

"It wouldn't be practical to return without knowing what we faced first," she corrected. "And with Rhodes on the hunt for you, I'd say you'd be facing a return to Tarass's dungeon, and if there is no way out of our marriage, Tarass may find it more prudent to make me a widow, thus eliminating the problem. Now that that is settled, please answer my original question about the woman you were kissing."

"There is no easy explanation to that," Slatter said, focusing on the flames as he stretched his long legs out to them.

"We have nothing but time at the moment," Willow said.

A knock interrupted them and Slatter went to the door and opened it.

The lad Willow had seen walking with the old woman stood there.

"Sorry to disturb you, Slatter, but my *seanmhair* isn't feeling well and I thought your wife, our healer, might be able to help her."

Willow was impressed by the lad. He had not only shown Slatter respect by referring to her as Slatter's wife, but he had also expressed acceptance of her by referring to her as *our healer*. He was a wise lad for his young years.

She joined her husband at the door. "I'd be only too glad to tend your grandmother."

"I'd be most grateful," the lad said with a bob of his head.

"Does Corliss know you're fetching the healer for her, Crofton?" Slatter asked, crossing his arms over his chest.

Crofton shifted his eyes to Willow. "My *seanmhair* can be stubborn, but I know when she doesn't feel well."

"Of course you do," Willow said and grabbed her cloak off the peg. She smiled sweetly and hurried her words out when Slatter went to speak. "We'll continue our talk when I return."

Slatter grabbed his cloak from the peg as well, letting her know she wouldn't be going without him.

The snowflakes were big and falling fast, covering everything. Winter had a few weeks before it officially arrived and this early snow warned of a possible harsh winter. Willow couldn't help but think that some of the structures here would not survive such unforgiving weather. But what could be done? Her mind started working on possibilities.

"*Seanmhair*, I brought the healer," Crofton announced when he stepped into the cottage.

The old woman turned from the hearth where she'd been stirring something in a pot that hung over the flames and wagged a crooked finger at Crofton. "You should not have done that. I told you I am fine."

"Sit, *Seanmhair*," Crofton said gently, going to his grandmother and helping her to a chair. "I will see to the cooking."

Willow smiled softly. "The cold brings the aches to your bones, doesn't it?"

The old woman grinned and nodded. "A wise healer. It has been too long since I have met one." She looked to Slatter standing in front of the closed door. "You did well. She will make a good and kind wife."

Aye, she would, he thought, *but not to me... some other man*. Anger pierced him as sharply as the blade of a sword and he wanted to roar with fury. He got angrier over his reaction. What did it matter? She meant nothing to him. She had tended him gently and with kindness once and now he returned the favor, keeping her safe. It was nothing more than that.

Willow turned to her husband. "Why don't you and Crofton wait outside while I see to his grandmother."

Crofton was shaking his head, ready to object.

"Come, lad, we leave the women to themselves," Slatter said in a tone that was meant to be obeyed, and Crofton obeyed, although reluctantly.

Corliss smiled as the door closed behind Crofton. "My grandson worries over me. I know he fears me dying and I pray I can last until he is a grown man and has found love. My passing would be less difficult if he had someone who loved him. We only have each other now. His mum, da, and sister lost to an illness that claimed all but five in the clan. I had been too weak to leave with the other three and though I urged Crofton to go with them, he wouldn't leave me. Slatter came upon us and brought us here. It is a good man you wed."

Willow was beginning to believe that, but it was hard to reconcile this good man with the man who had been called a whoremonger, a thief, and a liar.

"Have you tried a heather brew for your aching bones?" Willow asked.

"No, I haven't, though I do recall my mum rubbing *'the ache',* as she called it, from her limbs with ash leaves."

"An ash bark poultice would work better," Willow said. "I will teach Crofton how to prepare it."

Corliss shook her head, her wrinkled-framed eyes filled with sadness. "A young lad doesn't need to be tending his granny."

Willow reached out and rested her hand over the old woman's. "Let him do this for you. It will help him worry less about you."

Corliss smiled. "You are a wise healer. You were taught well."

"My mum," Willow said with pride, realizing for the first time just how much her mum had taught her. She recalled her mum telling her that it wasn't always the illness, the wound, or the injury that needed to be treated. And sometimes it wasn't only the ill person in the family that needed tending. "I'll fix you a heather brew and hopefully that will ease your aches some."

Willow got busy preparing the brew while she continued to talk with Corliss.

***

Crofton stood quiet, staring at the cottage door.

"Women get lost in talk," Slatter said, seeing the concern on the lad's face. He'd been impressed with Crofton since he had found him and his grandmother alone in a village that had been ravaged by illness. His grandmother had insisted Crofton go with him, but the lad refused to leave her and Slatter had no intentions of leaving the old woman behind. The lad looked after his grandmother without a word of complaint. Slatter actually thought it was the old woman who had more to complain about, not that she did, since her grandson was forever on her to be careful, not to do this or that. But she just smiled at him and nodded at his loving orders and did as she wished.

"I don't mean to be ungrateful, Slatter," Crofton said a bit of a tremor to his voice, "but you did say you would be moving all of us to a safer and permanent home. Will that be soon? I fear our small cottage will not do well in a winter storm."

"I agree with the lad," Devin said, joining the two. "It's time for you to leave here, time for you to return home, where it is safe."

The door opened and Crofton hurried to Willow, concern drawing his brow together in deep lines for one so young.

"Your grandmother does well and I'm going to show you how to prepare a poultice to help ease her aches." After Crofton entered the cottage, a smile of relief chasing his worry lines, Willow looked to her husband. "You need not wait. I will be a while. I will see you at the cottage."

Slatter nodded and stood there a few moments after the door closed.

"My wife tells me she saw me kissing a woman in the market before chaos broke loose," Slatter said.

"He slipped through your fingers again. He's as good at vanishing as you are. This has gone on far too long. You've come close to losing your life because of him and almost losing your freedom. And damn Beck for getting hold of you before we reached you. This devil-in-disguise has to be found and made to pay for what he's done. This has to end."

"I've noticed that this foe of mine vanishes for extended periods of time only to surface and create havoc again. I wonder if he does this of his own accord or if he has no choice and must return somewhere? Then when he gets anxious to play his little games again, he surfaces."

"You need to make your wife aware of this," Devin advised.

"I have little choice after what she saw."

"It is better she knows what goes on, keeping her ignorant could harm her. Besides, once you return her home, this evil-doer could show up at her door and claim her as his wife."

***

Slatter sat staring at the flames in the fireplace after Devin left. He could not get his friend's words out of his head. If this man, so intent on making it appear Slatter an evil scoundrel, discovered he had wed, what evil deed would he attempt with Willow? Anger surged in him at the possibilities and made him all the more determined to keep her safe and by his side until the culprit was caught.

The door creaked open and he turned to see his wife enter the cottage. He did what seemed natural and stretched his hand out to her.

She responded as if out of habit. She went to him and his hand closed possessively around hers. He gave a tug to land her on his thigh, his arm going around her waist to keep her steady.

"All goes well?" he asked.

"It does and Crofton has calmed, knowing there is something he can finally do to help his *seanmhair*," she said, her thoughts not on their words but how easily she had responded to him. She rubbed at the deep wrinkles that worried his brow. "Something troubles you?"

Her gentle touch was meant to soothe, but instead it aroused him, but then he had been finding, since their time together, that he aroused easily around her. He found her attractive, so why wouldn't he grow aroused? Yet there was something different about her and he couldn't quite reason what it was.

He hadn't realized his eyes held hers and silence had grown heavy between them, not to mention the passion that sparked around them. It was easy to sense, to see, though difficult to ignore. He'd be in trouble if he wasn't careful. He was relieved, or was it regret he felt, when she hurried off his leg and went to stand at the end of the fireplace, the farthest distance from him.

Willow struggled to temper her feelings for her husband. She worried that he had awakened her passion when they had been in the hole in the ground together and now she was having a difficult time controlling it when too close to him. She had to quash her feelings, since if she surrendered to him, consummated their vows, they would be stuck together forever. And Slatter was still a stranger to her.

"You never explained about the woman you were kissing in the marketplace," she said, a change of subject the best way to divert her rousing thoughts.

"We should talk. There are things you need to know," Slatter said, glad for the diversion. He'd been close to kissing her and with how fast he had gotten aroused, he feared it wouldn't have ended with a kiss and he could see in her passion-filled eyes she felt the same.

He pointed to the other chair, not trusting himself to step near her.

Willow hurried to sit across from her husband as he turned his chair around to face the table and waited eagerly, though somewhat apprehensively, to hear what he had to say.

"That wasn't me you saw kissing that woman."

Willow shook her head, not expecting a denial. "My eyes did not deceive me. It was you I saw."

"I'm sure you believe that, but I'm telling you it wasn't me." Slatter raised his hand when she went to protest again. "Let me explain." Her silence let him continue. "It started about two years ago, though I wasn't aware of it then. It wasn't until a man accosted me and accused me of fornicating with his wife. I had no idea what he was talking about, since I refuse to bed married women. I was also accused of stealing and lying in a particular situation I had no knowledge of. It took time, but I discovered that someone had claimed my name and was passing himself off as me."

"There is someone you believe resembles you?" she asked startled by the revelation.

"Your encounter with him proves that, since as I said, it wasn't me you saw kissing that woman."

Her brow scrunched.

"You wonder if you should believe me."

"Of course I do since you're known to lie easily." She bit at her lip, wishing she could take back her remark.

"I see it dawns on you that perhaps it isn't me who lies."

Willow voiced her concern. "How do I know if this is truth or tale you tell? It could be nothing more than an excuse to vindicate you of your poor deeds."

That had been the problem all along. How did anyone believe him when the person claiming to be him lied with ease and apparently without guilt? Why when so many believed him a liar, should anyone believe his story?

"And how is it that there is someone out there that resembles you with such exact detail that I had mistaken him for you?"

"I don't know who he is or how it is that he resembles me or why he does what he does," Slatter admitted. "It is a puzzle and one that has many missing pieces."

She narrowed her eyes as she gave thought to his strange explanation. "Why didn't you explain this when you were caught, accused, and imprisoned?"

"I tried that once and it didn't go well. It was then I realized that unless I caught this culprit and made my innocence known, I would continue to suffer from his misdeeds. And the only way to do that was to pretend to be him, when the occasion called for it, and find out what I could about him, in hopes it would lead me to him."

He could see that she wasn't sure if she should believe him and that troubled him, though he couldn't blame her. It sounded a poor excuse to his ears as well. He didn't like that she doubted his word. He wanted her trust. He'd believed he had it when they had been snug in the hole together, but she had had little choice then.

"You could have said something to me when I tended your wound."

"You would have believed me, after I had attempted an escape?"

"I suppose if you speak the truth, that you are innocent, yet made to suffer punishment for another's misdeeds, it would be a good reason to attempt an escape."

He wanted to wipe her doubt away, return that small bit of trust she had had for him, but mostly he wanted to kiss her. And that would help nothing. She would think he wanted to charm her into believing him when all he wanted was another taste of her lips. That, in itself, was a dangerous thought as was prolonging her time with him. But what choice had he?

Devin had been right about the danger to her now. If he returned Willow home before this problem was solved, how could he be sure this culprit wouldn't show up on her doorstep and claim her as his wife? How long would it take her to realize the difference? Or would she?

"It is good you see reason," Slatter said, "since it isn't only solving the problem of our unexpected marriage that needs to be settled that keeps us together. We also need to remain together until I capture this culprit and lay this problem to rest."

"Why would that be?" she asked, wondering how it could possibly matter.

"What if for some reason you arrived home before our marriage was disavowed and I claimed you were my wife and that you would stay my wife? And what if it wasn't me, but the man you saw at the market? Would you be able to tell the difference?"

"You make a good point, a worrisome point," she admitted. "Still, how do I trust that you speak the truth to me?"

The old woman's voice sounded in her head. *It is a good man you married.*

She had begun to believe that, had seen it for herself with the people that Slatter had gathered here, by the way he had helped her when he could have walked away and left her to Beck's greed. Then there was the way she felt in his arms, that she belonged there. Or how his lips had brought hers alive, or the way her body had responded to his gentle, intimate touch. She felt something for this man whether she wanted to admit it or not.

And she wasn't ready to admit anything, not with her recent, unexpected thoughts. A new voice had chimed in, a devilish one, tempting her to do things she would have never considered even giving thought to. So how then did she see reason in this situation?

"How long do you think this will take?" she asked, worried that too much time spent with him could prove far too challenging. If she responded so easily to his offered hand, how would she respond if he kissed her again?

"It is difficult to tell."

"My family will be worried, more so when news of the market incident reaches them. And a message will not suffice, since they will think it comes from you. And what of Tarass? He will continue to search for you. We will be hunted as we hunt your culprit."

"Regret not going with Tarass's warriors when you had the chance?" Slatter asked, it sounding that way to him.

"No, I don't regret it."

That she didn't hesitate in her response brought a slight smile to his face.

"I would suggest you make sure that I don't regret it or regret joining you on your quest to find this culprit and clear you of the harm he has done you. And also to make sure our marriage is absolved so that we both may go our separate ways."

Her last few words wiped the smile from his face. It was inevitable they part, and yet, the thought disturbed him, which troubled him even more. Why should it matter? She would never fit into his life, and she would never want to.

Chapter Nine

Willow stretched herself awake and wasn't surprised to find herself alone in bed. A sniff of the spot beside her, a bold woodsy scent, told her that her husband had joined her some time during the night. It was better that way, the narrow bed forcing them to sleep wrapped around each other, leaving them open to temptation.

So she would be less likely to fall sway to temptation, she had slept fully dressed last night, the cold making it an easy excuse to do so. But there was no excuse to lie abed any longer. She wanted to check on Erna and Corliss and see how both were doing, though she imagined if there were any problems she would have been summoned by now. She hoped it would remain that way.

The evening had proved a bit fruitful, she, Slatter, and Devin discussing what might be done to catch the culprit that was causing her husband a multitude of problems. No conclusion had been reached, but ideas were brewing and she believed it wouldn't be long before they formed a plan.

She straightened her garments, but couldn't rid herself of all the wrinkles, then freed her hair of the braid and ran her fingers through it repeatedly. The braid had left her hair to wave more than it usually did, and she raked her fingers through it one last time, pulling it away from her face to fall along the sides.

With her cape thrown over her shoulders, she headed out the door to almost collide with Crofton.

"Is Corliss all right?" Willow was quick to ask and his wide smile was answer enough.

"She does well today, less aches, and her walk more confident. I make certain she drinks the brew and I'll apply another poultice to her knees later today," he said, proudly and held up a small sack. "Food, not much, but Slatter told me to make sure you got something to eat. He and Devin left early to hunt. Hopefully, we will all feast later. And hopefully, we leave here soon. Slatter promised he would move us from here to a far better place, a permanent home."

"Where is this place?" Willow asked, wondering over it since her husband had made no mention of it to her.

Crofton shrugged. "I don't know, but Slatter is a man of his word. He'll take us there and we'll be safe." He handed the sack to Willow. "Visit with my s*eanmhair* today and see how well she does."

"I will," Willow assured him, knowing he was seeking reassurance that his grandmother actually did do well.

Not hungry, she left the sack on the table and after turning from closing the door saw her husband and Devin rush out of the woods that surrounded the small area, not a fresh kill in sight. They both stopped and spoke to several people who quickly rushed off, a look of fright on their faces. Something was wrong and when she saw how pale Crofton turned after speaking with Slatter, she knew something was seriously wrong.

Willow hurried to her husband and when he spotted her, he rushed to make his way to her.

"We leave here now. Rhodes and his men head this way."

"Are they close?" she asked, her heart pounding with fright in her chest.

"A day at least." He shook his head. "There's no time for talk, we must go. Gather what blankets and clothing there is in the cottage, and any food."

"Corliss nor Erna can walk," she reminded.

"Devin has a cart. They can ride in that. Do what you must to make them comfortable in it, but hurry, there is no time to waste."

"Tarass's warriors are well-trained. They will pick up our trail."

"Aye, they will, and that's why you and I will be taking a different trail."

There was no time for questions. They would come later and so Willow hurried and did as her husband asked.

Roanna was upset at the prospect of moving her daughter and Crofton was worried for his grandmother. Willow did her best to reassure both that Erna and Corliss would do fine and the two seemed to settle until they learned she wasn't going with them.

"What if fever rages in my daughter?"

What if my grandmother's pain worsens?"

"Enough worry," Slatter said, approaching the complaining pair. "Willow has instructed you in the care of Erna and Corliss. You both will do well and it won't be long before we join you again. Be grateful that you finally go to a permanent home."

Crofton and Roanna were quick to offer their appreciation for his generosity and Willow went with them to see that Erna and Corliss were settled, along with Pell, the man missing part of his one leg, in the cart.

Willow waited by Slatter's horse when all was done. She watched her husband talk with Walcott. The man paid heed to his every word, gave a nod, and went to the front of the small ragtag group and led them away from the worn and battered shelters that had been their home.

Devin walked beside Slatter, talking as the two men approached her.

"You know what to do. I will see you soon," Slatter said when he came to a stop near his wife.

Devin reached out and hugged Slatter, giving him a firm slap or two on the back. "Return home safe."

"I always do," Slatter said with a confident smile.

"That you do," Devin said and turned a nod on Willow. "But you've got a wife to worry about now, so remember that. And don't do anything foolish."

"I won't let him," Willow said, the words slipping out and wondering where they came from. She truly had no say over him, just as he had no say over her.

Devin laughed. "I've never known a woman who could bend the will of this one." He turned a nod on Slatter this time. "But you just might be different."

"It's women who submit to me, not me to them," Slatter boasted with a smile. "Now go, we both need to be on our way."

"I'll see you soon and I'll have your word on that," Devin said.

"You have it. Now go and stay safe."

As soon as Devin turned and hurried to join the others, Slatter scooped Willow up and deposited her on the horse and was up behind her in an instant. She'd never seen anyone as quick in movement as him or so confident in all he did. He never seemed to falter in decision or action.

They hadn't gone far when she asked, "Where do we go?"

"Away from the others so we don't bring them harm," he said, his arms snug around her as he led the horse through the woods, no obvious path to follow.

"This will delay your search for that man who causes you grief," she said, his dark eyes more intense than she had ever seen them. They seemed to take in his surrounding without shifting his glance and that he was highly alert she felt in his taut body that he kept her cradled against.

"He's not going anywhere and I've no doubt he'll make himself known before long. Right now, it is more important to keep you safe as well as those people who have come to depend on me."

"How did that come about?" she asked, taking advantage of this time alone with him to find out more about him, since he still, in some ways, was a stranger to her.

"They needed help," he said, his eyes remaining steady on his surroundings. "Like you when you were lowered down into the hole to join me. You were in need of help."

So he thought of her no differently than all the others in that conclave of needy people? He rescued her like he had the others. Had she been foolish enough to expect something different?

He had no interest in marriage, no interest in having bairns, no interest in love. She had to remember that or she just might find herself suffering the pain of caring for the wrong man.

She stiffened her resolve to keep her thoughts and actions sensible. She needed to think things through, not jump at impulses that would only complicate their situation.

"I hope to repay you for all the help you have given me."

"That's not necessary, you're my wife."

His annoyed response surprised her as did his reminder that they were wed, as if somehow that changed things.

"Perhaps, but I will not stand by and see you imprisoned again by the Lord of Fire or given to barbarians."

"Worry not, that won't happen."

He sounded far too confident and she had to ask, "How can you be so sure?"

"I told you, *leannan*," he said with that cock-sure grin. "There isn't any place or anyone that can hold me, or any place or one I can't escape."

Even marriage to me. Willow was foolish to allow the thought to hurt her, but it did. She would remember that, remember that this marriage of theirs was temporary, that it would eventually end. She would go home and life would return to the way it had been.

A thought struck and she asked, "If you can escape from anywhere, why didn't you escape the hole in the ground?"

He hesitated and kept his eyes on the path ahead.

His silence made her realize something. "You were going to escape, weren't you? My arrival stopped you."

His eyes met hers then and he made sure to keep her from seeing his shock. She was far more observant than he had thought. He definitely had to keep that in mind going forward. "I wasn't quite sure of success, which is what caused me to delay my plans."

"Now you lie," she accused. "You don't strike me as a man who doubts his skills."

"Believe what you will. I will not debate the matter with you."

She could tell by his stern tone that she would get nothing more from him on the matter. It made no difference to her, since she had gotten what she wanted. He had remained in the godawful hole with her purposely and his gallantry touched her heart.

"Where are we going?" she asked, seeking a more neutral discussion.

That she didn't pursue the matter gave him pause and made him wonder why, since she could be tenacious when she wanted to be. But he let it go and answered, "We're taking a bit longer way home."

"Don't you worry that Rhodes will pick up our trail?"

"I'll make certain he doesn't."

His confidence far surpassed hers and so she reminded, "But he picked up your trail from the last time."

"He never found *my* trail. He heads in the direction of where we just left, but that doesn't mean he will reach the now deserted place. If he does, he will follow the obvious trail, the one the group left, and when or if he comes across the group, they will give no indication I was ever part of them."

"What if his tracker picks up our trail?"

"Not possible. Devin will see that our tracks are covered."

"But you said we would travel a different trail so as not to bring harm to anyone, as if we were leading them away from the others," she said, feeling he talked in circles.

"Aye, I did. If we remained with the group and were caught, what might the consequences be?"

"I'm sure Rhodes wouldn't harm them. They are a harmless lot," Willow said.

"So it would appear under the circumstances, but change those circumstances and what happens?" He continued, not expecting a response. "When forced into certain situations, we do what we must to survive and to protect those we love."

Willow thought of her and her sisters' situation when their da had taken ill and their mum had died. Life had changed rapidly and they had had to adapt. Sorrell had to do the same when she had discovered her husband was a far different man than she had believed.

Slatter kept his focus on the road as he spoke. "Corliss is old and her bones protest more often than not, but nothing stopped her from protecting her grandson when a lone man tried to do him harm. She smashed his head with a rock and continued to do so until there was no breath left in him. She knew if she didn't, they both would die. Corliss did what she had to do to keep them both safe."

"I would have never thought she had the strength."

"Strength often comes when needed. Roanna found her strength when her brother-in-law told her either she or her daughter would warm his bed or he would put them out of their own home. She knew even if she submitted to him that he would eventually have her daughter as well. She chose to leave and face the unknown. It took courage to do that."

"She told me differently," Willow said, imagining how horrible the situation must have been for the woman.

"She thought it better to keep the truth to herself. Her brother-in-law is a respected man and she doubted anyone would have believed her. Then there's you," he said, a teasing smile surfacing. "You were the most challenging to rescue."

"Was it me who was a challenge or the situation?" Willow asked with a lift of her chin.

"A bit of both, I believe, but I'm not one to give up easily."

"And obviously you're a man with a kind heart."

His smile vanished in a flash. "Remember as with Corliss and Roanna, things are rarely what they appear to be." A teasing sparkle in her green eyes and a slight smile pushing at the corners of her mouth, returned his smile. "Do you have a sensible response to that?"

Her smile broke free. "Only that while Corliss and Roanna have secrets, you're charming, though often less-than-honest tongue is not a well-kept secret."

"Perhaps it's a ruse for a much darker secret," he whispered as if hinting otherwise.

She turned a puzzling look on him. "That would make sense of why there are two sides to you; a man with a kind heart and a man with a misleading tongue. Now I'm intrigued to solve this mystery."

Slatter laughed. "I'm no mystery. Who you see is who I am."

What Willow saw, though mostly heard, was that his usual lightheartedness was missing from his laughter. It gave her pause to think a moment. Could it be possible? Did Slatter keep a secret? And if so, what was that secret he guarded with laughter so that people would not give thought to it, brush it away, ignore it.

"Then I will have to look closer at you," Willow teased with a smile that dripped with sweetness.

"I'm right here for you to see, wife, look as closely as you like," he said and wished he could retrieve his words. Her smile and tone might appear sweet, but there was a determination to them that warned this was no teasing matter. She had set her mind to it, a pragmatic mind at that, and she would now look more closely at him. But she would see only what he let her see. Or would she see what others didn't?

Silence followed after that, Willow's thoughts weighing heavily upon her until she found her head bobbing with the weight of them. Having grown accustomed to resting her head on Slatter's shoulder or chest when she slept, instinct had her lowering her head to his chest.

Slatter adjusted his wife in his arms as her body grew limp with sleep. It was strange how easily he had grown accustomed to sharing a bed with her to the point where he looked forward to it. Of course, sleep wasn't the only thing on his mind when he'd join her in bed. That he wanted to make love to her had his loins aching more than they ever had. But he could be wise when wisdom was called for, though it was getting more difficult to remain wise when his wife snuggled so close that she roused his manhood throughout the night. And forget the morning when he woke with an aching need for her that had him rushing out of bed to avoid surrendering to it.

She was his wife and he had a right to couple with her, but that would make an already difficult situation worse. As much as he enjoyed her company, sleeping with her, holding her, sneaking a kiss now and then, sharing his life with her was out of the question. He had to return her home to her family.

His chin shot up and his thoughts vanished in an instant upon hearing a sound. He listened again and was relieved to realize it was an animal in the forest. He had learned at a young age to distinguish sounds. Lander had taught him well. He had taught him most everything he knew.

He had always thought of Lander as his father, called him da for as long as he could remember, not that he and his mum ever wed, though they had been like a married couple and more loving than any married couple Lander had known. Lander had been at a loss when Blair, Slatter's mum, died three years ago and it wasn't but a year later that he died as well. He had claimed his heart had been too broken to live without her. His mum had told him that she knew when she had first laid eyes on Lander that she loved him and Lander had said the same about Blair. They had been inseparable. Slatter missed them both and he better understood how they felt about each other since meeting Willow.

He couldn't say he had loved her at first sight, though it might be that he didn't want to admit it to himself since he had to let her go. She had told him that he couldn't give her what she wanted most... love.

He couldn't help think that that might be the easiest thing he could give her.

***

They stopped to rest and eat a short time after midday. The skies were overcast and the air more than chilled. Willow wished she had a hot brew to warm her insides, but was grateful for the food they did have.

"The scratches on your face heal well," Slatter said, handing Willow another piece of bread.

"As do the others since I've been applying what bit of honey I have left."

"I'm glad they heal well for you, not that even the slightest scar can distract from your beauty."

She smiled, shaking her head at him. "Compliments roll off your tongue so easily."

"The truth rolls off my tongue easily," he said with a smile of his own and a slight tilt of his head.

"I would think lies roll off with greater ease."

Slatter's grin grew. "Lies take greater care to tell. They must convince and be kept to memory so that one does not get caught in it at another time. To be a successful liar takes skill that few if any master."

"And are you a master liar?"

"I am a master at everything, *leannan*," he said and leaned in and kissed her quick on the lips.

"You respond without responding," she said, his light kiss sending flutters through her stomach. "I would say you are skillful at manipulating as well."

"You are getting to know me well," Slatter said, trying not to let his smile falter with the lie he had just told.

This time Willow leaned in close and brushed her lips softly against his before saying, "I'm getting to know you far better than you realize."

Her words disturbed him while her not-so-innocent kiss aroused him. He got the overwhelming feeling that she had seen past his lie.

"We need to get going," he said, stuffing the remaining food in the cloth sack and rushing to his feet. He hooked the sack to the saddle and turned to Willow.

Her eyes lit with concern when she saw how his brow had narrowed and his dark eyes turned on her with an intensity that sent a shiver through her.

She was getting to her feet when he reached her and yanked her up by the arm the rest of the way.

"You will stay behind me, say nothing, and do nothing that will put you in danger, and on this you will obey me, wife."

She barely had time to nod when he continued.

He lowered his head and his voice to a whisper. "There are three of them. I will see to them and again you will hold your tongue and do nothing."

"Is she yours or can we share?" a man called out.

Willow held herself with courage, but took a step closer to her husband when she saw the size of the one man who walked in front of the other two who approached. He was big, not in height, but in girth, barrel chest and arms that looked as if he could easily crush a man. The other two were slim compared to him, though all three seemed to wear similar grime on their garments and skin.

"I warn you now. Take your leave or suffer the consequences," Slatter said with that cock-sure confidence of his.

The three men laughed.

"Three of us and one of you." The big man laughed. "I don't think it'll be us suffering the consequences. But don't worry, we'll let you watch as we enjoy the woman before we kill you."

Willow shivered against her husband as the three laughed heartily.

His arm tightened around her as he whispered, "Trust me, I won't let them hurt you."

She recalled the last time he had told her to trust him and he had kept his word, while it didn't seem possible he could keep his word this time, something inside her told her he would.

"I trust you," she murmured and watched as the large man rushed at them.

Chapter Ten

One minute Slatter was beside her and the next he was gone. Willow stood frozen barely able to comprehend what was happening. She hadn't even seen her husband reach for his dagger in a sheath tucked somewhere she hadn't noticed at his waist. She only saw the hilt protruding from the one man's throat, his eyes wide as he dropped to the ground dead. Slatter's arm hooked the big man around the neck as he grabbed the fellow's dagger sheathed at his waist and flung it, lodging it in the other slim man's throat. His eyes turned wide and his hands rushed to his neck but never reached it. He toppled over dead.

"Your time has come," Slatter said.

Willow thought it odd that the man's eyes bulged from his head as if at that precise moment he somehow recognized Slatter.

"Mercy, Sla—"

Willow stared in disbelief as Slatter snapped the big man's neck with ease and let him drop to the ground. She continued to stare at him as he went and retrieved his dagger from the one man's throat and wiped it clean of the blood on the man's garment before wiping it clean again on the grass. He retrieved the other dagger as well, cleaning the blade in the same fashion.

Willow was speechless when he stopped in front of her.

He reached his hand out, his arm resting against her chest as his hand closed gently at her throat, his fingers stroking the side of her neck. His hand was warm, his touch tender, and she couldn't believe that only moments before that same hand killed three men with ease.

"I will never fail to protect you, *leannan*, not ever," he said and kissed her, sealing his words as if they were a vow.

Willow latched onto to his arm, accepting his pledge, accepting that he would always be there for her, and it calmed her pounding heart and laid her fears to rest.

"Time to leave," he said softly.

He had her up on the horse and they were a distance away before she realized he had kept his body positioned so that the dead men were blocked from her view after the altercation had ended.

"You are a skilled warrior," she said, turning her glance on him.

He was glad his words held some truth as he responded, "I owe that to my da. He taught me well."

She quieted briefly in thought before saying, "It appeared as if that the large man recognized you there at the end, your name almost slipping from his tongue. I wonder if he had mistaken you for the man you search for." She shook her head. "But then he would have recognized you right away. So how would he know your name if he never met you? And why would he suddenly know your name."

"You probably heard him wrong," Slatter said, offering a more reasonable explanation.

"I suppose I could have, since everything happened so fast," she agreed, though something told her not to dismiss it so easily.

There had been such bravado in the large man until something happened to change it all. She recalled the instant shock had claimed his face, but it wasn't only shock she had seen on it, there had been fear as well. What had caused him to suddenly fear Slatter?

Your time has come.

Slatter's words. It was after that, that fear had gripped the large man, but why?

"I'm sorry you had to see that," Slatter said.

His brow deepened with concern and Willow was touched that he should worry over her. "I am grateful to you for saving me from another horrible fate. That is twice now you have rescued me." She chuckled softly. "I wish you had been there when I was smashed on the head and my sister abducted."

His body turned rigid, the muscles in his arms and chest feeling like solid rock against her.

"Who did that to you?"

His rough tone demanded a response and Willow quickly gave it.

"Lord Ruddock saw that the person responsible would never bother anyone again."

Slatter said no more, though Willow got the impression that he wanted to. He kept his eyes focused straight ahead and said nothing, though only for a moment.

"I will never let anything like that ever happen to you again."

"I appreciate that you will keep me safe, at least until we part," she said, needing to remind him they would not be together forever. Or was it she who needed reminding?

"*Ever, leannan, ever!*" he said so empathically that Willow simply nodded.

***

Evening found them camped by a stream. Slatter got a good fire going and they sat, shoulders pressed together, as they ate, the night air cold.

"We stop tomorrow where more food will be available to us and we'll be safe," Slatter said and handed her what was left of the bread.

Willow broke the piece in half and handed the other half to him. "I'm not that hungry."

He looked about to argue with her, but forced himself not to by taking a bite of the bread.

Willow was more tired than anything. She wanted to sleep or perhaps it was that she wanted to escape into sleep if only for a while. The day's troubling events had worn on her mind and body, and she needed to rest and refresh both. She always thought clearer, more reasonable, after a good night's sleep.

Her yawn confirmed how she felt.

"You're tired," Slatter said, his arm going around her to find her slipping comfortably into the crook of his arm.

"My body aches with fatigue," she said on a sigh.

"We'll sleep and get an early start."

"When will we meet up with Devin and the others?" she asked, longing for the warmth of a cottage no matter how small it might be.

"A day or two," he said and went to move away from her.

"No," she cried out softly, "don't leave me. I need your warmth."

He realized then how much of a toll the day had had on her. Willow was not only practical, she was brave. It wasn't only the cold that trembled her tonight; it was that she had witnessed him kill three men. As much as she knew it had to be done to protect them both, it was not something that was easily forgotten.

"I'm going to get some pine branches and fashion a pallet for us to sleep on, so the cold ground doesn't seep into our bones," he said.

She used him to lean on as she slowly and with a few gentle moans began to get to her feet. "I'll help."

Slatter helped her to her feet as he got to his. He'd argue with her that he didn't need her help, but it would be pointless. It would go faster if he just let her have her way, since she would anyway.

They were done in no time and Slatter spread a blanket over the narrow pallet.

"Keep your back to the fire and your chest pressed to mine and you should stay warm," he said as he helped her down on the makeshift bed.

She turned on her side, facing her back to the fire as he suggested, then stretched her hand out to him. "Hurry we need each other's heat."

Slatter spread another blanket over her, then slipped beneath it, easing his cloak around her as he went to tug her close against him. He didn't have to, she pressed herself so tightly against him that he thought she'd slip inside him. Her arm went around his waist and her one leg pushed its way between his two, not that he objected. They both needed the warmth to battle the cold. She tucked her head into the crook of his neck, seeking a spot to keep her face warm.

He worked his hand beneath her cloak to stroke along her back when she continued to shiver and silently cursed himself. He should have let Tarass's warriors take her home where she'd be safe and kept warm. But no, he didn't and why? When he had seen them take her, a fury had raged through him. He would return her home and no one else. After all, she was his wife.

His wife.

He had to stop thinking of her that way. Their marriage had been born out of necessity and it would end the same way. And he couldn't let himself forget that.

Willow lifted her head to look at him. "I'm so cold."

He acted out of instinct and brought his lips down on her trembling ones. It didn't take long for him to chase the cold and quiver from her lips, though that didn't stop him from continuing to kiss her. Why would he when she responded so eagerly?

He had ached for this, ached to kiss her, hold her close, feel something other than the emptiness that consumed him. She tasted of sweetness, kindness, and something else, something he fought to deny, something he thought he'd never find... love.

The thought poked at him. Lingering there, tormenting him... love. It wasn't possible. At least not for him. Still though, she tasted so good, warm and inviting, and she pressed against him with a passion that couldn't be ignored.

She wanted him as much as he wanted her.

He fought against the maddening passion and tore his lips away from hers with great difficulty.

"I'll take you here and now if we don't stop," he said with feral growl.

Willow clamped her lips shut, sound reasoning rushing up to grab hold of her as she fought to control the response that had rushed to spew out.

Take me; I'm yours.

What was she thinking? This couldn't be. It could never be. Could it?

Until she could make sense of things, she'd have no answer and without an answer, without reasonable thought how could she trust herself to do anything?

She spoke what she felt. "You sway me too easily."

Slatter rested his brow to hers. "That is not something you should say to me, *mo ghaol.*"

Did her tired mind hear him correctly? Did he just call her *my love*?

Be sensible, Willow, you're tired and are hearing what you think you'd like to hear, she warned herself. *Your marriage is a lie. Your husband is a liar. And most importantly, he doesn't love you.*

"I'm tired," she said as if it explained all.

"Sleep," he urged.

Please sleep or else I'll wind up sealing our vows, sealing us together for the rest of our lives.

A thought that was more appealing than he ever would have imagined, but not at all possible.

When her body went limp with sleep and her breathing turned light, he couldn't have been more relieved. Of course, it didn't help the ache in his groin or ease his thoughts of making love to her. He wanted his wife with a passion he had never known.

He'd have his need of a woman. It was like an itch that needed to be scratched and when that itch struck, he'd go find a willing woman. This was different. It wasn't an itch he had for Willow, it was a thirst he feared would never be quenched. He'd always want her and not only to make love to, but to hold, to kiss, to wrap himself around her and sleep more contentedly than he had in a long time.

Mo ghaol.

He had called her *my love* and he had meant it.

He was in serious trouble.

***

Willow woke beyond cold, shivering after rubbing at her eyes to make certain it was a light dusting of snow she saw that covered her and Slatter.

She smiled when she heard him mutter several oaths.

"We need to be on our way before this snow worsens," Slatter said and got to his feet, reaching his hand down to help her up.

Willow stood with a shiver and her husband was quick to wrap his arms around her. She felt tearful, though no tears sprang to her eyes. She loved the way he always took her in his arms without question. It was as if he knew what she needed from him and gave it to her without hesitation. She would miss that when they parted and the thought rushed a single tear to one eye.

"We need to go," he said, releasing her reluctantly. "This snow could worsen."

She nodded as she pretended to rub the sleep from her eyes so he wouldn't see the tear that trickled down her cheek, then gathered the blankets as Slatter turned his attention to the fire that had died out hours ago. They were soon on the horse and on their way. The snow remained light, but after traveling about three hours, the snowflakes seemed to consume the sky as they fell rapidly over the land.

After another hour, Slatter stopped and guided the horse beneath a tall tree. He didn't dismount. He brushed what snow covered Willow off as he said, "It's about another hour to our destination, though with the snow worsening it will probably take longer."

"Then we should not waste another minute," she said, realizing he was letting her know the remainder of their journey would not be easy.

"It is a warm cottage, good food, and a friendly face that will greet us," he assured her.

She smiled. "Then why do you wait? Let's be on our way."

"Keep your cloak up around you and I will keep my cloak over you as well. And keep yourself snug against me for warmth."

"What of you?" she asked with concern.

He leaned down and brushed a kiss across her lips. "You will keep me warm."

Willow did just that. She kept herself cuddled tight against him and she periodically rubbed along his arms and back, encouraging warmth to his flesh, as they battled the snowstorm together.

Slatter had been caught in many a snowstorm but never one as enjoyable as this one. His wife was intent on keeping him warm and she did, more ways than she realized. She had a caring touch, but it was her green eyes, bold with concern when she looked upon him as her fingers gently brushed the snow from his face that touched his heart the most.

She truly cared for him and God help her, for in the end he would bring her pain.

Snowfall made travel difficult. Heavy snow could make travel impossible. Visibility was poor, the path disappearing, markers as well. But he had learned how to combat the snow and so he preceded with confidence.

It was almost two hours when he recognized the area and was relieved since they wouldn't have been able to travel much farther.

"Not long now," he said, leaning down to let Willow know.

Shortly after, he spotted the small cottage through the falling snow. He directed the horse to the enclosed shelter that once was home to a horse, but no more. Once close, he dismounted and helped his wife off the horse. He led the horse inside the shelter and saw to his care, smiling when his wife arranged one of their blankets over the horse.

When done, he took her hand and led her to the cottage, eager to see the woman inside.

Slatter opened the door, a smile on his face, ready to call out a greeting and stopped.

The fire was nothing but embers and in the front of the hearth lay a woman with gray hair, the strands having fallen loose from her long braid. Slatter rushed to her and when he turned her over gently, it was to see that blood soaked the front of her garment.

Willow approached to see the woman's eyes flutter open and see the worry on her face as she looked upon Slatter and struggled to speak.

Slatter shook his head at her. "Don't try and talk. I'm here now. All will be well."

From the look on the old woman's face, Willow didn't think she believed him.

Slatter looked to Willow. "Please help her. She's my grandmother."

Chapter Eleven

"No, don't move her yet," Willow said, stopping her husband from lifting his grandmother in his arms as she hurried to his side.

"The earth floor is cold and so is she," Slatter argued and Willow laid her hand on his arm to prevent him from moving her.

"If she still bleeds, she could lose more blood as you move her, which will not help her. If we stop the flow of blood before we move her it will serve her well. And while I see to that, you can get a fire going and get the room heated which will also benefit her."

Slatter was about to argue when he nodded. "Whatever you say, wife, you're the healer."

"Her name?" Willow asked softly.

"Sara," Slatter said almost reverently.

Willow gave his arm a gentle push and he moved and let her see to his grandmother as he got a fire going, though he kept a watchful eye on the two women that meant more to him than he would ever admit.

"Sara," Willow said, running a gentle hand across the older woman's brow and worried over the slight warmth she felt there. "I'm Willow and I'm going to help you."

Sara's eyes fluttered as she struggled to open them, but failed.

Willow took her hand. "You can squeeze my hand to let me know you hear me."

She was relieved to feel a slight squeeze. "Your grandson is here. He'll take your hand in a moment. He's getting a fire going and you'll soon be warm and in bed. But first I'm going to see to your wound."

Another light squeeze to her hand told Willow the woman understood, a good sign.

From what Willow could see the shoulder wound had stopped bleeding, but blood still trickled from a wound to her side. She needed to get both cleaned before she could see what damage it had left.

Willow looked to her husband. "Lift her gently and place her on the bed just as gently."

Slatter took hold of his grandmother's hand before taking her in his arms. "You must get well, *Seanmhair*. I want to you meet Willow not only the woman who will heal you, but my wife."

The older woman's eyes fluttered madly, trying desperately to open them.

"Heal, *Seanmhair,* heal, so that you can meet the beautiful woman I married," he said and gently lifted her in his arms.

Once on the bed, Willow went to work, sending Slatter to collect snow in a bucket and melt it by the fire. When he returned and placed the snow-filled bucket by the hearth, she took his hand and stepped over by the door.

She spoke in a whisper to him. "The shoulder wound isn't too deep and has stopped bleeding. I have some, hopefully enough, sphagnum moss to pack the wound. It's the side wound that concerns me, though I believe if seared, she may survive. I have some *fluellen* to help treat her fever, but I fear it will not be enough. Do you have a healer at your home?"

"No, there is no healer there, and not much of a home either," Slatter admitted.

"I'll do my best, but if we got her to my home, she'd have a better chance of surviving. For now, I need your help in getting her out of those bloody garments and searing the wound."

"Whatever you need from me," he said, thinking he might not have any choice but to take her to Willow's home and if his grandmother knew the consequences to him if he did that, she would tell him to let her die. And he would not let that happen.

Willow couldn't get over the tenderness of her husband toward his grandmother or how he shared her pain, his face grimacing every time she winced. But that was not all she saw in his dark eyes. She saw anger bubbling there and it was obvious that a time would come when he would find the one who did this to his grandmother and she had no doubt he would kill the culprit.

When the time came to sear the wound closed, Slatter bent over his grandmother, kissed her cheek, and whispered in her ear, "I'm sorry to cause you more pain."

Willow took hold of the old woman's hand and was surprised at the strength of the fingers that locked tight around hers.

The old woman let out a cry and her eyes opened wide and before a faint grabbed hold of her, her eyes found her grandson, and she smiled.

"I'm going to kill the bastard that did this to her," Slatter said as if committing to a vow that would be kept at all cost.

"Help me get her settled comfortably before she wakes and suffers more pain from us moving her," Willow said and Slatter didn't hesitate to help.

When they finished, Slatter sat beside his grandmother on the bed, holding her hand while Willow went through her healing pouch to see what she had left.

"What's wrong?" Slatter asked, catching the troubled look on his wife's face.

"I have less than I thought to help your grandmother. I gave most of what I had to Roanna for Erna and to Crofton for his grandmother. Sara needs more than I have to help her heal and her healing is going to take time. She will need attention and care, and she is not safe here. What if the culprit returns?"

"I have thought the same myself, though what I can't understand is why someone would do this to her." He shook his head.

"Something else bothers you," Willow said, seeing the troubling look in his dark eyes.

Slatter looked down at his grandmother, sleeping peacefully, and though he should be relieved, he wasn't. She was far too pale and looked more like death had claimed her than healing sleep.

He turned to his wife. "As you see for yourself, my grandmother is a wee bit of a thing. She couldn't defend herself against a warrior let alone one with a weapon." He chuckled. "Not that she wouldn't try. She's a feisty one."

Willow heard not only the pride he had for his grandmother but the obvious love he had for her.

"So why two wounds? Why not one wound that would end her life? Unless…" He let his words drift off and let his thoughts simmer before speaking again. "Unless there was something he had wanted from her. The wounds weren't meant to kill. They were intended to make her surrender whatever it was this person wanted. But what?" He scanned the small room. "Nothing looks to have been touched and she has nothing of worth."

"Your grandmother can tell you all as soon as she wakes."

"Will she wake?" Slatter asked.

"I wish I could tell you she will do well, but I honestly don't know. She has grown warmer to the touch from when I first felt her brow and I don't have enough of the leaves to brew what she needs, or clean cloth to dress her wounds properly."

"Could she survive the two-day journey to your home?" he asked, his glance going to his grandmother. "I could fashion a carrier for the horse to pull. We could bundle her in blankets."

"It wouldn't be wise to drag her through the snow. She needs rest. Let's see how she fairs in a day or two."

Willow got busy preparing a brew from the few leaves she did have, hoping it was enough to help until they could get more. When she finished, she searched the small room for food and found some root vegetables stored in a basket. They would be enough to make a soup, one that would serve the old woman well.

She cast a glance at Slatter every now and then. He remained by his grandmother's side, holding her hand as if sharing his strength with her. He may have debated her a time or two over whether he was kind or not, but seeing him now confirmed to Willow that kindness did reside in him and love as well. Not that he would admit it.

He was a man who would be a good husband... only if a wife could trust him not to lie.

It was over an hour later when Willow was bending over the hearth, stirring the soup that bubbled in the pot over the flames, that her husband came up behind her and slipped his arm around her waist to turn her to face him.

"I owe you much," he said, gently pushing the long strand of her dark red hair away from her eye to tuck behind her ear.

"You owe me nothing. It is I—"

He pressed his finger to her lips, stopping her from speaking. "You are a good woman, *mo ghaol*—" He paused, letting the words that followed remain in his thoughts... *and you deserve a good man.* "I am forever grateful to you for looking after my grandmother."

Willow smiled softly. "She's my grandmother now too."

"Aye, that she is," Slatter said and wished that could be so.

He almost shook his head at the thought. He couldn't keep thinking this way. He couldn't keep getting used to having her with him. He couldn't allow himself to believe he was falling in love with her. If he did, he'd never let her go.

Willow gently rubbed at the deep crease in his brow. "Do not worry so. We will take good care of her."

We.

She did the healing but she talked as if they did it together, a couple, a pair, a husband and wife. How was it that he felt so joined with this woman? Or how was it he felt that she belonged to him and that he belonged to her, and that no other should ever come between them?

He was sounding like Lander when he talked about Slatter's mum. The man had commented time and again how he had lost all common sense and sane reasoning when he had met Blair. Slatter would often laugh and Lander would chuckle and say wait until it happens to you.

Had it happened to him?

A moan from Sara had them both rushing to her side and when Willow felt her head, worry twisted her stomach. Fever had set in.

"Fill the bucket with snow," she ordered Slatter and he didn't hesitate to do as she said.

As soon as he returned Willow placed handfuls of snow on her forehead and around her neck. "My mother did this a few times when fevers got high. I hope this helps to keep the fever away."

Slatter looked at his grandmother, fearful for her as she lay there as if lifeless. He rested a firm hand on his wife's shoulder and she turned to look up at him with worry in her green eyes. He wasn't sure who the worry was for, his grandmother or him?

"I need to leave for a bit," he said and wasn't surprised that Willow seemed to expect it.

"You're going to see if the culprit still lingers about. I had the same thought." The worry grew in her eyes. "You will take care."

"Is that an order, wife?' he asked with a teasing grin.

"Aye, it is and you'll obey if you know what's good for you," she said with a twinkle in her eyes that seemed relieved to share a light moment with him.

He folded his arms across his chest. "And what's my reward for this obedience?"

The twinkle left her eyes replaced by a loving softness he feared he could drown in.

"Welcome arms, a warm hug, and a kiss," she said, a reward she would favor herself.

He was speechless for a moment, then he leaned down to bring his face close to hers and said, "For such a fine reward I would battle the devil himself." He brushed his lips over hers, then grabbed his cloak off the chair, and turned when he reached the door and returned to her, pulling his dagger from its sheath at his waist as he did. "If it's the devil who walks through that door and not me, use this on him."

Willow took it, nodded, and sent a silent prayer to the heavens as he closed the door behind him that she wouldn't have to battle the devil today.

She returned her attention to Sara and wondered about the woman. Why did she live so isolated from family? Why didn't she make her home with her grandson? Could she be hiding from something or someone? If she was, Slatter certainly wouldn't have had knowledge of it, since he would have seen to the matter post haste.

Willow shook her head. Sometimes she cursed the way her mind worked, always looking for reason, always trying to make sense of things. She wished she could let some things be, not question or probe to find a reason behind it, not be practical.

A smile hurried to spread across her face. She certainly hadn't been practical when she chose to stay with Slatter rather than go with Tarass's warriors, though she tried to convince herself otherwise. She questioned it at times, but hadn't regretted it.

The problem now was that the more time she spent with her husband, the more time she wanted to spend with him. A dread filled her when she thought of them parting, of never seeing him again, and yet, what other recourse was there for them? And what of how easily he lied? How could she spend her life with a man whose tongue she constantly questioned?

So many hurdles for them to cross, perhaps too many.

With her smile gone, she returned to working on Sara, applying more snow as it began to melt. She was relieved when the snow chased the fever. But how long it would keep it at bay, she didn't know.

It wasn't long before she was pacing the floor in front of the fireplace, wondering what was keeping Slatter. Had he run into the culprit? Could he be in trouble? Or was it worry that had her thinking he'd been gone longer than he truly had been?

What if something happened to him? What would she do? How would she get Sara to safety? She shook her head. There was no point wasting worry on something that had yet to happen. Besides, having seen how skillful a warrior her husband was there was no reason for her to think something bad may have happened to him.

Unfortunately, that did not stop her worries. They lingered, poking and pricking at her like the thorny bush she had gotten caught in while hiding from the battle that had started this adventure.

A moan drew her attention and she went to Sara's side and saw that she shivered. It could be from the snow or the fever could be working its way through her. She decided to see if she could get some soup into the woman.

She filled a wooden bowl with the hot liquid and after grabbing a wooden spoon, she went and sat beside Sara. She was careful to let each spoonful cool some before gently placing it at her lips to dribble in. Once Sara tasted it, she lapped at it eagerly. A good sign that brought a smile to Willow's face.

She was just wiping at Sara's face when she heard someone at the door. She hurried to exchange the bowl for the dagger on the table all the while praying for it to be Slatter who walked through the door.

The door swung open and for a moment, she wasn't sure who stood there. The hood of the dark cloak was pulled too far down for her to see the person's face and the cloak was covered with snow.

The hood was suddenly tossed back and Willow's hand fell away from the dagger with relief.

"The snowfall makes it impossible to see much and covers whatever tracks there might have been," Slatter said, after closing the door and was quick to shed his cloak and hang it on the peg in the wall. He went straight to the fire, stretching his hands out to warm them. "How does my grandmother do?"

Willow wanted to run into his arms, let him know how relieved she was that he had returned safely, hug him tight, feel his arms wrap around her, but he had sought the fire's warmth not hers. And she can't say she wasn't disappointed, foolish as it felt.

"The snow has eased her fever and though she hasn't fully woken yet, I was able to feed her some soup, which she eagerly ate."

"That is good to hear," he said, rubbing his hands together vigorously.

"I'll get you a bowl of soup. It will help warm you."

He turned to her. "Not before I get my reward. Knowing I would claim it upon my return, did much to keep me warm in the cold." He spread his arms out to her. "Come to me, *mo ghaol*."

Her heart seemed to flutter in her chest and she lost all common sense every time he called her *my love*. He sounded so sincere and it was far too intoxicating to ignore. Besides, she had promised him a reward.

Poor excuse, Willow, poor excuse. You just want to be in his arms.

Her admonishing thoughts couldn't have been more right, and she eagerly went into his arms.

A chill still lingered in him, seeping into her as soon as she pressed her body against his, but his hands were warm when they came to rest at her back as he hugged her tight against him.

She was home.

A crazy thought, and yet, it felt right. She was at home in his arms. He held her with strength and confidence, and with a possessiveness that let one know he'd never let her go. Which was fine with her, since she was right where she wanted to be.

Their eyes held briefly, "I'll have that kiss now."

"And I'll gladly give it to you," she whispered and brought her lips to rest on his.

Slatter assumed that she changed her mind when her lips made no move to actually kiss him. When suddenly, as if released from a trance, her lips delivered a stunning kiss that had him quickly responding.

It was as if something had broken free in her. That she threw caution to the wind without a second thought. That she kissed him with a passion that was new to her. That she kissed without doubt or reserve.

He ran his hand down along the curve of her back, craving that small touch of intimacy, warning himself not to go any farther, reminding himself it wasn't the time nor the place. But there was an ache in him he didn't know he had and it grew every time he touched his wife. It could be the simple way her fingers wrapped around his hand when he took hold of hers, as if she welcomed him home. Or the way she fit so perfectly in his arms. Or how he had never truly tasted passion until he had kissed her.

Aye, there was an ache in him. An ache for a woman he could never have.

He ended their kiss with a tender tug of her bottom lip, fighting with himself to let go of her.

"I'm not the right man for you, *leannan*," he whispered.

The kiss had stolen her breath and though she didn't want to admit, had tried to ignore it, deny it, she feared he had stolen her heart.

"Isn't that for me to decide," she found herself saying.

"Trust me when I tell you that I'm no good for you." he stepped away from her.

"You can't tell me you're not a good man, not after I've seen you suffer along with your grandmother or how I've seen the fear of losing her spark in your eyes."

He turned a deep scowl on her. "I've asked for your trust when it was most important. It's more important now than ever that you trust me on this. You would regret remaining my wife."

"Why?" she demanded. "Is it that I'm too plain for you, you don't find me appealing? Or perhaps I'm not strong enough. Is it a more courageous woman you want? Or is it that I'm a virgin and wouldn't know how to satisfy a man as experienced in poking as you are?"

Willow's eyes shot wide and she jumped. But she had no time to move, her husband was upon her so fast, his hand at the back of her neck gripping it firmly. And anger simmered in his dark, fathomless eyes.

"Hear me well, wife, I see a timeless beauty every time I look upon you. Most times I cannot take my eyes from you or have a thought in my head that doesn't include you." He stopped and a growl-like sound rumbled from him before he continued. "And you appeal to me like no other woman and you have since I first laid eyes on you. Strong? Courageous? I've met no woman that can compare with your strength and courage." He lowered his face closer to hers. "I believe

I told you once that it wouldn't be a poke I'd give you. We'd make love and once we did, I'd never let you go."

His mouth came down on hers in a punishing kiss, almost as if he was trying to frighten her away, but it didn't work, not after hearing his last few words.

I'd never let you go.

His kiss stopped abruptly and that's when Willow heard Sara moaning.

His hand released her as soon as she turned and he followed her to the bed.

"Her fever rises again," Willow said, her hand on the old woman's brow.

Slatter reached the bucket before he finished saying, "I'll get more snow."

It was a difficult night. They took turns watching over his grandmother. They got little sleep, but when the day dawned, her fever had broken, leaving them both much relieved, though not completely worry free. Willow knew her fever could return and there was still the possibility of her wounds turning putrid. And while she made no mention of it to Slatter, she could tell he was already aware of it.

Once he saw that the snow had stopped, he had told her he would go hunt, in hopes of finding them a more substantial meal.

With Sara sleeping peacefully and Slatter hunting, Willow decided to freshen herself with a quick wash. She grabbed the empty wooden bucket, not bothering with her cloak, since she'd be but a moment in scooping up some snow to melt by the hearth.

She cast a glance at Sara, checking on her as she opened the door and kept her head turned to make sure she closed the door good, not wanting to let any cold air in the cottage. She turned and took a step, halting abruptly, the bucket falling from her hand.

A few feet away stood not only Rhodes and his warriors, but Ruddock's warriors as well.

Chapter Twelve

"You're a difficult woman to find, but now that I've found you, you won't be escaping me again," Rhodes said, taking a step toward her and stopped when her hand shot out in front of her.

"Don't bother to come near me, since I'm not going anywhere with you," she said with worry for her husband filling her every thought. If he returned now, he would be captured. What then? And what of Sara? She needed care.

"We have orders to see you safely home."

Willow was pleased to see it was William who spoke. He wore a clean bandage around his head and looked much better since she'd last seen him.

"You do well, William?" she asked.

"Thanks to you and I'd like to repay that kindness and see you home without any problem."

"That is very nice of you, William, but I'm not ready to go home just yet," she said, chasing her worry as best she could so that she could think more clearly and find a hasty solution.

"Whether you're ready or not, you're going home," Rhodes commanded.

A quick and stinging response rushed off Willow's tongue. "Lord Ruddock's men were charged in seeing me returned home. This has nothing to do with you."

"Wrong," Rhodes said and marched toward her, though William brought him to an abrupt stop with a curt shout of his name.

"Rhodes, give me a moment to speak with Willow."

That William spoke to Rhodes as if the man was in charge disturbed her. Had Tarass's men been directed to lead the mission to rescue her?

"What is there to say?" Rhodes asked with annoyance. "She is to come with us and you and your warriors are charged with finding Slatter and returning him to Lord Tarass to serve his punishment."

"Who has given such an order?" Willow demanded.

"The Lord of Fire," Rhodes all but snarled.

"He has no say over me," Willow said with a defiant lift of her chin.

Rhodes grinned. "James, Chieftain of the Clan Macardle, gave the Lord of Fire say over you when Lord Ruddock's men arrived at the Clan Macardle wounded. William," —he gave a nod toward the warrior— "gladly accepted our help, since I doubt he wants to return home and tell Lord Ruddock that a Northwick troop failed to see you home safely. I received word what was to be done and William confirmed it once he joined us. Unlike, William, I will see my duty done without incident." His grin had long faded. "Get your cloak. We leave now."

Did she go with him to draw them away from here, so that her husband would be safe? But how safe would he be with William and his men searching for him? She threw reason aside and did something, she never did before. She threw caution aside and stood her ground.

"I don't care what orders you were given, I'm not going with you," Willow said, squaring her shoulders, ready for a fight.

"It's not your choice," Rhodes said and rushed at her.

Willow reacted, picking up the bucket she had dropped and throwing it at Rhodes.

He batted it out of his way with his arm, and grabbed her arm, his fingers clamping like a shackle around it before she could move out of his reach.

"See if anyone hides in the cottage and get her cloak," Rhodes ordered and one of his men went to obey.

"There is an injured, old woman in there with fever, leave her be," Willow demanded, while struggling to free herself.

Rhodes nodded toward the cottage and the young warrior walked to the door.

"Harm her in any way and I'll see you suffer the fires of hell for it," Willow threatened Rhodes.

He ignored her, as if her threat meant nothing, was futile, and that fired Willow's temper even more.

"Let go of me now," she demanded, yanking her arm as hard as she could and not realizing that the snow was pushing up beneath her shift and tunic as Rhodes dragged her toward his horse, her boots digging into the snow to try and stop him.

Willow's anger grew. She wished her husband was there, and then she wished he wasn't. He'd be caught along with her and what would happen to Sara?

"You can't leave the old woman alone. You have to take her back to my home with me," Willow demanded.

"She's not my problem," Rhodes said.

"But she's mine," Willow argued, hating the man for being so heartless and annoyed at her herself for being so helpless.

What would Sorrell do?

With the silent question came an answer and Willow fisted her hand and brought it around so fast that it actually stunned Rhodes when it connected with his jaw. Unfortunately, it didn't stun him enough to free her, though it did anger him.

Rhodes gave her arm a sharp yank and Willow stumbled almost falling to her knees, and yelping in pain when he yanked her arm again to keep her from falling.

"Let go of *my wife* or *I'll kill you*."

That stunned Rhodes enough to loosen his hold on her and she took immediate advantage and broke free of his grip and ran to her husband where he stood on the side of the cottage.

Slatter caught her up in one arm, his sword gripped in his other hand. "Are you harmed?"

She shook her head and while relieved to have his arm firm around her, she worried for his safety.

William was the one to ask, "Willow is your wife?"

"She is and she'll not be going anywhere with you," Slatter said, the strength of his voice leaving no doubt that he meant it.

"This presents a problem," William said, turning to Rhodes.

"What problem? I was tasked with bringing Willow home and you were tasked with finding Slatter and returning him to the Lord of Fire. That can now easily be accomplished," Rhodes argued.

"What can easily be accomplished is returning both Willow and her husband, Slatter, to James of the Clan Macardle and have him discuss the matter with the Lord of Fire. The decision is theirs to make," William explained.

Willow was relieved to hear some common sense being made, but it also annoyed her that a decision would be made for her, then she remembered.

"It is no one's decision but mine," she said, drawing both men's attention. "Lord Ruddock claimed that I was free to pick a husband of my choosing and I picked Slatter."

Rhodes's brow creased in annoyance and he looked to William. "This is nonsense. He's charmed her and now she lies for him. He's a scoundrel, liar, and thief, and I refuse to believe they're wed or if for some outlandish reason they are, that James Macardle would approve of their union."

"Evidently you didn't hear what I said," Willow said caustically. "It's no one's decision but mine who I wed."

"If you are wed," Rhodes challenged.

William spoke up. "We have only one choice, return them home and let James Macardle and Lord Tarass decide what is to be done with them."

Rhodes didn't hide his deepening anger. "The Lord of Fire will see it made right."

That was what Willow was afraid of, that Tarass would have his way no matter what, and the thought made her shiver.

"Worry not, *leannan*, all will go well," Slatter whispered near her ear.

His words only worried her more, since she recalled how he'd talked with pride of how he could escape anyone or anyplace. Would he eventually make his escape and leave her? She shivered again.

His arm coiled tighter around her waist. "The only ones to make this right between us will be *you and me*."

Something about the way he said you and me as if no one else mattered, only the two of them and that only they would decide their destiny, vanquished some of her worry.

"Get yourselves together, we leave shortly. I want this mission done," Rhodes said.

"We're not leaving until it is safe for the old woman to travel," Willow said, turning to Rhodes.

"Who is this old woman to you?" Rhodes demanded.

Her husband gave her side a squeeze and she understood, though she had had no intention of telling Rhodes the truth, fearful it could hurt Sara.

"She was a good friend of my mother's," Willow said, since neither man would know if that were true or not.

Rhodes conceded with a complaint. "We can't wait long or they'll send another troop out after us and if it snows again and we get stuck here, it will not bode well for mine and William's warriors."

"I will let you know after I see how she fares," Willow said and stepped away from her husband, expecting him to follow her into the cottage. When she saw that he headed toward Rhodes, she stopped, fearful for what might happen.

Rhodes didn't wait for Slatter to reach him, he walked straight at him.

Willow worried this would end poorly and as she'd seen him do on other occasions, her husband moved with such speed that Rhodes didn't even see the punch coming. He was flat on his back, his eyes stunned wide, his lip bleeding and already swelling.

His men went to go at Slatter and he shook his head. "You truly wish to embarrass him even more, by all of you coming to his defense against a man he should have been able to defend himself against."

"Stay!" Rhodes shouted, weak as the shout was, still lying flat on his back in the snow.

His men backed away.

"A reminder," Slatter said, standing over the fallen man. "Lay your hands on my wife again and I will kill you."

He turned his back on Rhodes, an action that made it clear he did not fear the man, and joined his wife at the door, reaching past her to open it and with a gentle hand to her back entered the cottage with her.

Willow went immediately to Sara. Thankfully, she was sleeping peacefully and a tender touch to her brow told Willow that the fever hadn't returned. She turned to her husband, standing directly behind her, worry in his dark eyes. "She does well."

His worry faded as he settled his hands on her waist. "And you? Do you do well?"

Her response surprised her. "When you're with me, I always do well."

His teasing grin surfaced. "I do always seem to be rescuing you."

When he had heard her yell as he was returning to the cottage, fear twisted at his heart and gut, feeling as if they'd be ripped out of him. And when he had seen how Rhodes had hold of his wife, dragging her in the snow, he was ready to kill the man. He was still trying to temper his anger so he wouldn't go out there and run a dagger through him.

He didn't like that she wasn't smiling in return.

"But will I be able to rescue you?" she asked, more of herself than her husband, and the thought made her shiver.

"You're cold. Come by the fire," he said, easing her over to the hearth, moving a chair in front of it, sitting, and taking her in his lap as he did.

Willow rested her head on his shoulder. "You know what this means, don't you?" She raised her head to look at him.

"That we remain husband and wife or chance the Lord of Fire taking me prisoner once again." He ran his finger along her chin. "I'm not good for you, *mo ghaol.*"

She didn't think that at all true, but kept that to herself. "Perhaps, but do we have a choice? And what of your grandmother? She would fare much better at my home than here. She could ride with you. You would keep her warm and safe."

She could see he was giving it thought, though she wondered if it was his grandmother's well-being that swayed him to consider it.

"And where would you ride?" he asked.

She hadn't thought he'd ask that, but she was quick to say, "With William." Her answer seemed to appease him.

"Is my grandmother strong enough to make the two-day journey?"

"I can't say with any certainty. What I do know is that I will have much more at my disposal to help her heal at my home than here. She'll have a warm room, a comfortable bed, and enough food to aid her in healing."

"It appears it would be a wise choice," he said, yet didn't sound entirely convinced.

"Something troubles you about it?"

"No, that doesn't trouble me. I see the wisdom in what you say."

"Something else troubles you then," she asked, seeing something in his dark eyes, but not quite understanding what she saw there.

"I'm not the man you think I am. Rhodes said it well... I'm a scoundrel and liar. We can play at being husband and wife, but only for so long. One day you will wake and I will be gone because that's who I am."

An ache settled around Willow's heart and she asked the one question that mattered the most to her. "Do you care at all for me?"

"That's the problem, *mo ghaol*, I care too much for you."

Chapter Thirteen

Willow sat silent in front of William on his horse since leaving Sara's cottage more than an hour ago. She had checked Sara's wounds and all seemed to be well and with no signs of fever, it was decided they would take their leave. The old woman had stirred when she and Slatter had wrapped her in three blankets. Slatter had spoken softly to her, telling her that he was taking her to a safe place where she could heal without worry or fear. Her eyes fluttered open and she nodded.

Willow's mother had taught her that rest was best when a person needed to heal, but it was no good if a person slept and didn't stir. Then it was too deep of a sleep, one that many never woke from. So she was relieved that Sara responded when spoken to even if it was only a shake or nod of her head.

Willow's silence, though, wasn't due to any worry over Sara. She was in the best place she could be, her grandson's arms. Her silence was due to what Slatter had said to her earlier.

That's the problem, mo ghaol, I care too much for you.

She had been ready to ask him… why then would he leave her if he cared for her? But Rhodes entered the cottage letting them know a light snow had begun to fall. That was another reason they had hastened their decision to leave. It wouldn't have been wise to remain there with barely enough food to feed one person.

Willow more than cared for him. She believed she had fallen in love with him. It made no sense and she questioned the wisdom of her feelings for her husband. She'd even made excuses as to why it was a foolish thought, but her heart ignored every one of them. Common sense cautioned her against thinking Slatter would make a good husband. And yet, the warning went unheeded.

Love can blind. That was what her mum had once told her.

When she had asked how not to be blinded by love, her mum had smiled and told her that was a mystery she doubted would ever be solved. Was she letting love blind her to the truth?

I'm not the man you think I am.

Was Rhodes right? Was Slatter nothing more than a scoundrel and a liar? Would he leave her brokenhearted?

Willow was suddenly eager to know what William thought of Slatter.

She turned a soft smile on him. "What do you know about Slatter, William?"

"I only know that his lies caused great pain and heartache to the Northwick Clan. He also had many a lass enthralled with him and some surrendered to his charm and lying tongue."

"You agree with Rhodes then?"

"I do. Slatter is nothing more than a scoundrel and a liar. You can trust nothing he says."

Why when everyone warned her against Slatter, did she not see it for herself? Had love blinded her that badly? Had she become one of those women who refused to see the worthlessness of her husband?

But what of the other man who resembled Slatter? Was that truth or tale? Devin had known of the man. Or did he lie to protect his friend? And why? Why? Why did she miss being in his arms?

She turned silent again and felt relieved she was on her way home. She'd be in familiar surroundings with people who loved her, perhaps once there she would see things differently.

***

They arrived at Willow's home late past mid-day on the second day of their journey. Thankfully, only a light snow had followed them on their way home, though it had turned heavier about an hour ago.

Rhodes and William followed her and Slatter, his grandmother cradled in his arms, into the Great Hall, where James, Snow, and Eleanor waited.

"Explanations will have to wait, I have an old, ill woman who needs tending," Willow announced upon seeing her family and got the results she wanted.

Snow, with Eleanor's help, hurried toward her. Thaw, Snow's pup, yapped as he followed along.

Willow was quick to reach out to her sister and hug her tight. "I am well, do not worry. We will talk later and I will explain all."

"I am glad you are home safe," Snow said, tears lingering in her eyes.

They both turned to their brother as he spoke.

"I'll speak with Slatter while you tend to the woman, Willow."

Slatter issued his own command. "I speak to no one until I've seen my grandmother settled."

Willow shocked them all when she said, "And you'll not talk with my husband without me present."

"Husband?" James, Snow, and Eleanor asked in unison.

"Aye," Willow confirmed. "That he is and that he'll stay."

"You let your wife dictate to you?" Rhodes said, sounding as if he issued a challenge.

The man was itching for any reason to fight Slatter ever since he had laid him low with one blow. Willow hoped her husband wouldn't oblige him.

"Keep it up, Rhodes and the next time you feel my fist, it will be the last time you feel anything," Slatter warned in such a deadly tone that it had people turning wide eyes on him.

"That's a threat I won't take lightly," Rhodes said and took a quick step forward.

"Enough," James bellowed, looking to Rhodes. "I'll talk with you and William in my solar." He turned to Willow, but Slatter spoke before he could.

"I'll join you as soon as my grandmother is settled in bed." Willow went to protest, but he stopped her. "I will see to this and you will see to my grandmother. We will talk afterwards."

In his own way, he was letting her know he would share what was said with her, but would he tell her everything?

There was no time to argue. Sara needed tending.

Eleanor had been placed in Sorrell's bedchamber to be close to Snow if she needed help. Willow had no choice but to have Sara taken to her own bedchamber. She would find a place for Slatter and her to sleep later.

Slatter placed his grandmother on the bed and went to release her from the blankets that had kept her warm.

"Leave her to us," Willow said, placing her hand on his forearm to stop him.

Slatter saw that Snow had entered the room along with the other woman. The pup had entered as well, though this time he sat quietly, leaning against Snow's leg. He wasn't very big, though the size of his paws was evidence enough that he would be a big dog and it looked like he'd be protective of Snow.

Slatter rested his hand to his wife's cheek, thinking he was a lucky man to have her as his wife, though unlucky that he couldn't keep her. "I trust you."

"As I do you," she whispered, "so please don't do anything to make me think otherwise."

He turned a teasing smile on her and grabbed at his chest. "You wound me, wife, to think I would do such a thing."

She loved his playfulness, but sometimes she wondered if it was meant to do more... distract or perhaps hide something.

Snow joined her sister along with Eleanor at the bedside as soon as Slatter left the room.

"He is so handsome that he startles the eyes," Eleanor said.

"How did you ever become wife to the man who set fire to the shed that in turn caused the fire in the keep?" Snow asked as she stepped next to her sister.

Willow was glad Snow didn't accuse, but rather was in search of an explanation. But then she knew Willow well and she was surprised Snow hadn't asked… *where did my responsible, sensible, sister go?*

"After I see to Sara," Willow said and Snow's response was just what she expected.

"What do you need me to do?

Eleanor was dispensed to gather the things Willow needed and Snow went and fetched one of her nightshifts since Sara was petite like Snow. Once Willow had everything she needed to tend the woman properly, she, with the help of Snow and Eleanor, got busy tending to Sara.

***

Slatter was shown to James's solar and was there only a few moments when Rhodes started on him again.

"He charmed Willow into marrying him to use her so he could escape punishment and like most women his good looks mesmerized her and his deceitful tongue charmed her into believing his concocted tale that someone who looked like him was responsible for all the evil deeds done in his name. How convenient for him."

"It does seem contrived," James admitted and turned a question on Slatter. "How did you and Willow come upon each other?"

"I rescued her from the man who took her from the Northwick troop," Slatter said, leaving out the part that he had been abducted as well.

James continued to probe. "How did you wind up wed so fast and who wed you?"

"It was a moment we couldn't resist and a cleric was close by to see us wed properly." That sounded good to Slatter and was as close to the truth as he could get."

"And Willow consented to this?" James asked.

"We both eagerly did," he said, recalling how they both wanted to be on their way and as far away from Beck as possible.

James shook his head. "Willow is the most sensible woman I know. It makes no sense that she would wed the man who caused damage to the Clan Macardle."

"I had nothing to do with the fire," Slatter said, though it was a futile attempt. They hadn't believed him before, so why would they believe him now?

"That tale again," Rhodes said with a sneer. "You expect us to believe that some phantom man who resembles you is the true culprit. A tale more suited for the storytellers and minstrels."

"Doubt all you want, Rhodes, it's the truth," Slatter said, though knew he wasted his breath. He would not be believed.

"A likely declaration from a liar," Rhodes accused.

"Truth or tale, either way it presents a dilemma," James said.

"What dilemma?" Rhodes asked. "Disavow the marriage and return Slatter to Lord Tarass."

"How can the marriage be disavowed when Willow may be with child?" James asked and turned to look at Slatter. "Is there a possibility she can be with child?"

"A strong possibility," Slatter confirmed without giving a moment's thought to the consequences. If Willow's brother thought any other way, their marriage would end and he didn't want that as foolish a thought as it was.

"It is your decision, not Willow's," Rhodes argued, his anger not only flaring in his eyes, but his tone flaring with it as well.

"Willow would have informed you immediately that Lord Ruddock had granted her and her sister Snow their choice of a husband," James said. "Are you telling me she didn't explain that to you?"

"She did," Rhodes said curtly, "but who am I to take her word for it?"

"You have my word now and I suggest you go and inform Lord Tarass about what has happened. Also advise him that I will speak with Willow first and send word when he can speak with her."

Rhodes glared at James. "Lord Tarass follows no man's dictate." He turned and left the room, swinging the door open with such force that it slammed against the wall.

James looked to William who had remained silent. "You have nothing to say."

"I don't speak for Lord Ruddock. My task is accomplished with Willow home safely. My men and I will take our leave on the morrow and inform Lord Ruddock what has happened. I am sure he will send a missive to you as soon as he receives the news, though weather may delay it. So it could be weeks before you hear from him." William gave a nod and left, closing the door behind him.

"I don't like this at all," James said, concern in his voice. "Something doesn't ring right about this, and yet, Willow isn't one to lie. If she claims you are her husband and will stay her husband, then I have no choice but to believe her." He looked over Slatter with a questioning glance and shook his head. "Still, I find it difficult to believe she would choose you for a husband."

"I can understand your misgivings, but I give you my word... I would never harm Willow and I would never allow harm to befall her."

"Why should I believe the word of a liar?" James asked apprehensively, though caught a gleam in the man's eyes that couldn't hide his feelings for Willow.

"I can't make you believe it, nor do I care if you do. I know it's true and that's all that matters to me." Slatter turned a defiant glare on James. "Willow made it clear that I am her husband and I will remain her husband."

James stared at Slatter and he knew why, so Slatter wasn't surprised with what James said.

"Why then does it sound like you doubt your wife's words?"

***

"You are tired and need to rest. We will talk tomorrow," Snow said and gave Willow a hug. "I am so glad you are home."

"I am too," Willow said, returning the hug and realizing the truth of her words. She also hadn't realized just how much she had missed her family.

"Eleanor had Mum and Da's bedchamber freshened for you. James has still to make use of it." Snow chuckled softly. "Though, I think we were right about him being taken with Eleanor. He seeks her out more than necessary."

"Do you think she feels the same?" Willow asked, recalling how she and Snow had seen how the two seemed to be drawn to each other almost from the day Eleanor had arrived here.

"I do. She grows giddy every time their path crosses and he finds chores for her to do that keeps them near," Snow confirmed.

"I'm glad for them both. He deserves a good woman and Eleanor has proven to be one. She has been a great help here and…" A yawn stole the rest of her words.

"You need to rest," Snow said, though it sounded like an order.

Willow was surprised and pleased by the strength she heard in Snow. Her absence had been good for Snow. Even though Eleanor had been here to help her, it wasn't the same as one of her sisters she had grown dependent on.

Eleanor entered the room. "Your husband is bathing. He says when he is done, he will come sit with his grandmother so that you may bathe and rest. I will have a fresh bath prepared for you as soon as he is done. Food and drink also awaits you in your parents' bedchamber."

"I am most grateful for that, Eleanor," Willow said, looking forward to finally having a good washing and donning clean garments.

"Come, Thaw, it's time for supper," Snow called out and the pup got up with a stretch from where he slept by the hearth, gave a quick bark, and hurried to Snow's side.

Alone, Willow went and sat by Sara, her legs and feet far too tired to remain on them. Sara rested comfortable. Willow had redressed her wounds with clean cloths and had washed her and got her into a soft wool nightdress. Eleanor had helped, combing and plaiting Sara's hair. She had sipped a good portion of the brew Willow had ordered prepared, and thankfully her fever hadn't returned. Slatter had been right about his grandmother. She was a strong, stubborn woman.

She wondered about the conversation that had taken placed in James's solar. What had James said to Slatter and Slatter to him? And what nonsense had Rhodes spouted?

"Slatter."

The soft whisper had Willow moving from the chair beside the bed to the bed itself. She sat beside the old woman and gently took her hand. She was about to let Sara know that her grandson would be there soon and that she was Slatter's wife when words rushed out of the old woman's mouth.

"Not safe," she said, squeezing Willow's hand. "Not safe."

"You're safe now, Sara. There is nothing to fear," Willow said, trying to reassure and calm her.

Sara shook her head and grew more agitated. "Not safe. Not safe."

Willow stroked Sara's arm. "It is safe, worry not. Rest and grow strong."

Sara's restless stirrings eased and once again she fell into a peaceful slumber.

Willow returned to the chair and sat. The warmth of the fire soothed and the crackling and spitting of the logs was like a comforting melody that lolled her, and she soon found her head bobbing as she dozed on and off.

A gentle hand on her shoulder had Willow turning her head.

"Your husband is finished and a bath awaits you," Eleanor said. "I will sit with Sara until Slatter arrives."

Willow didn't argue. She longed for the hot water to soak away her aches and wash away the dirt of her journey. She thanked Eleanor and hurried up the curving staircase to her parents' bedchamber.

The door opened as she reached for it and she almost fell into her husband's arms, but righted herself before she did. His appearance stunned her speechless. She didn't think he could look more handsome than he already was, but he did. He was dressed in a Macardle plaid, a tan shirt beneath and his dark hair was damp from its recent washing, the shoulder-length strands curling some at the edges.

"Your turn," he said, drawing her out of her musings and he stepped aside for her to enter.

A round wooden tub sat near the hearth and Willow almost ran to it.

"I will return after spending some time with my grandmother," Slatter said. "She does well?"

"She does. Her fever hasn't returned and she rests comfortably. Though, she did speak, repeatedly saying, 'not safe, not safe'. I assured her she was, but you might want to reassure her yourself."

Slatter reached out, his arm circling her waist. "There are no words to let you know how much I appreciate what you've done for my grandmother. She has been a vital force in my life and continues to be. I don't want to lose her."

"I understand and I'll do all I can to make sure that you don't lose her." Willow couldn't stop the yawn that slipped out.

"You need to rest. You've done enough," he said, seeing the exhaustion in her eyes that appeared to fight to remain open. "I will see you later." He released her and stepped past her out the door.

Willow shook her head, fatigue fogging it, but recalling what she wanted to ask him. "What did you say to James?"

Slatter turned, a grin surfacing. "It's not what I said but what your brother asked of me."

"And what was that?"

"He asked if there was a strong possibility that you were with child."

Shock turned her eyes wide. "What did you say?"

His grin grew. "I told him there was a very strong possibility."

Willow's response stole his grin. "Then you best get started to make it so."

Chapter Fourteen

Slatter stood, staring at the door his wife shut in his face, and mumbled several oaths. What game did she play with him? He shook his head. Willow didn't play games.

He's my husband and he'll stay my husband.

Did she mean that? Or had she said it to protect him until they could absolve their marriage? What difference did it make? He couldn't remain wed to her. Could he? He was better off asking... could he let her go?

He shook his head as he took the stairs down. It was as if she had become part of him and there was no existing without her.

He stopped abruptly on the stairs.

Damn, could it be possible? Did he even dare admit it? Had he actually fallen in love with her?

He smiled at the absurd yet truthful realization. What did he do now?

You better get busy making it so.

Was she inviting him to seal their vows, seal their fate?

Once he made love to her that would be it. He'd never let her go. Had she been telling him that it was her wish to remain his wife?

Still, there was much to be settled. How did he offer her any kind of life without laying the past to rest? And could he?

He shook his head, feeling at war with himself. Part of him told himself to let her go, he was no good for her, and the other part urged him to return to the bedchamber and plant his seed deep inside her, sealing them together forever.

He continued on to his grandmother, needing time to think and wishing she was lucid. She was a wise woman his grandmother and she had offered him endless advice through the years, that he had benefited from. He could use her wisdom now.

Eleanor left shortly after he entered the room. He moved the chair closer to the bed and took his grandmother's hand in his. Her hand, while small, had always held such strength, felt fragile now and caused him to worry. But he trusted Willow. She knew about healing, though she didn't consider herself a healer. In time she would realize her skills as her mother probably had recognized her latent talent and had taught her well.

"I need to talk, *Seanmhair*," he said. "I need your wisdom." He proceeded to tell her all and every now and then he could have sworn she had squeezed his hand, though it might have been that he had wanted to believe that she did.

Eleanor returned a couple of hours later. "It has been a tiresome journey for you and Willow. Go sleep. I will watch over Sara for the night."

He consented, though with guilt. He felt he should stay with his grandmother, but he wanted to be with his wife. Though, it might not be wise to join her in bed, especially a decent, comfortable bed, that accommodated more than one person.

After thanking Eleanor for her help, he rushed up the stairs and to the bedchamber he would share with Willow. He found her asleep in bed, lying on her side hugging her pillow.

He was relieved or so he told himself. He hadn't wanted temptation poking at him and temptation was surely poking, though more like jabbing hard at him. A thought brought an image to mind of him sliding gently between his wife's legs and burying his manhood deep inside her and leaving her… with child.

What was he thinking? He couldn't do that. Not yet at least. He wouldn't do that to her. He wouldn't let her wake one morning to find him gone.

He told himself not to remove his garments, not get in bed naked, but he paid no mind to his own warnings. Besides, she wore a nightdress, one he itched to remove, but warned himself against doing. He eased himself up against her, his arm going around her waist to draw her slowly back against him. She was toasty warm, her flowery scent ridiculously tempting, so much so that his manhood roused considerably.

He buried his face in her slightly damp hair and enjoyed its fresh scent. She smelled so good and felt so good that he could devour her, except… she snored lightly.

She was exhausted and he couldn't bring himself to disturb her, even if his manhood urged otherwise.

He settled comfortably around her, thinking how easily he had grown accustomed to sleeping with her. He'd never felt that way about a woman. A woman had meant nothing more to him than a way to satisfy a need and a warm body to wrap himself around on a cold night.

With Willow, it was more than a need. It was a feeling of being content when he was with her, and suffering an empty ache when separated from her. And being wrapped around her warm body felt like a welcoming hug after being away from home.

Damn, he did love her, and he had no idea what he was going to do about it.

***

Willow woke alone, though she hadn't slept alone. She had woken during the night to find herself snuggled against her husband. She had never felt as content as she had at that moment. She had been tempted to stir him awake with an intimate touch, but she had asked herself if that was what she wanted, to take advantage of their situation? It had been an easy decision. She wanted her husband to decide for himself if he wished to remain wed to her. She would not have passion decide their fate.

There was much to be done today and with a long, easy stretch, she eased herself out of bed. She donned her garments, combed and plaited her hair, slipped her boots on, and left the bedchamber to see how Sara had fared the night and certain that was where she'd find her husband. Afterwards, she'd speak with James. She owed him that and she knew exactly where he'd be at this early hour… in his solar. It was a habit of his to go there in the morning upon rising and plan what needed to be done that day.

Willow was surprised that her husband wasn't with his grandmother when she entered the bedchamber, though more surprised to find James there and to see that he and Eleanor were asleep. He had placed his chair beside hers and her head rested on his shoulder while his head rested atop her head. It appeared James was more than smitten with Eleanor and obviously she felt the same.

Willow hated to disturb them, but she had to see to Sara.

"Eleanor," she said softly and the young woman and James's heads shot up.

James quickly got to his feet and turned to face Willow. "We fell asleep."

"It was generous of you to keep Eleanor company," Willow said.

Eleanor's cheeks blossomed red. "We were talking and must have grown tired."

Willow almost chuckled at the way they both attempted to explain what happened.

"I must see to my chores," Eleanor said, appearing eager to take her leave.

"I as well," James said, looking toward the door.

"I am most grateful for your help... both your help," Willow said.

Eleanor gave a bob of her head as she hurried and left the room.

James stopped halfway through the open door, casting a hasty glance after Eleanor before turning his attention to Willow.

"When you are done here, a word, please, in my solar," he said.

"Aye," she said a smile breaking free, watching James inching more and more out the door as he cast another glance toward the stairs. "I'll be there soon."

"Good. Good, see you there," he said and rushed off.

Willow had been tempted to ask James if he had seen Slatter, but being she had found him and Eleanor asleep, she doubted he had seen her husband.

She walked over to the bed and saw that Sara still slept. She placed a gentle hand to her brow and was relieved to find it normal to the touch. That the old woman didn't stir worried her some. She would ask Eleanor and James how Sara had fared during the night.

A young servant lass, Carna, appeared at the open door just as Willow was adding logs to the hearth. She knew all the servants' names, not that there were that many to remember, most all were trustworthy and dependable. A few got into their cups too often, but James dealt with those.

"I've been sent to help with whatever you need," Carna said, hurrying over to help Willow with the logs.

"I need you to sit with Sara and watch over her until I return. I need to know if she stirs much or remains still," Willow explained.

Carna nodded and once done with the hearth went to sit in the chair by the bed and keep watch.

Willow hurried down the stairs and to the kitchen to have cook prepare the brew Sara would need when she woke or stirred. She was surprised and pleased to find Eleanor already there seeing to it.

With that done, she made her way to James's solar. She half expected to run into Snow, her sister an early riser, but then she recalled before going to see Sorrell that Snow had been taking the pup out in the morning for a walk, which was probably what she was doing now. She would find her later and talk with her in their mum's solar, a place she and her sisters would gather to talk, laugh, and cry together. It was a place that brought them comfort and camaraderie.

James had left the solar door open for her and she entered, closing it behind her.

He pointed to the chairs by the hearth. "Hot cider awaits us on this cold day. Yesterday's snow stopped, though I think it will fall again before the day ends."

They sat, both stretching their legs out toward the flames lapping at the logs in the fireplace.

James finally spoke. "Tell me why you wed this scoundrel."

Her answer slipped out without thought. "I love him." She smiled upon hearing herself admit it aloud. It felt good to say, to let someone know what her heart had been telling her. "And he's not the scoundrel he professes to be."

"You are the most sensible woman I know, Willow. You can't tell me that you believe his outrageous tale about a person who resembles him being responsible for all he's accused of."

"I understand how you doubt that, and if I hadn't seen the man with my own eyes, I would be skeptical myself."

"You saw this phantom man?" James asked anxiously.

"I did and I would have sworn, if asked, that it was Slatter I saw."

"You saw the two at the same time?"

"No, but where I saw the man and then saw Slatter," —she shook her head— "he would not have been able to get to that place so fast."

"I would like to believe you, I truly would, and if you had seen them together, then there would be no denying it."

"I believe him," Willow said, defending her husband.

"I'm sure you do. He has a charming, though rather conniving tongue and can convince most anyone of anything. Do you truly want a husband you cannot trust?"

"I trust my husband. He speaks the truth to me."

"Slatter doesn't know how to speak the truth," James said frustrated. "He lies to benefit himself and uses people until they are of no use to him, then walks away. Do you want to live each day wondering if it will be the last you will ever see of him?"

"Let it be, James. Slatter is my husband and will remain my husband," Willow said firmly.

"But for how long?" James asked.

"As long as she'll have me."

Willow and James turned to see that Slatter had entered the room and had closed the door behind him.

"I didn't hear you knock or enter," James said.

"I heard my wife's voice and since we don't keep secrets from each other, I knew she wouldn't mind me joining you both." Slatter went to his wife and placed his hand on her shoulder, giving it a squeeze.

James looked to Slatter, then to Willow. "If this is what you want, Willow, I will not object, though I must admit it makes no sense to me and I fear you will regret it. However, there is the issue of his past deeds and my concern of the potential for future questionable deeds."

"So what you're saying is that you want to make sure that I'm going to behave properly," Slatter clarified.

"The Clan Macardle is recovering from *difficult* times. I don't want that recovery hampered in any way," James explained.

"Are you asking for my word that I will behave properly?" Slatter asked.

"I would if I could trust your word."

"James," Willow said in a scolding tone. "I will not have you speak with such disrespect to my husband."

"You would be the first to tell me that men earn respect. Do you truly believe your husband has earned respect after knowing what problems his lies have cost others and what he has cost the Clan Macardle? And please don't tell me it was someone who resembled him who is responsible for it all. That is a poor excuse unless it can be explicitly proven."

"Then I suppose we'll just have to prove it," Willow said, standing. "But until then I will not have my husband disrespected, especially in my own home."

James stood as well. "I gave your father my word that I would take care of his daughters and that is why I question this marriage. I don't want to see you hurt or suffer any regret over a hasty decision."

"When have you ever known me to make a decision that I hadn't thought out? Believe me when I tell you that I wanted this marriage."

"I believe that, Willow. What I question is the reason you married Slatter."

A knock at the door interrupted any response.

"Sorry to disturb," the servant said after entering, "but the Lord of Fire approaches."

"The devil has come to collect his due," Slatter said with a laugh.

Willow scowled at him, more from fear than annoyance, worried that Lord Tarass would demand Slatter be returned to him for punishment.

James openly admonished him. "This is not funny. Lord Tarass is a formidable man. You would do well to beg his forgiveness."

Slatter's joviality vanished in an instant. "I beg no man's forgiveness and most certainly not the man who wrongfully imprisoned me."

"It would be best if neither of you were present when I meet with him," James said.

"No!" Slatter and Willow said in unison and Slatter took his wife's hand.

"We will face Lord Tarass together," Willow said and felt her husband's hand close tight around hers.

The three went to the Great Hall to wait for Lord Tarass, James ordering food and drink brought to the table.

"Let go of my arm, you idiot!"

Willow's mouth dropped open and James rolled his eyes and shook his head. Slatter smiled seeing it was Snow who called Lord Tarass an idiot.

"What did you just say to me?" Tarass demanded.

"You're not only more blind than I am, you're deaf as well," Snow said and Thaw, cradled in the crook of her arm, agreed with several barks.

"You walk blindly about the village and almost get run down by me, yet I'm the one who's blind?" Tarass argued.

Snow yanked her arm free of his grasp, though truth be told he let her go, his grip having been too firm to free herself when she had first tried.

"You are when you carelessly ride through a village with no thought of anyone but yourself," she accused, shaking a finger in his shadowy direction.

Tarass grabbed her finger. "Not only does that annoying pup of yours need a leash, but so do you."

"A leash would be best served on you," Snow said with a heavy scowl.

Gasps were heard from those in the Great Hall, all except Slatter... he smiled.

Tarass yanked her against him, the little pup snarling and snapping at him. Tarass paid him no heed. "Don't ever, *ever* point a finger at me again and as far as a leash, if you were mine, I'd keep you on a short one."

Snow could make out the shadow of his face and she planted her own face close to his. "Then I thank the heavens that I'm not stuck with an idiot brute like you." Thaw snarled in agreement.

"Snow!" James called out in a reprimanding tone as he approached her.

Tarass appeared ready to explode. "If you weren't blind—"

"What? What would you do to me?" Snow challenged.

Tarass planted his nose against hers. "Trust me, you don't want to find out." He gave her a slight shove and stepped away from her.

Slatter leaned down and whispered to his wife, "You Macardle woman certainly have courage."

Willow had been worried for Snow, fearing what Lord Tarass might do to her, but Slatter was right. Snow had gained much courage in her absence and she was proud of her sister. She was about to hurry over to her when her husband stopped her.

"She can make her way to us, just let her know you're here," Slatter said.

"Snow, over at our table," Willow called out, realizing habit would have had her going to Snow.

Snow made her way to Willow, leaving James to speak with Lord Tarass.

"You need to deal more firmly with the Macardle sisters. First, you allow Sorrell to ruin the marriage arrangement made for her, then you let Snow, a blind woman, wander around without anyone looking after her or chastising her for being disrespectful, and now Willow arrives home with Slatter, my prisoner, now her husband. This will not do, James. Husband or not Slatter needs to pay for his crimes. I received a missive from Lord Ruddock before I learned of Slatter's escape from my men, letting me know that he played a part in the devastation his family suffered. Slatter needs to pay and I intend to see that he does."

"My husband did nothing wrong," Willow said, Tarass having spoken loud enough for all to hear.

"You are a fool if you believe his lies that a man who resembled him is responsible for his dastardly deeds," Tarass said.

"But what if it is true and you condemn an innocent man?" Snow asked.

Tarass shot Slatter a look. "You let women speak for you, Slatter?"

Slatter grinned. "Intelligent, courageous women can speak for me anytime."

"You'll not take my husband from me," Willow said with a defiant toss of her head.

"He will suffer the consequences of his crimes," Tarass said as if declaring it already done.

"Prove he committed the crimes," Snow challenged.

Willow reached out and squeezed her hand grateful for her sister's support.

"I leave this in your hands for now, James," Tarass said. "Find out the truth and if Slatter isn't responsible, then I care not about him, but if he is, I will see him punished. You have until the end of winter. If nothing has changed by then, he will be returned to me for punishment," —he held up his hand when James went to protest— "and I have no doubt Lord Ruddock will agree with me on this."

"I have your word on that?" James asked.

"You do," Tarass said.

James nodded, wearing his worry for all to see.

The door burst open. "Lord Tarass! Lord Tarass! Rhodes is dead, a stab wound to the chest."

Chapter Fifteen

Willow gripped her husband's hand tightly as she, James, and Tarass stood looking down at Rhodes. The warrior was dead, blood covering his chest from what looked to Willow to be two stab wounds. He lay inside the woods, not far from where Clan Macardle land met Clan MacLoon land.

Fear ran through Willow. Her husband would be blamed for this. Too many had seen the animosity Rhodes and Slatter had for each other. And there were those who had heard Slatter threaten to kill Rhodes. This did not bode well for her husband at all and she did her best to calm her fears and think sensibly. Not an easy task with the fire she saw blazing in Tarass's eyes. And when he turned his eyes on Slatter, Willow's stomach twisted with such fear that she thought her legs would fail her.

"Slatter killed him! He killed him!"

They all turned to see Owen, another of Tarass's warriors and one who rode with Rhodes, rushing toward them.

Pain and fury mixed in the warrior's dark eyes when his glance landed on Rhodes. He turned his anger on Slatter.

"Slatter killed him," Owen said, his curt remark leaving no room for doubt. "Rhodes told me that Slatter asked to meet with him at sunrise, that there was something of great importance he needed to tell him and only him. I wanted to go with him but he ordered me to remain at camp with the men."

Tarass turned heated eyes on Slatter. "You'll hang for this."

Willow went to step in front of her husband, but he pushed her behind him. "Do you want the truth of what happened to Rhodes or would you hang an innocent man and let the one who took Rhodes's life walk free?"

"You lie, you coward," Owen yelled. "You set a trap, lured him here, and killed him."

"I never asked to meet Rhodes, and watch who you call coward," Slatter threatened with a snarl.

"Liar," Owen yelled and took quick steps toward Slatter.

Slatter didn't hesitate, his hand went to the hilt of his dagger.

Tarass's hand shot out stopping Owen from taking another step toward Slatter. "You deserve to die."

"The one who did this deserves to die," Slatter corrected.

"You gave your word we'd have until the end of winter to prove Slatter innocent," Willow reminded, stepping from behind her husband and wishing he had been beside her in bed when she woke this morning. Then no one could dispute his innocence.

"My word I gave you concerned his other deeds, not killing one of my warriors," Tarass argued.

"This can easily be settled," James said, stepping forward. "Dawn, the time of the meeting, would find Slatter in bed with his wife. Willow need only confirm that."

"His wife would lie for him," Owen accused.

"My wife does not lie," Slatter said, defending her. "She would speak the truth and tell you she woke alone this morning."

Her husband was right. She wouldn't have lied for him. There would be no reason, since she believed him innocent. Her husband knew her well, just as she did him. He didn't do this, but would anyone but her believe him?

"Where were you around sunrise?" James asked.

Willow didn't draw a breath waiting for her husband to answer.

"With Snow," Slatter said. "I met her in the Great Hall after having looked in on my grandmother." He gave a nod to James. "I saw that you and Eleanor had fallen asleep in chairs beside each other and, so I left, not wanting to disturb you or my grandmother who slept peacefully."

Willow let a quiet breath out, knowing the truth of his explanation since she had come upon the same scene with James and Eleanor.

"Snow was alone when I came upon her," Tarass said.

"I left her, knowing my wife probably had woken and would be seeing to my grandmother. The servant watching her told me that Willow was with James in his solar and I went there. Snow can confirm it for you."

"You will hide behind a blind woman?" Owen accused.

Slatter turned harsh eyes on him. "Is it the truth you want or blame you seek for failing to protect your fellow warrior?"

Tarass's arm once again stopped Owen from lunging forward and none failed to see the strength it took to stop him, Owen stumbling back from the impact.

"You lead the troop now, Owen. Return to the warriors and assure them that Rhodes's death will be revenged and appoint men to come and get Rhodes and see him taken home for a proper burial," Tarass ordered and Owen obeyed, though not before sending Slatter a nasty look.

"I'll hear what Snow has to say and will decide then what to do," Tarass said.

"What is there to do but find the culprit responsible for killing Rhodes," Willow said, worrying that Tarass would forcibly take Slatter and see him hanged.

Tarass turned to head back to the keep, saying as he went, "Maybe your husband didn't kill Rhodes, but I have no doubt he was someway involved with his death, and I intend to see him hang."

***

Snow confirmed what Slatter had said and was quickly dismissed from James's solar along with Willow who protested vigorously until her husband ordered her to leave to her surprise.

Leave now, wife.

His words still rang in her head as she sat with Snow in their mum's solar.

"Let the men do what they will," Snow said, petting Thaw, asleep in her lap. "And we will do what we will, search for the truth ourselves."

Willow snapped out of her musings. "You're right. I know the man who resembles Slatter exists." Willow sat up straighter in the chair. "So does Devin, a longtime friend of Slatter's and so does Walcott, another friend, though often pessimistic, but faithful to Slatter. Then there are all the people he has helped who would defend him."

"They need to be here to help him. No one believes another like Slatter exists and, therefore, will not bother to search for him. But he must be close if he convinced Rhodes to meet him in the woods."

Willow gasped. "I never thought of that, but you're right. That man must be close by if he met with Rhodes under the pretense of being Slatter."

"Have James send a small troop of men to escort them here. At least then you'll have some who will defend Slatter," Snow explained.

Willow laughed softly. "And here I thought I was the sensible one."

"Love distracts," Snow said, laughing herself. "And don't bother to deny you love your husband. I can hear it in your voice when you speak about him just as I can hear it in his voice when he speaks about you."

"You think Slatter loves me?" Willow asked.

Snow tilted her head at her sister. "Isn't that why he wed you?"

Guilt poked at Willow for not telling her sister the truth. The three had always trusted one another, knowing anything they shared would not be shared with anyone else.

"I need to tell you something," Willow said.

"I was wondering when you were going to get around to it." Snow lowered her voice, though the door to the room was closed. "So tell me why you truly wed Slatter."

It didn't take long for Willow to explain it all and finish with, "How I fell in love with him I'll never know."

"Fate, I suppose. And truth be told when I spoke with him this morning I couldn't seem to align him with the man who had set fire to our shed or did the many things said of him. I know his tongue can charm but he doesn't strike me as a scoundrel."

"I have seen him kill without hesitation," Willow said, recalling the men who had meant them harm and explained to Snow.

"He killed to protect you. That is different from luring a man into the woods and murdering him."

A soft rap on the door and Eleanor calling out that she had hot cider for them had Willow hurrying to open the door.

"Join us," Snow offered. "We are trying to find a way to keep Slatter from hanging for this killing. Another's thought is always helpful."

Eleanor looked hesitant.

"The truth is, Eleanor, Snow and I know that you and James are falling in love."

Snow giggled. "I so enjoy hearing you two tread lightly around each other, complimenting and finding reasons to be with each other. I don't understand why James doesn't admit he loves you and be done with it."

Eleanor's cheeks blushed red. "I think I lost my heart to him when I arrived here and he caught me after

I almost collapsed once off the horse. He was so gentle yet strong. I never had a man treat me with such kindness. But it isn't me we should discuss."

"You have a thought on the problem with Slatter?" Willow asked anxiously.

Eleanor spoke hesitantly and in a whisper. "I overheard the Lord of Fire speaking to one of his warriors as he walked through the Great Hall."

"Do share," Snow urged.

Willow pointed to the chair, her sister Sorrell usually occupied, for Eleanor to sit, and she did.

As soon as Willow saw Eleanor worry her hands, she asked, "What's wrong?"

"What is it? Did something happen?" Snow asked, leaning forward in the chair and causing Thaw to pop up out of his sleep to give a yawning yelp.

Eleanor spoke reluctantly. "I fear what I overheard."

Willow's stomach knotted. "What did you overhear?"

"Lord Tarass ordered his warrior to send a message to a man. That he would pay handsomely if he could get here as soon as possible and handle a disturbing matter."

"Are you familiar with this man Lord Tarass sends for?" Willow asked, her apprehension growing.

"I know the name. A man showed up at the abbey one night begging for help. He insisted that one of the devil's strongest demons was after him and the only place he'd be safe was on sacred ground. Mother Abbess allowed him entrance, thinking him ill of mind and once he calmed down she'd send him on his way.

He ranted for two days, begging God to protect him, not to let the mighty demon get him." She stopped and shivered. "One night the whole abbey woke to agonizing screams that seemed to come from the stone walls themselves as if they suffered along with the man. Mother Abbess had me and another postulant lead the way to the man's room, her and only two other nuns following. I knew she meant to sacrifice the two of us if necessary."

Willow listened intently, fear tugging at her stomach.

"When we reached the room, Mother Abbess ordered me to open the door and go inside. She kept the door locked at all times, according to the man's instructions, but she didn't hand me the key since we had all assumed someone had already gotten inside. I tried the handle, shocked to find the door locked. How did someone enter a locked room? Mother Abbess's hand trembled when she handed me the key and she hurriedly stepped far away from the door with the others.

"My hand shook so badly that it took me several minutes to unlock the door. The room was dark, since the man had insisted on a room without a hearth. He lay on the ground dead, his body misshapen by all his broken bones, his eyes wide with fright, and his mouth open in his last scream. I could still hear the name he screamed over and over. I never wanted to hear that name again, but I did when Lord Tarass said, 'send for the *Slayer*.'"

Chapter Sixteen

Willow wanted to run from the room and warn her husband, tell him to get as far away from here as possible, but she feared that wouldn't be far enough from what Eleanor had said.

"We need to solve this problem before this demon descends on Slatter," Snow said.

"The man was right. The Slayer is a demon. How else could he enter past a locked door?" Eleanor said, a tremble running through her.

"You need to get Slatter's friends here, and maybe his grandmother knows something that might help," Snow suggested.

It didn't surprise Willow that she had thought the same. The three of them, Sorrell, Snow, and herself often shared identical thoughts on a matter, though her approach had always been the most sensible. She didn't think being sensible now would help her, especially if she was to face a demon to save her husband. Though she questioned the validity of demons, the horror that some men perpetrated on others made one wonder if perhaps the devil actually did capture souls to serve him.

"Did Sara say anything last night?" Willow asked Eleanor.

"No, she was restless but silent. I wondered if she was fighting to wake, but she settled to my touch."

"It worries me that she hasn't fully woken," Willow admitted.

"Don't you remember that I barely woke after the accident that took my sight? I could hear Mum and you talking, and Sorrell when she came and sat and talked with me. But I didn't want to wake and talk with anyone. I was in pain and sleep was the only thing that made it tolerable," Snow said.

The door opened and Slatter filled the doorway. "A word with my wife."

After a quick hug from her sister, Snow left the room with Eleanor, Thaw yapping at her heels as he followed her out.

Slatter shut the door and stood there looking at his wife.

"I know what you're going to say and don't even think of it," Willow warned. "You're not leaving. We will fight this together and clear your name."

"You're confident I am innocent?" he asked.

"Without a doubt and if we don't clear your name Lord Tarass will forever hunt you. No, you must stay and see this done," she insisted and walked over to him. "You also need to send for Devin and the others. You made mention that you didn't have much of a home. Well you have a home now and so do your friends… here with the Clan Macardle."

His first thought was to deny her, but that wouldn't be fair to the others. He had promised them a home and they deserved a good one. They would find that here with the Macardle clan.

Willow began to pace back and forth in front of him. "Lord Ruddock left some of his warriors here to help with repairs and to protect us. They won't do for this task. The Clan Macardle does have a few warriors of their own. We'll send two or three of them to escort your friends here."

His wife spoke as if they had decided this together, that they worked as one. That he was not alone. That they were family. The thought that she fought for him stabbed at his heart. He didn't deserve her trust, and yet, he ached for it.

Willow stopped pacing. "What was discussed in the solar?"

"That they trust me less than before Rhodes was killed and that I'm not to go anywhere. That I'm not to venture off the grounds of the keep. That Lord Tarass's men will keep close watch on me. And that if I harm you in any way I'll hang for it. Lord Tarass made quite the point that hanging would be the easiest way to absolve our marriage."

"So it didn't matter what Snow said, Lord Tarass and James believe you guilty and the meeting consisted of nothing more than warning you."

"Every minute of it," Slatter confirmed, "though I was more concerned with what other horror this dastardly fellow has planned. I believe he wants me to suffer the blame. If I suffer no consequences for this killing, who then would he choose next to kill?"

Willow shook her head when she saw how his dark eyes focused so intently on her. "No. No. He would not come after me."

"You don't think if you were found dead that I wouldn't be blamed and hanged almost immediately?"

"We'll find him," Willow said.

He stepped closer to her. "How?"

"As I first suggested, a trap," she said. "We'll think of something and when Devin and Walcott get here, they can help us execute it."

"I'll not see you put in harm's way," he said, reaching out to take hold of her arm and gently tug her toward him.

"Nor I you," she said softly, her hand going to rest on his chest. "Have you ever heard of a man called the Slayer?"

His eyes shot wide with anger and his fingers tightened around her arm. "Where did you hear that name?"

"Eleanor heard Lord Tarass tell his warrior to send for the Slayer. She knew the name due to an incident at the abbey where she had been a postulant. She believes that the Slayer is one of the devil's demons."

"Come to claim the souls of the damned," Slatter said.

His words sent a chill running through Willow. "You've heard of him?"

"Aye, his name is whispered in places where good men don't frequent, but send men to hire heartless men, or soulless men as some believe the Slayer to be."

"He must be soulless from what Eleanor said he did to the man at the abbey, which is why we must prove your innocence before he arrives."

"You don't doubt, not even a little, my innocence?" he asked, releasing her arm to slip his hand to rest at her back, nudging her closer to him.

"Not a trickle or hint of a doubt," she said, easing into the comfort of his arms.

"Be careful, wife, with the way things are going, you may be stuck with me for the rest of your days," Slatter warned with the hint of a smile.

"I could think of a worse fate."

"And what would that be?"

"Never having met you at all," she said softly.

Words failed him, though instinct didn't. He kissed her, a gentle kiss, as tender and heartfelt as her words. But the ache for his wife that seemed to forever linger in his loins flared, demanding more. His kiss paid heed to the passion that flamed in him and demanded more as well. He might have been able to harness it and keep it at bay if his wife didn't respond with an eager passion of her own.

His hands ran down along her back to cup her backside and squeeze it tight, pushing her up against his manhood that was growing hard with impatience.

He tore his mouth away from hers. "Once I make love to you, wife, our fate is sealed. Is that what you want?"

"Sensible or not, it is what my heart tells me... I love you," she said a soft smile surfacing as she brought her lips to his.

A rap at the door sounded before a voice called out, "Sara is awake and asking for her grandson."

Slatter felt pulled between the two women who meant so much to him. How did he brush aside what his wife had just told him and go to his grandmother and how did he not go to his grandmother who had to be frightened upon waking in a strange place?

Willow grabbed his hand. "Come, we must see to *Seanmhair*. Afterwards you can tell me how much you love me."

Slatter shook his head and snagged his wife around the waist with one arm to lift her off her feet and kiss her quick.

"Damn it, wife," he snarled playfully, "You don't tell me to tell you how much I love you. I say it of my own free will."

Willow chuckled, feeling good she had admitted what was in her heart. She grabbed his face in her hands and brought her lips near his, though didn't kiss him. Instead she whispered, "Then show me of your own free will how much you love me."

That brought a rumbling growl from him before he teasingly nipped at her lips. "That's a challenge I can't refuse."

He placed her on her feet, took her hand, and wondered with things appearing so bad how he felt such joy.

His wife.

She had not only brought joy to him, she brought something much more… hope. Something he hadn't felt in years.

Sara smiled as soon as she saw her grandson, her one arm reaching out to him with some difficulty.

Slatter hurried to her side, taking her frail hand, and sat on the edge of the bed and leaned over to kiss her pale cheek. "You are safe here, *Seanmhair*. You have nothing to fear."

She shook her head and her smile quickly dissolved.

"Aye, you are safe," Slatter assured her, wanting to chase the fear he saw rush up in her eyes that had aged through the years, lines framing them and wisdom buried deep in them.

Sara tried to speak but coughed instead and Willow quickly grabbed a goblet, off the small table, filled with a chamomile brew, to hand to her husband.

Slatter slipped his hand beneath his grandmother's head and held the goblet to her lips to drink. He was surprised and pleased with how much she drank. Before he placed her head back on the pillow, Willow braced another pillow beneath Sara's head.

The old woman smiled her thanks.

Slatter took his wife's hand. "This is my wife, Willow, *Seanmhair*. She is a healer and tends you well."

"Beautiful," Sara said with a smile stronger than either Slatter or Willow expected.

"I am so pleased to meet you and tend to your care. With rest and some healing brews, you will do well. I look forward to talking with you about your grandson."

"Many tales to tell," Sara said with a soft chuckle.

"That's not fair, two against one," Slatter complained playfully.

His grandmother slipped her hand out of his and held up two fingers, then pointed one finger at Slatter. "Protecting one."

His grandmother had always been there for him, had always listened to him, and had never preached to him. She had advised one thing over and over... *heed your thoughts and your words, they make you who you are.*

"I protect you now, *Seanmhair*," he said.

Her eyes went wide. "Not safe."

He was about to assure her that she was safe when she pointed to him.

"Not safe," she said, jabbing her finger toward Slatter.

Slatter took her hand and leaned down as he brought it to his lips to kiss. "It's all right. I understand. You feel it's me who's not safe."

She nodded.

"Did the man who caused you harm come looking for me?" he asked, trying to keep his rising anger out of his voice.

Sara nodded again.

"He wanted to know where I was?"

Another nod gave him the answer and his temper flared even more. The man who had stolen his identity had caused her suffering and he couldn't wait to get his hands on him.

Sara gave barely a shrug, her eyes starting to flutter with sleep.

He knew what she tried to tell him. What she told the ones who harmed her. She didn't know where he was. He visited when he wanted, but where he went when he left her, she never knew, and he had purposely kept it that way. He hadn't wanted her to know what he did.

Slatter felt a hand on his shoulder and he looked up at his wife, knowing what she would say, and agreeing.

"She needs to rest."

Slatter laid his grandmother's hand on her stomach, then leaned over and kissed her brow. "Sleep. We'll talk again."

Slatter moved off the bed and Willow followed him to stand near the hearth. He leaned down to add more logs to the fire.

"I don't want her to get cold."

Willow ached for her husband, seeing the worry and anger swirling in his dark eyes as he looked up at her.

He stood. "She suffers because of me."

"She suffers because of the man who stole your identity. He's the one who needs to be found and punished for what he's done to so many."

Slatter knew the man's punishment... death, at his hands.

"Right now *Seanmhair* does well and that's what matters. She will heal and grow strong and she will make her home here with us. And we shouldn't waste a minute in seeing that happen. We need to send that message to Devin."

Did he deserve this woman's love? She put all else aside to help him. Deserve her or not. Wise or not. He finally admitted to himself that he never wanted to let her go. And he intended to seal their vows so nothing could keep that from happening.

"I'll have someone sit with her," she said and headed to the door, hearing a small bark and stopped, knowing any moment Snow and Thaw would appear. And they did.

"What is it, Thaw?" Snow asked and the dog brushed against her leg, his tail wagging, hitting the hem of her garment. "Someone we know is here."

"He is learning well," Willow said. "Slatter and I just finished speaking with Sara and I need someone to sit with her."

"I was just coming to do that," Snow said. "Go. I will keep Sara company."

Slatter rested his hand on Snow's shoulder after she sat in the chair by the bed, Thaw settling at her feet. "I appreciate your help with my grandmother."

"She's family," Snow said with a pat to his hand.

Slatter followed Willow out the bedchamber door and as they descended the stairs, he said, "I think we should consult James on our decision before we send anyone to collect what little family I have. He is chieftain of the clan."

"The Clan Macardle needs to grow. I'm sure he'd be only too pleased to accept them into the clan."

"Let's make certain of that before we send for them. I don't want them to arrive here only to be turned away. They have suffered enough."

They each slipped on a cloak, having been told that James was checking the storage shed."

A cold wind whipped at them when they stepped outside the keep as did a light falling snow, and Slatter was quick to take his wife's hand in his, covering most of it to keep it warm.

His considerate gesture did more than warm her hand, it also warmed her heart.

It wasn't lost on them that not only a couple of Tarass's warriors lingered near as they walked, but a few Ruddock's warriors' kept steady eyes on them as well. A good watch was being kept on Slatter.

Willow thought Slatter might complain, but he said nothing. His glance, while appearing to remain straight in front of him, took note of every warrior that marked their path, just as his eyes had seemed to take in everything around them when she had ridden with him.

James greeted them with a nod. "Thanks to Lord Ruddock finishing the building of the shed, *lost to a fire*, we have a sturdy food shed."

"I know I waste my breath, but I will say it again. I didn't set fire to your shed. Whatever possible reason would I have for doing so?" Slatter asked, having grown exceedingly tired of taking the blame for something he didn't do.

"The offer of coin is a good reason," James said.

"Aye, and when we catch the fellow he can tell us how much he was paid for his heinous crime," Willow said.

She could see she perplexed James, but then he had always been able to count on her to see reason and do the right thing. He had lost her dependable nature and she hadn't given thought to how it might have upset him. But she could see now that it did and while she felt a tug of sadness, as strange as it seemed, she also felt a sense of freedom.

"You've often said how you wished to see the Clan Macardle grow in size—"

"You're with child already?" James asked not even trying to hide his shock.

Slatter smiled and rested his hand to Willow's stomach. "It will be soon enough that Willow grows with child."

"But not yet," Willow was quick to say, seeing the teasing look in her husband's dark eyes and brushing his hand away before someone saw and set off wagging tongues that would have her with child by nightfall. "Slatter has a small group of people that is like family to him and I'd like to send for them so they can make their home here with the Clan Macardle. I've met a few and they are good people."

"Are they much like Slatter?" James asked, casting a glance at him.

"Life has treated them poorly, some more poorly than others, but they are honest, good people and would prove grateful for the opportunity to have a good, permanent home and be part of a good clan. There are young and old alike among them, and all will do their share," Slatter said with a pride for the small group he had gathered.

"I will gladly accept them into our clan after your innocence is proven," James said.

Willow turned such an angry glare on James that it had him drawing his head back in shock.

"I can't believe you would refuse us this," Willow said.

"These people you speak of no doubt owe their allegiance to Slatter. They would protect him and possibly lie for him. There is enough lies being spoken and spread without more people to attest to them," James said.

"Are you accusing me of lying?" Willow asked.

"You are an honest woman, Willow, but you have changed since being with Slatter and I must do what is best for the clan, and at one time you would have advised me to do just that."

Willow couldn't argue with his logic. She would have done what he said, advised him against it. And she would have thought the woman foolish for believing a man who was known to lie. She could beg him to trust her on this, but again there'd be no logic to it. James would be right in refusing her. So what did she do?

"I understand, James. Your clan counts on you to protect them, keep them safe as do my people," Slatter said.

Willow heard a low warning in her husband's voice that she doubted James recognized.

"Once your innocence is proven, I'll gladly offer your people sanctuary," James said.

Sanctuary, not a home, Willow thought and from the way her husband tensed beside her, he thought the same. Which meant that James didn't expect Slatter to be proven innocent. He was placating her, letting her believe he would accept her marriage to Slatter, when he agreed with Tarass. Both men would see her husband dead.

"Now if that is all, I need to get done with this chore before the heavy snow falls," James said, dismissing them.

Slatter nodded and Willow turned with him, their hands having remained joined, to take their leave.

"A private word, Willow," James said, stopping the couple.

Slatter kissed his wife's cheek. "Go speak with your brother. I will be in the keep."

Willow didn't want to leave Slatter's side. He wasn't pleased with what James had said and she wasn't either. James and Tarass thought Slatter guilty and they intended to see him punished. That was why Tarass had sent for the Slayer.

Willow returned to James and didn't give him a chance to speak. "You lied to me. You want my husband dead."

"What I want is the truth and for you to be safe and not regret a decision made on a whim in a moment of madness," James argued.

"If you believe one thing I say, James, believe that my decision to wed Slatter was not decided in a moment of madness, nor did I fall in love with him on a whim. He won my heart just as you won Eleanor's heart, by being a good and kind man to her. And I hope you do not waste time in letting her know that you love her and make her your wife. Time with the one you love is too precious to waste even a moment not acknowledging it."

James stood staring at her, his mouth open but no words coming out.

"Though Snow is blind, I think she sees more clearly than any of us. She knew from the start that you and Eleanor were drawn to each other just as she could tell how much Slatter and I love each other, just as she senses Slatter is a good man regardless of what is being said about him." She shook her head. "I am sorry I'm not the sensible woman you had come to rely on, but I'm not sorry for allowing myself for once in my life not to listen to reason, but follow what my heart tells me. I love my husband and I will not see him hang," — she shuddered at the thought— "when he is an innocent man." She went to turn and stopped. "And just so you know. I think Eleanor is a wonderful woman and would make you a good wife."

She hurried off, worried what her husband might do.

Chapter Seventeen

Willow had grown suspicious of her husband when she realized he was avoiding her. Every time he spotted her, he smiled, sometimes winked, and turned in another direction. He kept his distance from her until evening when the Great Hall filled for supper. He was up to something and he was taking no chances she'd find out about it.

James requested to speak with her in his solar after supper, a more jovial meal than she had anticipated. Her husband had everyone laughing at the table with tales he had heard in his travels and James even shared a tale or two of his own. It was a pleasurable time, one Willow wished could be repeated more often.

When Willow went to follow James out of the Great Hall, Slatter stood and took her in his arms. He kissed her cheek and whispered in her ear, "This may not be the right time, but I have a need to tell you that I love you. How you captured my heart I'll never know, but my heart belongs to you now and forever."

He stepped away from her then, far too fast for her to stop him, and while his words filled her heart with joy, a sense a dread fell over her. He may have told her he loved her, but she got the distinct feeling he was also saying good-bye.

Willow hurried to James's solar, worried about being away from her husband too long, worried she wouldn't find him there when she returned.

James was quick to speak with her. "I've rethought what you asked and I think it would prove beneficial for Slatter to have his people come here. Perhaps they can help shed some light on the truth."

Willow rushed to James and hugged him. "There's the understanding and kind brother I've come to know and love."

"My apologizes, Willow. You returned changed, though if I were honest with myself you returned happier than I've ever seen you and your confidence and courage just as strong as it's ever been. When you advised me about not wasting time when it came to love and how easily you accepted Eleanor—" He shook his head. "I should have known you would have never brought danger down upon your family. I will do all I can to help prove Slatter's innocence."

"You believe him?"

"I believe you and if you believe him that is good enough for me."

Willow hugged him again. "Thank you, James, and thank you for being a wonderful brother." She turned a soft smile on him as she stepped away from him. "So how long before you tell Eleanor how you feel about her?"

James laughed. "Not long. Not long at all.

***

Willow hurried into the Great Hall where she had left her husband, hoping he was still there. The hall room was full of a mix of people, clan members, Lord Ruddock's warriors, and some of Tarass's warriors. But she had yet to spot Slatter.

Chatter and laughter filled the room. Even Snow and Eleanor were deep in conversation and Willow kept her distance from them not wanting to be drawn into their chatter. She needed to find her husband.

She finally spotted him, talking and laughing with a couple of Lord Ruddock's warriors, then moving smoothly away from them to chat with some clan members. She watched how easily he engaged people while making his way toward a narrow hall that only the servants made use of and how those he talked with remained in conversation with one another, not noticing when he moved away.

If she hadn't kept focused on him, she would have missed how easily he had disappeared into the shadows without notice. She knew where the hall led and before hurrying off she stopped to speak with Snow.

"A moment with my sister, Eleanor," Willow said when she reached them.

Eleanor nodded and left them to talk.

"What's wrong?" Snow asked. "I can hear the worry in your voice."

"I have no time to explain. I may have to leave for a few days, or not. I'm not sure, but if I do I need you to make sure Sara is looked after. You know what to do."

"Slatter goes with you," Snow said.

"You're far too observant, but he doesn't know that yet."

"Stay safe and worry not about Sara," Snow said and hugged her sister. "And make sure you return home."

"You have my word on that," Willow said and hurried off as teary-eyed as her sister.

Willow grabbed her cloak she had left on a bench earlier in the day and made her way through the hall that led to the kitchen. She snatched a sack off the wall hook and stuffed it with bread and cheese.

When the cook looked at her oddly, Willow held the sack up, "A secret, late night rendezvous."

The cook laughed and nodded.

Once outside, she hurried to the stables, her booted-feet leaving footprints in the snow. She was glad the snow hadn't turned heavy, though the continuous light snowfall had left enough on the ground to leave an imprint.

She heard faint sounds coming from the stable where her husband's horse was sheltered and she kept her steps as light as she possibly could. The door stood open and she cautiously made her way inside.

She had taken only a few steps when an arm caught her around the throat and she gagged for a breath. She was released in an instant, spun around, her husband's arm going around her to steady her.

"Damn it, wife, what are you doing here?" Slatter demanded, then cursed at seeing his wife coughing as she breathed in air. "I could have hurt you." He was berating himself, not her. "You shouldn't have followed me, and how did you follow me? I never heard your footfalls."

She took a couple of more needed breaths before speaking. "I knew where you'd be going when I saw you sneak off. I took a different route." She coughed again. "And did you really believe you could tell me you love me now and forever, and not think I'd know you were bidding me farewell?" She didn't give him a chance to respond. "You're not going anywhere without me, though if you're leaving because James refused your people sanctuary, then your departure is no longer necessary. James apologized to me for refusing our request and offered your people a home here." She coughed again.

"Stop talking and give your throat a chance to recover," Slatter ordered, annoyed he had caused her discomfort. "And I appreciate James's change of heart, but I'll go myself and escort Devin and the others here."

"A foolish choice," Willow said, trying to fight back a cough. "Tarass will have his men chase after you in no time."

"I'll return before they can find me. Stop talking," he ordered again and this time continued, not giving her a chance to speak. "Besides, I need to go. If I can draw the culprit away from here and capture him, I can prove my innocence."

"And place yourself in danger." She shook her head. "You're not going anywhere without me."

His arm fell away from her and he laughed as he stepped around her and went to his horse, adjusting the blanket before turning to her. "You're staying put and don't think to argue with me on this. You're not going and that's that."

Willow scrunched her nose and tapped at her closed lips a moment, giving it thought.

"You'll not get your way on this, wife, no matter what reasoning you come up with," he warned.

She stopped tapping her lips. "So you think the culprit will go after you once he's realized you have left. But what if he sees that I remain here, lets a few people catch a quick glimpse of him, then kills me, leaving you to be blamed. That would be a reasonable and probably successful plan."

Slatter stared at her, an odd look on his face, then went to her, took her in his arms, and kissed her senseless.

"A good-bye kiss to your wife?" James asked, standing in the open door, his arms folded across his chest.

Willow had to take a moment to get her bearings when her husband ended the kiss and it took another moment for her to realize why he had kissed her. He had heard someone approach and was quick to make it look like they had snuck off together.

"A secret rendezvous," Willow said, turning with a smile.

"Your brother is wiser than to believe such a foolish explanation," Slatter said. "I didn't know who approached and anyone other than your brother might have believed we were having a playful rendezvous."

"And the truth is?" James asked.

"I was taking my leave. I thought the culprit would follow me and danger to your clan would cease. However, Willow pointed out a flaw in my plan. I also intended to go fetch my people and bring them here, since I worry that this madman may not stop at hurting anyone connected with me."

"Even though I ordered otherwise?" James asked.

"I respect you, James, but I don't take orders well and I protect the small group of people who have come to rely on me as you protect your clan. Willow told me that you changed your mind and I appreciate that, but I need to do what is best for my people."

"I'm a man of my word and I will not renege on it. Your people are welcome here. I would ask for your word, though I'm not sure how much it is worth, that you remain here until this matter is settled."

Slatter hesitated and he didn't miss the disappointed look on his wife's face.

"I ask for your word not for me, but for Willow," James said. "It would not bode well for her if you simply leave without an explanation. I will not see her hurt and humiliated in front of her clan and in front of Lord Tarass and also when Lord Ruddock learns of it."

Willow had been so willing to leave with her husband that she hadn't given the consequences of her actions thought of what it might have done to others. And the thought upset her greatly.

"I would never do anything to intentionally hurt Willow," Slatter said.

"It's never what we do intentionally that hurts. It's what we don't do, but what we should do. I could care less what happened to you except that if anything did happen to you, I know how much my sister would suffer. And my sister has suffered enough already. So I ask again, will you give me your word that you will remain here and see this matter settled?"

"I will see this matter settled, on that you have my word. As for remaining here, I don't know if this matter will take me away to see it settled and, therefore, I cannot give you my word."

"At least you give me the truth this time," James said. "I will have men leave tomorrow to escort your people here. And you know that now I have no choice but to place extra guards around you."

Slatter nodded.

"We should return to the keep before someone searches and cannot find you," James said.

Willow didn't hesitate, she walked past James and didn't stop, a worry creeping through her that she couldn't stop. It didn't take long for her husband and James to catch up with her and when her husband went to take her hand, she moved away from him.

"I need to return this food to the kitchen," she said, holding up the sack, not bothering to glance at either man.

She hadn't thought that her husband would leave and not return to her, but listening to what he said to James gave her pause to think about it. If he could tell her he loved her and leave without a word, what would stop him from ever doing so? Would he wake one day, tell her he loved her, and be gone forever? What if she got with child and he left them both? Was she a fool for believing him more honorable than he actually was? Had she let love blind her to the truth?

After she was done in the kitchen, she went to the Great Hall to find her sister to let her know she wasn't leaving and stopped when she saw Slatter talking to her.

He caught her eye and she could tell he was there purposely waiting for her.

She stopped Eleanor who was about to rush past her to James. "Would you tell Snow that I'll see her in the morning?" And before the young woman could respond, Willow hurried off.

Willow went to see how Sara was doing.

"Has she stirred, Carna?" Willow asked, after entering the room and going to rest a gentle hand on the old woman's brow and glad to find no fever.

"She has and she drinks the brew each time. She does well, I think."

"She does and you do well watching over her. I will look in on her in the morning."

Willow made it seem that she was retiring for the night, but that wasn't her intention. She wanted some time alone to think, something she feared she hadn't done enough of lately. She had allowed her heart to rule and she didn't know if that was a good thing. Being sensible had always served her well and she hadn't been sensible since the day she was dropped in the hole with Slatter.

It was time to be practical about her circumstances before it was too late, before she foolishly fell into bed with him, sealed their vows forever, and possibly got with child. She had to come to terms with what she believed since she had met Slatter or she had to let him go.

She went to her mum's solar where she'd always found peace. She added more logs to the low flames to chase the chill that had settled in the small room, slipped off her boots, and curled up in one of the chairs to think.

"How long did you intend to avoid me?"

Willow sighed, not glancing at the open door where her husband stood. "I was hopeful it would be a bit longer."

"I'm not going away," Slatter said.

Willow turned and looked at him. "But you were going away and without me and without telling me. It took my brother to make me realize that I could wake any day and find you gone, without even a good-bye."

Slatter entered the room, his steps slow, his manner relaxed. "I've warned you that I wouldn't make a good husband."

"Then why tell me you love me?" She tilted her head back and shook it. "Or did you tell me because I had told you that I love you?"

He walked over to her and leaned over her to look her in the eyes. "I didn't say I loved you because you had said it. I told you I love you because I do love you. I may lie more than other men, but I didn't lie when I said I love you."

She drew her head forward as she got out of the chair and turned to face him. "How do I believe you when you admit that you lie?"

"How do you question me now when I never hid who I was from you?"

She shook her head again, nothing making sense to her. "I don't know. I suppose I believed that we could do well together."

"That I would change?"

She stared at him, shaking her head again, though slowly. "No, people don't change easily. I learned that seeing my da grow ill and change through no fault of his own. I've also seen people change due to tragedy in their lives. I feel I changed after losing my parents. I found myself becoming more responsible, feeling the need to be a parent to my sisters. I wasn't looking for you to change. I was hoping the man you let me catch glimpses of would eventually reveal himself, the one that's somewhere deep inside you that you keep hidden, for whatever reason."

Slatter took a deep breath as if fortifying himself. "There is no other man inside me."

"That's not true and you know it. I feel him in the way he takes my hand so gently and lovingly in his. I feel it in his arms every time they wrap around me and make me feel as if I've come home. I feel it in his kiss that tells me more than words ever could how much he loves me and I felt it in the way you wed me—a stranger—to save me from a terrible fate."

"You don't know what you're saying," he argued.

"Actually, I finally know what I say is the truth and I do know that I love that good man with all my heart and as foolish and insane as it may seem I will love the other man who lives the lies until he realizes he doesn't have to lie anymore."

Slatter shut his eyes for a moment, his hands fisting at his sides. "I'm not who you think I am. I am not a virtuous man."

"I don't believe you."

He stepped closer to her. "Believe me, Willow, when I say I'm not a noble man."

"You are a decent man and nothing can make me believe otherwise."

He stepped closer, his arm coiling around her waist and drawing her close. "I'm telling you now—the truth—I'm not a moral man and one day you will learn that and it will be too late for you to walk away. So I'm giving you a chance to walk away now. If you don't I'm going to take you to our bedchamber and seal our fate. You'll be mine, bound to me until the day you die, bound with the lies and all that comes with them." He leaned down and whispered in her ear. "Leave while you can, *mo ghaol.* Don't let the devil get you."

Chapter Eighteen

Willow smiled softly and whispered, "I'm not afraid of the devil."

"You should be," Slatter said and scooped his wife up so fast that she gasped. "You just sealed your fate, wife."

He was wrong. *Their* destiny had been sealed the day she had been lowered into that pit.

He carried her to the bedchamber and, once inside, placed her on her feet. He barely shut the door when he began to disrobe. Willow on the other hand stood there, not moving, her eyes focused on his every movement.

He was an exceptionally well-built man, his body sculpted perfectly with every muscle and curve defined. It was humorous to her, though, that with such a beautiful body, it was his hands she favored the most. They were long, lean, and held such strength yet were tender. She loved when his hand closed around hers and held it strong, or the way he placed it to rest at her lower back at times, and she especially liked when his hand captured her face and held it still for him to kiss her.

"Do you need me to undress you?" he asked with a slight tease.

"Aye, I do," she said, wanting to feel his hands on her.

Pleasure grew in her as he walked with slow, lithe steps toward her and when he raised his hands and took hold of her tunic, she shivered.

"Is that from a chill or fear?" he asked softly.

"Anticipation," she whispered.

"You truly want this?" he asked.

"I truly want you and no other." She reached up to kiss him, but his lips reached hers first.

His kisses were always magical to her, stirring her senses, her passion, making her feel more alive than she had ever felt and this time making her feel even more—

His lips left hers briefly to whisper, "I love you, Willow, I love you so very much."

Loved. It was as if he had finished her thought. He made her feel more loved ever since he had said it aloud to her. She lost herself in the kiss and all it meant to her.

His hands didn't hurry to remove her garments after he reluctantly ended their kiss. He took his time gathering her tunic to bunch in his hands as he raised it up and over her head. He kissed her briefly, teasingly before his hands grasped her shift and began to pull it up.

"You're sure about this?" he asked when the hem of her shift brushed the tops of her thighs.

"I've never been more sure about anything." She pressed her fingers to his lips when he went to speak. "And I won't regret it, not ever. I love you and whatever life brings us as long as we're together that's all that matters to me."

"I'll never let you go, Willow. You're mine now and forever."

He quickly pulled the shift over her head, scooped her up once again in his arms, and carried her to the bed.

Willow had sometimes thought what it would be like making love with her husband when she married. Her mum had spoken openly with her daughters about the intimate duties of a wife, not wanting any of them ignorant of what they would face or what was expected of them. But never did she imagine how much she would look forward to consummating her vows. But then Slatter had given her a taste of the pleasure that could be shared between a man and a woman, more so between the two of them.

His hands began to explore her body and she responded to his every touch, his every kiss, some more so than others. She couldn't stop the moan that escaped from her lips when his mouth settled at her breast, teasing her nipple hard, and sending a pleasurable tremble through her that had her thinking she would climax there and then.

She gave him a little shove and he looked up at her with concern.

"I want to touch as well," she said a bit breathless and shoved him on his back, though he fell willingly.

"Touch all you want, wife. I belong to you and only you."

"Now and forever," she said with a smile and kissed him as her hands caressed his chest.

Her lips soon followed where her hands had touched and she couldn't seem to get enough of the taste of him. His flavor was warm, potent, and intoxicating and she was soon lost in exploring him.

Slatter had known since that time he had brought her to climax in the pit that there was a passion in his wife waiting to be freed, but he had thought it might take time to fully free it. He was wrong. It had taken no time at all.

He stifled the gasp that rose in his throat as her hand drifted down along his mid-section getting closer and closer to his manhood that was already screeching for him to slip into her. And the way she feasted on his nipples didn't help any, though he damn sure enjoyed it. Enjoyed it more than ever since he knew it was love that made her desire him and that made all the difference to him.

He almost jolted off the bed when her hand took hold of his manhood and began to caress it. He closed his eyes and got lost in her innocent playfulness until she began to instinctively tug on it.

His hands went to her waste and he gently flipped her on her back, covering her body with his. "Enough, wife, or this will be over far too soon."

She smiled. "But then we get to do it again and again and again."

He laughed softly. "As many times as you want, *mo ghaol*."

She rested her hand to his cheek. "I want you, husband, *always*."

All the intimate touches that had ever stirred him couldn't compare to how her words fired his passion.

"Love me. Love me now and seal our vows and bind us together forever," she whispered and faintly brushed her lips across his.

At that moment Slatter felt what it was like to be lost in love. He wanted nothing more than to join them together forever, seal them as one so that no one could ever tear them apart.

He wanted to be as gentle as possible with her, not bring her any pain, since this was her first time, but neither of them had patience. She was as eager as he and between their kisses and intimate touches there was no going slow.

"Now! I need you now!" Willow all but screamed.

Slatter felt the same, far too close to not being able to hold back any longer.

He entered her slowly, but that wouldn't do for Willow and she lurched up to meet him and that was it. Slatter drove into her and they both let out a gasp of pleasure. They were soon lost in passion, mindless of anything but the consuming pleasure building uncontrollably in them.

"Slatter!" Willow screamed as her passion erupted in a blinding climax.

Slatter joined her, an uncontrollable roar erupting from deep inside him, his release so powerful he couldn't contain it.

Passion rushed like a mighty wave through Willow, ebbing and flowing until it settled into a ripple that shivered her senseless. She shut her eyes, soaking in every last ripple and shiver and feeling overjoyed that this was something they could enjoy over and over again.

Slatter's limbs had never turned weak when he climaxed, but they did now. He barely had the strength to hold his weight so he wouldn't collapse on his wife.

He was still reeling from the intensity of his release and while he would have loved to remain inside his wife a bit longer, he feared he would collapse on her and he didn't want to hurt her.

He went to pull out of her.

"Not yet," she cried, grabbing hold of his arms and she wiggled as if unsettled, beneath him and suddenly shuddered, her eyes shutting tight as she let out a small gasping sigh.

He was surprised, though enjoyed seeing his wife climax again and he told himself to remember that for the next time and make sure to escalate her second climax.

When her hands fell away from his arms, he eased out of her and rolled off to settle alongside her, pulling the blanket over them as he did. They lay on their backs for a few minutes, gathering their breath and letting their rapidly beating hearts calm.

After a few moments, Slatter reached over to tuck his wife in the crook of his arm. She eagerly settled against him, resting her head on his chest and thinking of all the things she wanted to say, but remained silent, enjoying the pounding of his heart that had yet to calm.

Sleep claimed Willow quickly and Slatter lay there, an overwhelming sense of contentment washing over him. He'd found something he thought impossible... love. His wife actually loved him and he loved her so much that at times it frightened him. He couldn't bear to lose her. He'd be a broken man if he did with no wont to live. He had a duty now as a husband and it was that duty that he would see to before anything. It was that duty that would change his life more ways than his wife would ever know.

Sleep finally intruded on his thoughts and his eyes closed and he slipped into a contended sleep.

***

Slatter woke before his wife the next morning. He lay on his side wrapped around her. His body heat had kept her warm, what logs left in the hearth only giving off a small glow. He'd get up and add more logs soon, but first he wanted to linger with his wife, feel her warmth, and caress her soft skin. She felt so good and he warned himself to be good, let her sleep, don't stir her awake, but then his innocent touch had done more than stir him. He had grown aroused and if not careful, he'd be slipping inside her as she woke.

He was being good, keeping control of his growing need when he heard her moan softly, and he smiled. He was about to turn her on her back when a sudden rap sounded at the door and he silently cursed whoever was there.

"Wake up, Willow, and you too, Slatter," Snow called out and Slatter immediately rescinded his curse against Snow. "Sara is fully awake and wants to see you both."

That had both of them popping up in bed.

"We'll be right there," Willow called out and turned to give her husband a jab in the chest. "You better make sure to put out this fire you set in me sooner rather than later."

Slatter's smile teased. "Anticipation only makes it better, my love."

He got another jab in the chest for that before she scrambled out of bed.

"Wait," Slatter said, laughing and reached out to try and grab her. "I can put that fire out quick for you."

"It's burning way to hot," she said, placing her hand on her naked hip as she turned. "It will take more than a quick poke to extinguish what burns in me."

The smile Slatter's laughter had left vanished, staring at the seductive pose his wife had struck, not to mention how much she burned for him. Damn if he didn't get all fired up.

Seeing the passion that flamed in her husband's eyes had her donning her garments with haste. If he teased her with playful touches, she'd be lost, and since he looked about to lunge off the bed at her that seemed probable.

"Grandmother waits," she reminded. "You can finally learn what happened to her."

That stopped Slatter and dimmed the fiery passion in his dark eyes, though didn't extinguish it.

Slatter dressed just as hastily as Willow had while she hurried a bone comb through her hair and plaited it with fast fingers. They were done in no time and with the same haste made their way to Sara.

Slatter was relieved to see his grandmother's head had been elevated on two pillows and her gray hair had been combed and braided. And best of all she had a bit of color to her otherwise pale complexion.

"Slatter," she said, tears gathering in her eyes as she stretched her hand out to her grandson.

He hurried to her, his hand smothering her fragile one with tenderness as he sat on the edge of the bed.

"I knew you'd come and help me," she said, tears running down her cheeks.

"Always, *Seanmhair*, I will always be there for you," he said and kissed her hand. "You are safe now and you have a new home here with me and my wife, Willow." He turned to his wife standing behind him and Willow stepped around him.

"You feel well?" Willow asked and rested her hand to the old woman's brow, pleased it held no significant heat.

"Some pain and I fear I have little strength," his grandmother said.

"Rest and food will help grow your strength and I will give you a brew that will ease the pain some," Willow assured her.

"I am happy my grandson has found such a good and skilled woman," Sara said. "I wish you both much happiness. But I don't wish to intrude on your life together. When I am well I will return home."

"No," Willow said before her husband could. "Your home is here with us. You are family. Besides who will help me with the little ones when they come along?"

That brought a smile to the old woman's face and another round of tears to trickle down her cheeks.

Slatter wiped her tears away with his thumb. "It is settled, *Seanmhair*. Here you are and here you will stay."

"You are a good man, Slatter," his grandmother said.

Willow looked at her husband and tilted her head with a defiant smile, daring him to deny what his grandmother had said.

He grinned that cock-sure grin of his. "You've always known me better than I know myself, so I won't argue with you, *Seanmhair*."

Her husband truly could charm, and she'd learned a thing or two from him.

"You'll have to tell me all about Slatter when he was young. I want to be prepared for when we have a son and he turns out to be just like his father," Willow said, looking to Sara.

The old woman laughed. "Heaven help you if he does."

"I wasn't that bad," Slatter protested playfully.

Sara laughed harder, but it was abruptly ended with a sharp wince, her hand going to her side.

Slatter looked with haste and worry to his wife.

"You still have much healing to do," Willow reminded, "and rest will help you do that."

"Before I leave so you can rest and grow strong again, tell me who caused you harm," Slatter said.

"I don't know who the two men were. I never saw them before. They burst into the cottage and demanded to know where you were." She cringed. "The big one pulled out a dagger and threatened me." She shook her head. "How could I tell him what I didn't know? He thought a stab to my shoulder might change my mind."

Slatter's hands clinched, wishing he had the man, both men, in front of him. He wouldn't be swift to kill them. He'd make them suffer, which was exactly what he intended to do.

"I kept telling him that I didn't know where you were, not that I would tell the ignorant fool where you were if I had known. Doesn't the idiot know that a grandmother protects her grandchildren regardless of the cost?" She shook her head. "I think he stabbed me again out of anger."

"I would not want you to suffer for me," Slatter scolded lightly.

"Would you suffer for me?" she asked.

"That's different," Slatter said, though knew it wouldn't be to his grandmother.

"No, old or young, you protect those you love," his grandmother said and yawned.

"You need to rest," Slatter said and rested his grandmother's hand on her chest.

She grabbed his hand when he moved it off hers. "Who chases after you, Slatter, and why?"

"I can honestly say, I don't know. But I will find out." Slatter kissed her brow. "Rest and worry not."

His grandmother laughed. "That's like asking the heather not to grow on the hills." She turned her eyes on Willow. "Would you mind if I spoke with my grandson alone for a little while?"

"Not at all," Willow said. "Take all the time you want." She kissed her husband's cheek and she could see worry spring in his eyes as to what she might be up to when alone.

"Wait in the keep for me," Slatter said, turning to watch his wife saunter out of the room.

When she raised her hand and, without looking back, wiggled her fingers as if waving, he knew she had no intentions of doing as he said.

"I'll find you," he warned.

"I won't be hiding," she said with a laugh and closed the door behind her.

"She's a strong woman. She will be good for you," his grandmother said. "Now tell me what goes on and don't bother to run circles around me and convince me of any nonsense. I know all too well when that tongue of yours charms and when it lies. I'll settle for nothing less than the truth."

Slatter hadn't intended to burden his grandmother with his problem, but she had suffered because of him and it was only fair that she knew what was going on.

"Settle comfortably, *Seanmhair*, I have a tale to tell you and it has a puzzle that perhaps you can help me solve."

Chapter Nineteen

Willow entered the Great Hall to see Eleanor talking with Snow, both women wearing worried looks. Snow had left Sara's bedchamber when she and Slatter had arrived, leaving them to talk privately. She wondered what could be disturbing the two women and went to them.

"What troubles you both this grand morning?" Willow asked, feeling as if the joy she had once known before her parents had died had finally returned. And it was largely due to last night with Slatter. They had sealed their vows. They would stay husband and wife and she couldn't be more pleased.

"Eleanor has been telling me more about the man called the Slayer," Snow whispered.

Willow took the seat opposite the table from her sister and Eleanor, Eleanor filling a tankard with hot cider and handing it to her.

"Tell me," Willow said, taking the tankard as a chill ran through her worried for what she might hear.

Eleanor kept her voice low, though there were few in the Great Hall to hear her.

"It seemed strange to say what I heard, but then I thought you should know since Lord Tarass has sent the Slayer after your husband," Eleanor explained.

"I appreciate that, Eleanor. Please tell me whatever you know."

Eleanor nodded and hurried to say, "I remember hearing the older nuns talking about the Slayer being around for years far beyond what a human man could live. The one nun, Sister Agnes, old as the hills and has since passed, said that when she was young the Slayer had come for a man in her clan. All knew he had been marked, though I didn't know what she meant by that, and avoided him. Even the chieftain had kept his distance. No one did anything to help him. Sister Agnes had said that afterwards many a parent warned their children to be good or the Slayer would get them." Eleanor crossed herself. "Sister Agnes believed the Slayer was a demon who rose up from the depths of hell when called upon and did as the one who summoned him asked."

"Wouldn't that leave the person who summoned him obligated to the demon or the devil himself?" Snow asked.

"Demons are commanded by the devil, so if you call upon a demon for help, you owe the devil his due," Eleanor said and shuddered.

"That means that Lord Tarass is beholding to the devil," Snow said and shivered.

The Highlands were full of folktales and beliefs, some having a basis for them and others pure myths, not a truth to them. That was what her practical nature told Willow. Man didn't need the devil to make him evil. He did that all on his own. Her mum, though, had warned her not to dismiss folklore too lightly. That she should consider it and see what purpose the tale served. That within it, there was a lesson to be learned.

But what lesson could possibly be learned from the Slayer going around marking and killing people?

"Tell her the rest," Snow urged.

"I didn't know if it was worth telling, since I didn't know how true it was. It had been something Sister Agnes had heard through others, though she claimed it true. The Slayer didn't only kill men. He killed women as well, or at least one woman. Snapped her neck he did, or so said Sister Agnes."

This time Willow shuddered, a deep chill rushing through her.

"Did you know how a person who wanted help from the Slayer got in touch with him?" Willow asked.

"That's the part I found so strange," Eleanor said. "Sister Agnes said the trees in the woods delivered the message. That the deep roots delivered it to the devil himself."

"Eleanor."

Willow had to smile at the way Eleanor's face lit with delight at James's voice and her eyes expressed even more joy when they settled on him.

"I have need of your help," James said as he approached the table.

"As you wish, sir," Eleanor said with a smile and stood.

"I believe it is time you call him James, Eleanor," Snow said with a chuckle. "It's also time to stop hiding how much you favor each other and let it be known, since all in the keep and most of the clan know it already."

Eleanor blushed and James smiled.

"I agree," James said and reached his hand out to her. "It's time we talk more seriously."

"As you wish… James," she said, her smile growing as he closed his hand around hers.

"He took her hand," Willow whispered to Snow as the couple walked off.

"She's perfect for him," Snow said. "Hopefully, we'll be celebrating a wedding soon. There's no reason for them to wait if they love each other. I'm so pleased for them and you and Slatter. Soon the keep will be full of bairns I can spoil."

It always broke Willow's heart to hear her sister talk of others' bairns. That she no longer spoke of having bairns of her own. It was as if she accepted she would be blind forever. Willow hoped beyond hope that that wasn't true.

"You sound happier today," Snow said. "Did you have an enjoyable evening?"

Willow laughed. "I don't know how it is that you claim to be blind when you can see more clearly than others."

"I'm right. You and Slatter sealed your vows," Snow said with glee.

Willow had told her sister everything, but then there was little to nothing they kept from each other.

"When Sorrell learns of this she's going to be mighty miffed at missing it all," Snow said. Her smile faded some. "I do so miss her."

"I do too, very much, but she's happy with Ruddock and he loves her beyond measure. She told me it won't be long before she visits, but I fear the snowy winter will keep her away until spring."

"I don't want to lose you, Willow," Snow said, reaching her hand out across the table.

Willow was quick to grab it and give it a squeeze. "I'm not going anywhere. My home is here."

"That isn't what worries me," Snow admitted. "It's what you plan to do that frightens me and don't try to deny it. I know you too well. I don't want you beholden to the devil."

"You do know me well and you know that I would do anything to protect those I love," Willow said.

"Which is why I knew as soon as Eleanor said that a message was left with the trees that you planned to leave a message in the woods for the Slayer." Snow shook her head. "You can't do that. You'll owe the devil."

"That's nonsense just as it's nonsense that the trees will pass the message to the Slayer. And that's how I'll prove it. I'll go into the woods, whisper to the trees and when nothing happens, I'll at least prove that false."

"What will you whisper? The Slayer seeks to kill. Who will you sacrifice?"

"None. I will leave a message saying I need the Slayer's help and nothing will happen."

And if it does," Snow challenged.

"Then I'll ask him to protect my husband."

"He doesn't protect. He causes harm."

"We don't know that for sure? Maybe there is more to the Slayer than we know," Willow argued. She gave her sister's hand another squeeze. "Don't worry. You know I don't take foolish risks."

Snow gave a hardy laugh, though lowered her voice when she spoke. "You never did until you wed Slatter."

"In some ways, he opened my eyes to things I never bothered to see."

"I'm truly happy for you, Willow, but please, please be careful and don't go into the woods alone," Snow ordered.

"I'm just going to the edge of the woods where the oak trees appear as if they're hugging each other."

"Where we played when young bairns while Mum collected plants. And you won't be long," Snow ordered again.

"I won't be long since I've yet to eat this morning and I'm starving." Willow's stomach grumbled to prove it.

Snow chuckled. "I haven't eaten yet either so we can share the meal together. Where is Slatter?"

"His grandmother wanted to speak with him privately. I'm sure he'll be finished soon since she was growing tired when I was there and she needs to rest." She stood. "Which means I have little time to get this done before my husband shows up. I'll be back in a wink."

"Be careful," Snow called after her and Thaw raised his head where he slept at Snow's feet and gave a yelp.

***

Willow loved the woods and the way it dressed for the seasons. Today she wore a light mantle of snow, the ground and bare tree branches dusted with it, except for the pines. The snow clung to the pine needles making them appear as if they flickered with light against the dull gray sky.

She had spent much time here with her mum digging up nettles, wild carrot, wild rasps, and more. Her mum taught her about plants and the woods itself. Her mum had told her that the woods was a safe place if people were wise to its ways.

She made her way to a spot where a group of oak trees appeared clumped together, though there was space for a person or three young lasses to squeeze into the center.

She smiled at the enjoyable memories the trees brought her, the laughter she and her sisters had shared, and the tears, the three of them having gone there after burying their da. They had sought solace together and the trees had given it to them. She had to shake her head at the thought that some believed the tree roots could in anyway reach down to hell and the devil himself. They were far too lovely and comforting to be touched by evil.

Willow had little time so she didn't dally or squeeze between the trees. She simply rested her hand against the trunk of one of the oaks and asked for the Slayer's help. She didn't plead; she simply asked for help.

She let her hand linger on the rough bark as if drawing strength from it and found herself offering a silent prayer to keep her husband safe. She turned with a flourish when finished to hurry back to the keep, recalling she had assured her sister she wouldn't be long, and stopped surprised to see her husband standing a good distance away. She went to smile and wave to him, wondering how he had gotten past her without her noticing him, when she quickly drew her hand close to her chest.

It wasn't her husband who stood there.

A quick glance and one would think it was Slatter, but a second look warned his garments were different then what her husband wore, his dark hair slightly longer, and even from a distance there was an evil look in his dark eyes, one she had never seen in her husband's eyes.

He smiled and reached his hand out. "Come to me, wife. We finally have some time alone."

"You're not my husband," Willow shouted firmly, taking slow steps back.

He laughed. "What nonsense do you speak?"

"I speak the truth, unlike you who poses as my husband."

He lowered his arm to his side, his smile fading. "One look at you at the market and I knew there'd be no convincing you." His smile returned. "Not so others though. Unless they see me themselves they won't believe you."

"Believe that at your own peril," she warned.

His features turned harsh and she was reminded of her husband and how he looked when he got angry. How this stranger and her husband could look so much alike baffled her.

"You are the one in peril and you will learn that soon enough, *leannan*." He walked off laughing.

His echoing laughter lingered like a strong, foul odor after he had long disappeared and Willow shivered as she turned, hoisted the hem of her garment, and ran toward the keep.

***

Slatter had hoped his grandmother might help shed some light on his problem. He had thought perhaps he had a twin that his mother never told him about. But his grandmother had attended his birth and she assured him that he was the only child born to his mother that night. She knew nothing about his father and his mother had spoken little about him to Slatter, except to say he was not important to their lives.

At the moment, he thought differently. His father could very well hold the key to his problem.

He entered the Great Hall expecting to see his wife there only to find Snow sitting at a table alone, a worried expression marring her lovely features.

"Where is Willow," he asked, concerned his wife had gone off and done something foolish.

Snow didn't hesitate to tell him the truth since she was upset that Willow had yet to return. "She went into the woods."

"I would ask why, but she can tell me that when I find her. Where in the woods did she go?" he asked eager to go after her.

Snow explained, then reached her hand out to the shadow that was Slatter to her and he took hold of it. "She had said she would be quick and she's been gone longer than expected. Please bring her home safe."

"Worry not, Snow, I'll have her back to you soon enough."

He let several oaths fly as he hurried out of the keep and headed in the direction Snow had directed. He paid no heed to the warriors who called out ordering him to halt and he knew he took a chance not stopping when they realized his hasty pace had him headed for the woods.

He didn't care. He would not suffer any delay in seeing his wife safe.

"Halt!"

Slatter ignored the shout and when he saw his wife just inside the woods, her face pale and her feet pounding the earth as she ran toward him, he took off. He had to get to her. He had to keep her safe. His heart pounded viciously in his chest and fear twisted like a knife in his gut.

Willow spotted her husband and ran as fast as her legs would carry her. Her eyes sprung wide when she saw one of Tarass's warrior stretch his hand out about to clamp down on Slatter's shoulder.

She thought they would hit the ground in a tumble of limbs, but they didn't. Her husband grabbed the warrior's arm and with what seemed like the strength of ten men flung him over his shoulder and onto his back, then continued to run toward her. Another warrior was almost on top of him and Willow hurriedly jabbed her finger up in the air and over, letting him know another was behind him.

Even in her own flight of fear, she made sure to warn him, to protect him, to keep him safe whatever way she could. Love for his wife hit him at that moment like a punch in the face. He'd do anything for this woman, anything, he loved her that much.

He cleared his head and focused on one thing, reaching his wife. He heard the footfalls get closer behind him and at the right time sidestepped the warrior who had run up behind him. His momentum wouldn't let him stop abruptly and as he passed Slatter, he gave the young warrior a shove and sent him tumbling to the ground in a flailing of limbs.

Slatter didn't miss a step, he kept going, picking up speed, desperate to reach his wife and know she was safe and in his arms where she belonged.

Willow stretched her arms out to her husband, desperate to reach him.

From the time Slatter had been a young bairn, he'd always been fast and agile on his feet. No one could keep pace with him or catch him, but for the first time he felt himself far too slow. He needed to reach his wife, needed to get his arms around her and hold her tight.

The footfalls stopped behind him, the fools probably realizing he wasn't running away, he was running to his wife who looked like the devil was chasing her. When she stretched her arms out to him, though a distance away, he cursed beneath his breath and pumped his legs even harder.

Willow flung herself into his arms as soon as she was close enough to her husband and he caught her, swinging her up off her feet and into his arms.

She hurried her arms around his neck and pressed her cheek to his. "I saw him. He was in the woods. I thought it was you at first. He called me *leannan* just as you do." She shivered.

When Tarass's and Ruddock's warriors came up behind them, Willow shouted at them.

"He's in the woods. Go find him," she ordered.

They stood there staring at her.

"Did you not hear me? The culprit who killed Rhodes is in the woods. Go after him."

They still didn't move.

"They hear you well enough," Slatter said, turning to face the warriors, his wife tucked safely against him. "They just don't believe you." He walked right at them and they scrambled to get out of the way and let him pass.

"He has plans. He's not finished with you," Willow said and shivered, recalling his echoing laughter.

"That's good, since I'll be the one to finish him," Slatter said not a hint of doubt that he would fail. "You are unharmed, wife?" He saw no visible signs of harm, but unseen harm could sometimes be worse than the harm you could see.

"I'm unharmed," she assured him. "He kept his distance, though I don't believe it will be for long."

Though Slatter agreed, he remained silent, thinking what he would do to the man when he caught him. It was one thing to bring havoc to his life, but far different for his foe to approach his wife.

"He needs to be stopped before another life is lost," Willow said.

Slatter agreed again, but there was something that troubled him. "What were you doing going into the woods alone, wife."

Willow saw no reason to keep the truth from him. "I went to ask the Slayer for help."

He stopped abruptly. "You what?"

"Let me explain," she said.

"Definitely do."

She told him what she had learned about the Slayer and how the information had taken her into the woods. "So you see I don't expect him to respond to me at all since it's ridiculous to think that the trees carry the messages to him or that he's a cohort of the devil. He may be a man of wicked ways, but he's no more than that. And if Tarass can speak to him, then so can I."

"And what if he is a cohort of the devil? What will you do then? You summoned him so you shall owe him."

"Nonsense. Pure nonsense," Willow said confidently.

"Know this, wife," he said and planted a quick kiss on her lips. "I'll go to hell to rescue you if necessary."

"Of that I have no doubt, husband, though it does my heart good to hear you say it." She kissed him this time and her heart thudded when he smiled his wickedly handsome smile.

"I would take you straight to our bedchamber if Snow was not so worried about you or that we didn't need to inform James of what happened."

"Later," she whispered.

"Sooner rather than later," he whispered as if it were a secret and Willow laughed softly and kissed him again.

Chapter Twenty

"Why are you alone? Where is Devin and the others?" Slatter asked surprised to see Walcott when he entered James's solar. "And why has it taken a week for you to get here if you've traveled alone?"

"Devin wanted to be sure of your request and that he brought the group to a safe place. Also, a few in the group need to rest after their last journey before taking on another one. And Devin refuses to leave until all are well enough to travel, though he is appreciative of the herbs Willow sent along for Erna and the others."

"There is shelter, food, and safety here for your people," James offered.

"Is it a permanent home?" Walcott asked.

"My sister Willow believes so, but it is up to Slatter to decide that," James said, glancing at the man.

"Let the group know they come to a permanent home," Slatter said. "Now let's get you some food and drink and a place to rest before you must leave again."

Slatter walked with Walcott to the door.

"A moment, Slatter," James called out.

"I'll meet you in the Great Hall," he said to Walcott, then turned to James.

"Is this a permanent home for you?" James asked.

"Wherever Willow is… so is my home," Slatter said and walked off.

When he reached the Great Hall it was to find his wife talking with Walcott. He stopped and watched his wife. She was genuinely happy to see Walcott and talked with him as if he were an old friend. He could hear her ask about Erna, the young lass that broke her arm and Corliss the old woman whose grandson Crofton worried endlessly about, and about Pell, the old warrior missing one leg and endless others whose names she recalled better than he did.

His wife grew more beautiful to him each and every day. More so today watching her with Walcott.

Then there were the fresh memories of having woken early this morning and how he and Willow had made love slowly, exploring, teasing, laughing, and falling more deeply in love. It had been afterwards when she had settled comfortably against him that it had struck him.

He didn't want to live without this woman, not ever. He wanted her by his side every waking day until he woke no more. Fate had blessed him, first time she ever did, and he wanted to make sure he didn't do anything that would have fate take her from him.

That meant seeing his problem settled. Unfortunately, his hands were tied not being able to go anywhere without being followed, not that it would stop him. He could easily leave and return without being missed. It was his wife's safety that stopped him from doing so. He hadn't let her out of his sight for long ever since the incident in the woods.

The culprit that resembled him hadn't shown himself again, though it was only a matter of time before he did. He had no intentions of his wife being the evil man's second victim.

Willow's lovely smile forced Slatter to return it in kind as he approached the table, her outstretched hand reaching for him making him smile all the more. She never failed to reach for him, welcome him beside her, be happy to see him, and her eagerness to be with him always poked at his heart.

"Walcott was telling me about everyone. It is good Devin waits until all are rested and well before traveling here. And I'm glad Walcott can take back news of what a fine home they are all coming to."

"They will be pleased," Walcott said.

"You need to get a good night sleep yourself and leave in the morning," she said. "I'll have a cottage prepared for you."

"I should leave after I eat," Walcott said.

"Nonsense," Willow said, shaking her head. "You'll do better with food and rest. Morning is time enough for you to leave. Besides, nightfall is not far off." She turned to her husband. "Right, Slatter?"

"My wife does make sense. A good sleep will see you more fit for your journey."

"Then it's settled. I will leave you two to talk while I see a cottage made ready for you." Willow gave her husband a quick kiss on the cheek.

"I don't like you going off on your own," Slatter said, cupping his wife's waist with his arm so she couldn't rush off.

"Snow waits outside for me along with Thaw who favors the freshly fallen snow."

"Good, and don't take long. It's cold out there." He kissed her lips and reluctantly let her go.

Willow turned and gave a wave to him before hurrying out.

Snow was falling again. It had fallen periodically over the last few days. There was no great accumulation, but most feared it was a promise of a large snowfall to come.

She laughed when she saw the young bairns throwing snow in the air for Thaw to catch, the pup jumping up with delight and vigor to catch the flakes that melted as soon as they touched him. Snow laughed and looked as if she watched them, her head turning toward the different squealing bairns. But all she saw were shadows and when there were that many they often became a blur to Snow from what she had told Willow.

Willow prayed every day for her sister's sight to return and she hoped one day soon her prayers would be answered.

"Snow," she called out and her sister turned her head. "I'm in need of some help."

***

"He's here. He killed one of the Lord of Fire's warriors." Slatter said after making sure no one was close enough to hear him. "And I've been blamed for it."

The piece of meat Walcott had jabbed with his knife and was about to put in his mouth halted near his lips.

"He'll strike again and see that it's blamed on me."

Walcott shook his head. "Why?"

"I wish I knew and I wish I knew how he avoids being discovered. I have no trouble locating someone I wish to find, but he has evaded all my efforts in finding him and it puzzles me."

"Have you searched the woods for him?" Walcott asked and finally popped the piece of meat into his mouth.

"The woods are too vast of a place to search. It would be senseless to try."

"What will you do?"

"Keep my wife safe and bide my time until you return with Devin. Then I'll set a trap for him and make sure it's one he can't escape."

"What if he leaves before you can set the trap?"

"He won't," Slatter said with confidence. "He's a fool. He believes he has me trapped and that he'll finish me here. That will *never* happen."

"What kind of trap could capture such a devious man?"

"One that's more devious than him."

***

It was a quiet night in the Great Hall, most remaining settled in their cottages. Walcott had gone to the cottage Willow had made ready for him after eating and gone directly to sleep, wanting to leave with the dawn on the morrow.

"I'll leave you to talk with your sister, while I go spend time with my grandmother. I'll meet you in our bedchamber after that." Slatter winked and planted a quick kiss on his wife's lips, leaving his wife with Snow.

He was gone only a few moments when a woman entered the Great Hall, her cloak dusted heavily with snow.

"Teresa, is there something wrong?" Willow asked, seeing the worried look in her pinched expression.

"It's Brent, he gashed his leg today and didn't tell me until it pained him so bad tonight he finally showed me the wound and it looks awful. Can you help him, Willow?" she all but begged.

"I'll get my things and meet you at your cottage."

"You are a generous woman, thank you." Teresa turned, her steps quick as she left the Great Hall.

"Don't wait for me, Snow, go and sleep. Slatter will probably be in our bedchamber by the time I return."

The two women hugged and Willow went and fetched her healing basket and cloak, and stepped out of the keep.

The night was eerily quiet as she made her way to Teresa's cottage. Her footfalls didn't even make a sound in the soft snow. The night shadows seemed to appear larger than usual, making one wonder if someone was actually lurking there watching. Willow thought, too late, that she might have been wise to let Slatter know where she was going. Normally, she wouldn't think anything of being summoned to someone's cottage late, bairns often choosing the late hours to arrive. And she had never felt the slightest bit fearful of walking through the village at night, but the incident in the woods had her thinking differently. She hurried along. The cottage sat more toward the middle of the village and she was relieved when she reached it, and Teresa answered her quick rap at the door, feeling foolish once inside.

Extra sentinels had been posted to make certain her husband didn't try to take his leave while they should have been looking for the culprit truly responsible for Rhodes's death.

She shook her head. She was safe in her village, though she couldn't help but think she'd feel safer if Slatter was with her. She would remember that the next time she was summoned late.

"You should have come to me right away when this happened," Willow scolded, after having a look at Brent's wound.

Brent wasn't a tall man but he was thick in girth with good strength.

"I took care of it just like your mum did the last time I got a gash. I put honey on it and wrapped it," he argued.

"It's good that you tried but this gash is deeper than the last one and needs to be tended differently," Willow explained, not wanting to discourage him from ignoring an injury like most men did. "I'll get it cleaned and wrapped, and you need to stay off your leg for a few days so it can start to heal." She raised her hand when he went to argue. "Don't bother to tell me you can't. I'm going to speak to James and let him know you're not to work. Besides, with this snow there'll be little work to do."

Brent grumbled but finally agreed.

It didn't take long for Willow to finish.

"It's feeling better already," Brent said with a smile as Willow slipped on her cloak. "You've got the healing touch just like your mum."

His words touched her heart to be thought as skilled as her mum had been. "That's nice of you to say, Brent."

"It's the truth," Brent said with a firm nod. "You watch your step in that snow now."

Willow stepped out of the cottage to find the snow falling more heavily and the wind having grown stronger, whipping sharply at her and reminded herself to pay heed to Brent's warning and watch her step. She shivered, straining to see the keep through the swirling snow and having difficulty spotting it.

She pulled her hood up and stepped away from the cottage eager to hurry back to the keep and her husband. The swirling snow didn't allow for a hurried pace and she watched her steps as she wound her way back to the keep.

"You called on me," the deep sinister voice said.

Willow halted and turned, but could barely make out a shadow alongside a nearby cottage.

"Who's there? I've called out for no one," Willow said.

"You sent your message through the trees," the deep voice said impatiently.

Willow locked away the gasp that shot up to spew from her mouth. It couldn't be. It wasn't possible. "You're the Slayer?"

"What do you want from me?" he demanded.

She didn't have to think. She knew what she wanted and she didn't hesitate to say. "I want the culprit caught who pretends to be Slatter so that my husband is freed of the false accusations brought against him, and I want the one responsible punished."

"You will owe me for this," he said, though it was more a warning.

"What will I owe you?" Willow asked.

"Whatever I ask of you."

"That could be anything," she argued.

"You summoned me, therefore, you owe me."

"I owe you nothing unless I agree, and your terms are unreasonable," she argued.

"You summoned me, therefore, you owe me," he repeated as if it was done and could not be undone.

Frustrated, Willow stepped toward the shadow, wanting to confront whoever hid in the shadows. There was no one there.

"I will collect my debt when the deed is done."

The foreboding voice seemed to be carried on the falling snow as it fell around her, and she shivered at what that debt might be. But did it matter? As long as her husband was safe, that was all that mattered. Besides, she refused to believe she had just spoken to a demon. It had been a man. A man who she would negotiate with when the deed was done, if it was done.

She hurried off, even more eager to speak with her husband, though she wondered if it was wise to tell him. Though, it might be unwise not to. She would have to think about it.

"You shouldn't be out here alone."

Willow jumped, her hand flying to her chest." "You frightened me, Walcott."

"The snowstorm is too nasty, the night too late for you to be out here alone," he warned. "Danger lurks in the dark."

"I appreciate the warning, Walcott. I'll be in the safety of the keep in a few short steps. And you should be sleeping. You leave at sunrise."

"I am fine. Hurry and be safe," he said.

She rushed off, feeling a bit unnerved, thinking it strange that Walcott had suddenly shown up. Could he be the Slayer? Just as that thought caught her, she caught sight of a cloaked figure running to the keep. He was hunched over. Did he disguise his true height? He made his way around the back of the keep toward the kitchen.

Willow hurried to follow him, wondering if it was the Slayer. She stopped abruptly when she turned the corner of the keep and found no one there. Where had the figure disappeared to so fast?

She entered through a door near the kitchen, hung her cloak on a peg, and left her healing basket on a chest to retrieve later. She took guarded steps, peering suspiciously at any nook or cranny she passed and turned corners with caution. If the cloaked figure had entered here, he could be lurking anywhere in wait. Or had it been someone simply returning to the keep?

She finally entered the Great Hall and cast a quick glance around to find it empty, the only sound the crackle and pop of the fire burning strongly in the hearth.

"Looking for me?" came the whispery voice behind her.

She gasped and turned with such haste that she stumbled and fell against her husband.

He was quick to settle his arms around her. "You're cold," he said and anger flared in his eyes. "Where have you been?"

He was warm, not a chill to him and she pressed herself against him to steal a bit of his warmth. "Someone needed tending."

"You went alone? On your own? In the dark of night? Have you no sense, wife?"

She laughed. "I usually have too much."

"Not this time," he snapped. "I forbid you from ever again going out on your own at night like that. You will find me and I will go with you."

"That word *forbid* does not sit well with me, husband," she said and stepped away from him.

"A wife follows her husband's rule."

"Not this wife," she said with a grin.

"And here I thought you were a reasonable woman," he said, a slight smile teasing the corners of his mouth.

"Aye, I am, which is why I chose a decent man to wed and not someone who wishes to dictate. Though, I see he may need reminding of that now and then." She gasped when she found herself in her husband's strong arms. She still couldn't understand how he could move so fast that his movements could barely be seen.

"I'll not lose you due to your own stubbornness," he said and kissed her when she went to argue with him. "One thing you are not is foolish and until this culprit is caught it would be foolish for you to go out alone late at night and in a snowfall that has turned heavy. I ask if it is necessary for you to do so, then let me go with you so I don't worry needlessly." He grinned. "And if you think to refuse my heartfelt request then know that I will be your shadow day and night until I deem it safe for you."

She couldn't help but laugh. "You're still dictating."

"I beg you to humor me on this before my poor heart shatters, so frightful I am of losing you."

She laughed softly again. "Your tongue does charm."

He cupped her chin. "My tongue tells the truth this time. I wouldn't want to live without you."

He kissed her and Willow was glad he did, since his words left her speechless. It was no tender kiss and it left no doubt as to where it would lead and that soared Willow's passion.

Slatter rested his brow to hers after ending the kiss. "I have an insatiable aching need for you, wife."

"And I for you, husband," Willow whispered a hair's breadth away from his lips.

"I have no patience for slow and lazy tonight. I want you quick and hard."

"Then what are you waiting for?"

He scooped her up in his arms and they were in the bedchamber with haste, tugging each other free of their garments before falling on the bed together, his lips claiming her in places that soared her passion beyond reason.

Willow didn't waste time in spreading her legs, eager for him to enter her, feel him swell inside her, fill her, love her.

"Love me," she said, not realizing she did until the words had slipped achingly from her lips.

"Always," he said and claimed her lips in a kiss that almost sent her over the edge.

She moaned with intense pleasure when he slipped into her and her moans grew as he did as he said he would... he took her quick and hard.

She spiraled up and up, reaching and reaching with every forceful thrust until she reached the edge and burst with pure passion.

Slatter captured her mouth in a kiss, though it was her climax he wanted to feel as her moans rippled through him, sending him over the edge to join her. He tossed his head back and let out a rumbling roar that echoed throughout the room.

"Don't stop. Please don't stop," Willow pleaded.

She pleaded with him every time, though she didn't have to. He had become familiar with her ways and knew she would climax again not long after the previous climax. He loved how responsive she was and how easily her passion ignited for him... only him.

They lay spent beside each other, Willow reaching out to take his hand only to meet him reaching out to take hers.

After a few minutes, Slatter pulled the warm wool blanket over them and Willow settled comfortably against him, her eyes growing heavy. A light snore came from her husband and she smiled, content. As she drifted off she recalled that she hadn't told him about the Slayer or seeing Walcott up and about so late or about the cloaked figure she thought had entered the keep. Tomorrow she would tell her husband all that had happened and he could talk with Walcott and see if he had seen anyone lurking about.

Chapter Twenty-one

Willow woke to a pounding, not in her head, but at the door.

Slatter was already out of bed and slipping his garments on, the voice at the door frantic.

"Wake up! Wake up!"

Willow hurried out of bed as well and into her garments with haste, the fright in Eleanor's voice all too real, and a shiver ran through her.

Slatter yanked open the door.

Eleanor looked as pale as freshly fallen snow. "It's your friend Walcott. Someone has hurt him badly."

"Where is he?"

"The cottage he stayed in last night," Eleanor said tears threatening her eyes.

Slatter turned to his wife.

"I'll gather what I need to help him and meet you there," Willow said, knowing without her husband saying what he wanted from her.

He nodded and rushed past Eleanor.

Willow went to follow and Eleanor grabbed her arm. "He's hurt bad, too many stab wounds."

Willow paled herself, recalling last night and how Walcott had warned her of the danger that lurked in the dark. It had found him.

"Get Snow, tell her how bad Walcott has been hurt and that I've gone to tend him. She'll know what to gather together to help me. Then help her bring it to me," Willow ordered. "And see that Carna stays with Sara."

Eleanor nodded and took off and Willow rushed off after her husband.

She stopped and retrieved her healing basket from where she had left it last night and gathered more herbs and anything else she thought she might need from the small room off the kitchen where she dried and stored the healing herbs and plants.

The snow had stopped, leaving a bitter wind to whip it around and enough on the ground to reach just below her ankle. She tucked her cloak tight against her to keep it from flailing around her, and she kept her head down to keep the cold wind from nipping at her face. She jumped when a solid arm suddenly caught around her.

"I should have waited for you," Slatter said, drawing her tightly against his side. "I don't want you out here alone day or night."

Willow shivered, not from the cold, but from what his remark had implied. The attack on Walcott had to be bad for him to leave the man's side and come after her, worried for her safety. She also noticed several of Tarass and Ruddock's warriors nearby and how they followed close as she and Slatter continued to the cottage.

James was in the cottage when they entered and when his eyes caught hers, he shook his head.

Willow hurried to Walcott and saw his chest was covered with blood as well as the blanket beneath him.

He was still breathing and it wasn't a shallow breath so death was not near yet.

She rid herself of her cloak, placed her basket on the table and looked from James to her husband. "My sister and Eleanor gather what I need, please help them make their way here and then leave me to this. It will do me no good to have either of you hovering over me."

"I'll see they get here safely," Slatter said, "then I'll wait outside for you."

There was no point in telling him to wait in the warmth of the keep. He'd wait outside not only to see how Walcott did, but to see her kept safe.

Willow worked diligently on Walcott, wishing he would wake and spew his usual grumpy complaints. But she feared he might never wake. Several slash marks on his arms indicated that he had tried to protect himself from the attacker's knife. Two chest stabs wounds were not deep and if it were not for the two others that were, Walcott could very well survive. But two wounds were close to areas that her mum had explained more often than not proved deadly.

She did know stopping the bleeding was most important and keeping the wounds from festering was of the utmost importance. She feared it would be a difficult fight for Walcott and one she didn't know if he could win.

Snow lent support whatever way she could, whether it was encouraging her sister or seeing that water was kept hot at the hearth. Eleanor was of great help, assisting her to cut away Walcott's bloody shirt and get him cleaned up and settled in a clean bed.

It was some time later that her husband sat on a chair next to Walcott's bed, staring at the pale man.

"Do you know if he'll survive?" Slatter asked.

Willow was honest with him. "It doesn't look good, but Walcott just may be cantankerous enough to defy death."

"Did Walcott ever tell you how we met?"

"He made no mention of it."

Slatter settled his arms across his chest as his eyes remained focused on Walcott. "I came upon two men beating him bloody. They claimed he stole from them." He smiled. "Walcott, his lips and eyes badly swollen, complained how he refused to pay the two lazy lots for a chore they had failed to complete. And it wasn't him, the messenger that they should be beating, but the man who ordered the chore in the first place." Slatter's smile faded. "He lost two teeth that day, joining in the fight I started, even with how badly he'd been beaten."

"He remained with you after that?" Willow asked.

"He did, after staying with our small group, smaller than what there is now, and healing, he told me he felt free for the first time in his life and wanted to stay free. He may be grumpy, but he's loyal." He shook his head. "I'm going to make whoever did this to him pay."

The time might not be right, but her husband needed to know about last night. She placed her hand on his shoulder. "I should have mentioned this last night, but my thoughts were elsewhere."

He glanced up at her.

"When I was returning from Teresa's cottage, Walcott popped out of the dark to warn me about being out alone and how danger lurked in the dark. I wondered what he was doing out himself since he was to leave at dawn this morning. And that's not all. Before Walcott made himself known, a voice called to me saying, 'you summoned me' and it took a moment for me to realize it was the Slayer. He asked me what I wanted and I told him how I wanted you safe and the culprit caught and punished. He told me I owed him. I asked him what I owed him and he said, 'whatever I ask of you.'"

Anger flared in his dark eyes. "And you didn't think to tell me this last night?"

"You distracted me."

"That's no excuse and you know it," he snapped.

Willow nodded her head, knowing he was right. She should have told him right away.

"Again, that's not all," she said, needing to tell him everything.

Slatter's brow shot up and not in surprise, his anger had flared.

"When I got closer to the keep I spotted a cloaked figure heading around the corner of the keep, near the kitchen area. I chased after him, but when I turned the corner he had vanished."

Slatter bolted up out of the chair. "You followed him?"

Willow stepped back away from her husband, but he caught her arm and hurried her over to stand near the hearth, away from Walcott.

"Do you know how foolish that was following him?" He shook his head. "Of course not because you had lost all common sense and plunged head long into danger. You should have come to me right away or to

James, or to any of the warriors so they could have searched the area."

"You're right. I should have," Willow said. "It was foolish, but would anyone but you have believed me? No one takes me seriously when I tell them of this man who wears your face. They think I say it to make an excuse for you." Her head drooped. "I should have told you. You would have attempted to search for the figure, which would have alerted the sentinels, which could very well have frightened off whoever was prowling the village, and which could have prevented Walcott's attack."

Slatter lifted her chin for her to look at him. "It was me you saw sneaking back into the keep, though that still makes no difference. You shouldn't have followed after me, not knowing who I was."

Willow's shock showed in her eyes that rounded wide.

"Walcott was out in the night because of me. We had made a time to meet in case anything came up before his departure that needed to be discussed. It's my fault and he could very well die because of it."

"It's neither of our faults," Willow said, resting her hand on her husband's chest. "The fault is on this man who pretends to be you. And I wonder if Walcott came upon him, thinking it was you, the dark night and falling snow making it difficult to see. And what about the Slayer? Could he have seen something?"

Slatter pulled his wife into his arms and hugged her tight. "It could be you lying in bed, close to death. I don't want to lose you, *mo ghaol*, promise me you will not be foolish again."

"I promise, but you must promise me that you'll be honest with me," she said, turning pleading eyes on him.

"If only I could," he said and it pained him to see the disappointment that filled his wife's eyes.

A moan had them both rushing to Walcott.

"It's all right. You're safe, Walcott," Slatter said, placing his hand on his friend's limp one, letting him know he was there. "Willow tends you. You need to rest and grow strong."

Walcott moaned again, turning his head slowly from side to side.

"You're not alone. I'm here and I'll see you kept safe, my friend."

Walcott calmed and his moans faded.

"Time will tell," Willow said.

Chapter Twenty-two

"What do you mean some believe Slatter stabbed Walcott? How could they think such nonsense?" Willow threw her hands up agitated and shook her head at James. The last four days, my husband has sat by his friend's side a good portion of the day."

"A ruse some say," James said.

"Tell me, it's Tarass's warriors who spew such lies, isn't it?"

"They feel he attacked Walcott to make them think otherwise," James explained.

"That's nonsense and you know it. And how do they explain Slatter getting past them without being detected?" Willow asked.

"Lord Tarass wants to know the same, but he got no answer. Though, wagging tongues say your husband sneaks out at night and blends with the shadows and shapes of the darkness."

"That's ridiculous. His nights are spent with me in our bed. The warriors waste time thinking it's Slatter when they should be searching the area for the culprit."

"Searches have been going on and no one has been found."

Willow turned a glare on him. "What do you mean searches have been going on? Why wasn't I made aware of this?" She gasped. "Don't tell me you think I shouldn't be trusted with such news?

"It's Lord Tarass who has insisted upon the search and that no one be told about it."

"Particularly me," Willow said.

James's silence confirmed she was right.

Willow lost the will to argue. It would do no good. No one believed her. She felt James even held some doubt. And how could she or Slatter prove otherwise when he was confined to the keep and village. If he even dared near the woods, warriors descended on him.

How did she prove her husband innocent?

"One good thing," James said, trying to cheer her some. "I discovered that Lord Tarass has heard no word from the Slayer. So at least Slatter doesn't have to fear that."

Willow had no intentions of telling James that the Slayer had contacted her. That would be her and Slatter's secret. She hadn't even told Snow, knowing her sister would worry.

"There is nothing my husband needs to fear from the Slayer. He is innocent of all that has been said against him."

"I do hope that can be proven, Willow," James said, "or I fear Lord Tarass will take matters into his own hands, and there'll be nothing we can do to stop him."

James's warning followed her like a gray cloud overhead as she left the room. She felt so helpless. If only her husband was free to go and come as he pleased. She stopped suddenly, a different thought intruding on the others.

Her husband had managed to sneak out of the keep the other night without anyone seeing him and without her knowing it. Had he done so other times? Could the gossip be right? Had her husband been sneaking out of the keep at night? She shook her head. She would have known. Or would she? Sometimes after making love, she would fall into a deep sleep and didn't wake until morning. But she never woke alone. Slatter was always there wrapped around her. Or he'd wake her with gentle caresses and they'd make love. Could he have just returned to their bed on those occasions? She had to know and she hurried off in search of him.

She found him with his grandmother. She was doing well, getting out of bed to sit in a chair by the fire for a while each day. She ate good, slept well, and complained little. It was obvious she was content and Willow believed it had much to do with her grandson.

Slatter was helping his grandmother out of the chair, his strong yet tender arm wrapped around her, lifting her gently to her feet and supporting her as he walked with her to the bed and helped her in it. He tucked the blanket around her and pushed a stray strand of her hair off her face to tuck behind her ear.

It was a scene that would live long in Willow's memory, her husband so strong and powerful lovingly assisting his petite, frail grandmother with such care and patience.

"You will rest now. I will visit with you later," he said and kissed her brow.

"You must have important things you need to see to. Worry not about me," she said, patting his arm.

"You are the most important to me, *Seanmhair*," he said and kissed her brow again.

"I do so love you," she said softly as her eyes drifted shut.

"And I you, *Seanmhair*," Slatter whispered and turned to see his wife standing at the open door.

As usual, she was struck by how his smile could stir her senses or was it how lovingly he had been with his grandmother that had touched her heart.

His smile turned mischievous as his arms circled her waist. "I see a spark of desire in your eyes, *mo ghaol*."

Willow didn't deny it. "Aye, you spark an ember that forever burns within me for you with a smile or simple touch."

He squeezed at the sides of her waist. "Never is my touch simple. Every time my hand touches you it is with purpose, whether to let you know that I am there for you, that I love you, that I ache for you, or that I simply want to feel the comfort of your hand in mine. Purpose, *mo ghaol*, I always touch you with purpose." His hand moved off her waist to stroke along her back. "I think we should take this conversation to our bedchamber where I can demonstrate in great detail the purpose of my touch."

She almost surrendered, forgetting what she was going to ask him, and turned as he directed her, with a slight urging of his hand to her lower back, to the stairs. She was reminded of it with how silently he climbed the stairs behind her, almost as though he wasn't there.

"I have a question," she said after entering their bedchamber.

"Let it wait," he said, his lips already at her neck, teasing the sensitive spots he knew all too well would have her responding with soft moans.

Willow had to push him away and shake her head to gather her wits about her. "It can't wait."

"Be quick, I have an ache for you that won't be satisfied quickly."

For a moment she gave thought to wait to speak with him until after they made love, worried what she had to ask him might affect both their passion. But in the end she let her sensible nature prevail, especially since she wanted to put the worry to bed before he took her to bed.

"I spoke with James and he told me—"

"That many of the warriors believe me responsible for the attack on Walcott."

Willow looked at him befuddled.

"I'm not deaf to the wagging tongues around me."

"And do you know that many believe you sneak out at night and prowl the area?"

"I've heard that as well."

"Do you?" she asked.

He didn't answer and when he turned away from her, she felt a pang to her heart.

Slatter ran his hand through his hair and shook his head as he turned to face her again. "It is better you don't know some things."

"How can you say that?" she asked incredulously.

"Easily, since I don't want you harmed in any way."

She walked over to him, her hand shooting out to poke him in the chest. "You harm me by lying to me."

"I didn't lie to you. I just didn't mention it to you."

"So you keep secrets from me." She turned away. "It's time I do the same."

Slatter grabbed her arm and swung her back around to face him. "You'll keep no secrets from me, wife."

"If you can keep secrets so can I," she argued.

"I do it to protect you."

"Or is it that you don't trust me?" she challenged.

"What would you have said to me if I told you I was going to search the woods at night to see if I could find this culprit?"

"You searched the woods?" she asked.

"From the look in your eyes, it is more than a simple question you ask me, wife, and a good way to avoid answering my question."

"I would have gone with you," she said, "but then you knew that and tried to divert me from the real reason you snuck out of the keep at night."

"And what would that be?" Slatter asked with caution, knowing his wife was not one who could be easily fooled.

"You were meeting someone. Someone you trusted. Someone who could do what you couldn't, go wherever he pleased." She gasped. "Walcott. He hadn't just arrived. He's been here for a while. He's not someone anyone pays mind to. Doesn't want to pay mind to because of his constant grumbling." She paced, thinking, and stopped suddenly. "It's why he warned me about the danger in the darkness. He found something in the darkness, didn't he? That's why he was attacked."

Slatter went to her and gripped her wrists in his hands. "Listen well, wife. You'll leave this be. I'll not have you suffer Walcott's fate."

"You're my husband and I love you. We're in this together whether you like it or not," Willow warned. "I'll see you safe just as you do for me."

His eyes smoldered with anger. "I'll not lose you."

"You think I feel any differently. The thought of never seeing you again, never feeling your touch, your kiss, frightens me something fearful. Your lies frighten me as well."

"I lie to protect those around me," he said.

"Why not simply speak the truth?"

"The truth is not simple to tell," he said and released her and walked over to sit on the bed.

Willow went and sat beside him. "It is simple and I'm listening." She could see the struggle in his dark eyes as to whether to tell her or not, and she waited. It was a struggle only he could settle.

Her stomach twisted nervously about what she might hear when he looked ready to speak.

"Willow! Willow are you in there," Snow shouted frantically before a rap sounded at the door.

"I am and so is Slatter," Willow said and they both hurried to the door.

Snow didn't wait, she opened the door and spoke. "Lord Tarass arrives with more warriors and with an unknown chieftain or lord and his troop of men as well. James wants you to join him on the steps of the keep."

Willow helped Snow down the stairs since they all were in a hurry, Slatter leading the way.

"I only spoke with James a short while ago and he said nothing of Lord Tarass's arrival," Willow said as they descended the stairs.

"James wasn't made aware of Lord Tarass's arrival or told anything of the other man and his troop. He's as shocked as everyone else."

"You'll stay close to me, Willow," Slatter ordered sharply as if he worried she wouldn't agree.

"That I will," Willow said, fearful of what awaited them.

"And you, Snow, will stay to the side out of harm's way," Slatter said.

"As long as you protect my sister, that is all that matters to me. Besides, I have Thaw to protect me," Snow said of the pup, who was showing some growth, by her side and following her every step.

The Great Hall was empty when they entered it and so eerily silent that Willow shivered.

"Everyone waits outside to see who Lord Tarass brings here and why," Snow said as the three walked through the heavy silence.

People stood near their cottages watching the procession of warriors walk through the village. Lord Tarass led the way on his horse and a man atop another horse following behind him.

James stood on the top step, his eyes steady on the approaching men. Eleanor stood beside him, though she rushed over to Snow when she spotted her.

"James says I'm to stay with you and that we're to keep ourselves out of the way of things," Eleanor said, hooking her arm around Snow's.

"I make no promises," Snow said and went to stand to the side with Eleanor.

Willow was proud of her sister's courage and that even though she was blind, Snow would come to her defense no matter what.

It wasn't long before Lord Tarass drew close to the keep. It was difficult to see the man who brought his horse up alongside him, the hood of his cloak partially covering his face. He didn't toss it back until they both came to a stop in front of the keep and everyone gasped in shock.

The man could have been Slatter's twin brother.

At first Willow felt a sense of relief, thinking Lord Tarass had found the culprit. That soon faded when she realized the man was not treated as a prisoner, but with respect shown to either a chieftain or a lord. Her stomach knotted painfully fearful of what that meant.

"This is Lord Sterling of the Clan MacBlair from the Isle of Wakelin. He has some information you'll wish to hear, James," Lord Tarass said.

Lord Sterling dismounted and approached the steps, staring up at Slatter. "I wouldn't believe it if I didn't see it with my own eyes. You are the exact image of me."

Slatter grinned. "I wouldn't say exact, I'm much handsomer." His grin shifted to a glare. "Wakelin, you say, isn't Wakelin that piss-ass isle no one gives a fig about?"

Willow squeezed her husband's hand in warning. It would do no good to antagonize the man, at least not yet.

He returned her squeeze, though never took his eyes off Sterling.

"Your lack of manners and civility prove what a scoundrel you are without me saying a word. You're also a sly one, giving me the slip at every turn," Lord Sterling said.

"This is best discussed in private," James said.

"Why? Your clan should know that an evil man resides among them," Lord Sterling said, raising his voice and not taking his eyes off Slatter as if daring him to deny it. "This man has committed endless crimes, some unspeakable. He cares not who he harms or the damage he leaves in his wake. He is a common thief, a thug who does anything for a coin, a liar who charms his way out of things or charms his way into a woman's bed, mostly married women, then threatens that he will tell her husband if she doesn't pay him for his silence. And he murders anyone who threatens to reveal his true nature."

"You claim much detail about my supposed exploits," Slatter said. "How is that?"

James agreed. "Slatter is right. How is it you claim these accusations?"

Lord Sterling pointed to Slatter. "You cannot see why by just looking upon us? I have suffered greatly because of this miscreant. I have been accused of stealing, lying, bedding married women, and causing harm for a mere coin. I cannot travel far from home without someone accusing me of a crime and wanting me to suffer for it. I finally had enough and began my search for the man responsible for it all... Slatter." He pointed again to Slatter. "Now it's time for him to suffer." He looked to James. "And when you learn what else he has done, you'll agree with me." He turned and shouted. "Bring her to me."

Willow stood beside her husband more frightened for him than she had ever been. She wanted to shout out that Sterling was a liar. That it was he who had done all the things he accused Slatter of, but she held her tongue, though it wasn't easy.

Her fear grew when she saw Maddie practically dragged and dumped in front of Lord Sterling. Her one eye was badly bruised and the corner of her mouth swollen and the way she held her one arm, it was obvious it pained her.

Her husband tensed beside her and Willow feared he would rush forward to help the woman, but he didn't.

"Tell them. Go ahead. Tell them the truth," Lord Sterling ordered.

Slatter spoke up. "Where's your husband Kevin, Maddie?"

"You'll not be asking her any questions," Lord Sterling ordered. "She's my prisoner."

Slatter paid him no mind and said again, "Where's Kevin, Maddie?"

Maddie rushed to speak. "He's being held with the others. The ones who survived."

Lord Sterling raised his hand ready to bring it down on Maddie.

"Hit her and I promise you you'll lose that hand," Slatter warned in such an evil threatening tone that it halted Lord Sterling's swing and sent a heavy silence descending over everyone.

Maddie rushed to say more. "Beck is dead, so are most of his men. There's only a few of us left."

"You killed them?" Slatter asked with a nod to Lord Sterling.

"My warriors did. They were a motley crew of thieves and murderers and suffered a fitting punishment." His lip turned up in a snarl. "But then you know their kind well since you're one of them. Now tell them, woman," Lord Sterling commanded.

Maddie looked to Slatter, her eyes pleading.

"It's all right, Maddie. Say what you must, Slatter encouraged gently."

Tears rolled down her cheeks. "Beck paid a man to act as a cleric. You and Willow aren't truly wed."

Chapter Twenty-three

"Lies! You force her to lie," Willow accused with a shout. "Just like all your other words are lies."

"Watch your tongue, woman," Sterling cautioned.

"Don't ever threaten my wife," Slatter warned his look even more deadly than his tone had been.

"She is not your wife," Sterling argued. "And I have tracked you here and I intend to see you punished for your crimes. You will be hanged at sunrise."

Willow's legs almost buckled and she grabbed hold of her husband's arm, not to keep from collapsing, but to keep anyone from taking him from her.

James stepped forward. "That is not going to happen. You are not known to us and until this can be sorted out no action will be taken against Slatter."

Willow wanted to hug her brother for defending Slatter.

Sterling looked to Tarass. "You will let the man live who killed your warrior and attempted to kill one of his own?" He turned back to James. "And you would defend an evil man who lies for the pleasure it brings him?"

"You don't step foot on our lands and dictate to us what will be done," Tarass ordered, his potent tone leaving no room for debate. "I brought you here to have your say. Slatter's fate is not for you to decide."

"Then I will remain here until I am sure Slatter gets what he deserves," Sterling said.

"You will be my guest," Lord Tarass corrected with a look that warned him not to challenge his command.

Sterling looked ready to argue, but held his tongue, and calmed before saying, "At least lock the scoundrel away so he can't disappear and cause more havoc."

Willow's stomach churned as wickedly fast as her mind, her thoughts focused on various possibilities, the most important... how to help her husband escape if he was imprisoned.

James spoke up this time. "Slatter is confined enough here. He needs no further confinement."

"Yet you have one dead and another near death," Sterling challenged, "and you're still foolish enough to allow him his freedom?" He raised his arm and pointed to Willow. "At least keep him away from your sister so he doesn't fill her head with more lies or fill her belly with a bairn and leave her in disgrace."

Willow felt her husband ready to pounce on Sterling and she hurried to step in front of him. "I don't for one moment believe the lies you force others to spew for you. Slatter is my husband and my husband he will stay. You, nor anyone here, will keep him from me. You say that Slatter is an evil man and lies for the pleasure it brings him. Only an evil man who lies for the pleasure of it would know that, so tell me, Lord Sterling, how much pleasure have you gotten in using my husband's identity to enjoy your wicked ways?"

Sterling's face flushed red with rage and his lips curled in a snarl as he went to step toward Willow.

Willow felt the brush of her husband's arm as he rushed past her, but he was too fast for her to stop him. By the time her hand reached out to try, Sterling was flat on the ground, blood pouring from his mouth, and his lips already swelling.

"Dare to come at my wife again and I'll kill you," Slatter threatened, clenching his fists at his sides, fighting the urge to plummet the man senseless.

Sterling glared up at Slatter, his hand shooting up to point at him. "I demand you lock him away for the safety of all."

"Enough!" Tarass bellowed. "We finish this matter in the keep."

Slatter turned to Willow and kept his voice to a whisper. "Tend Maddie and see what you can find out."

Willow didn't argue, aware she would be excluded from the matter once the men retired to James's solar. And her husband was right. She needed to find out what Maddie knew.

She gave him barely a noticeable nod and as he went up the steps, she went down to Maddie.

"Leave her be," Sterling ordered when Willow reached Maddie.

Slatter swung around, his dark eyes still glaring with a molten fury.

Willow was relieved when Tarass spoke, fearful her husband would lunge at Sterling again.

"Willow will tend the woman and you will follow us inside," Tarass ordered, once again leaving no doubt his command was to be obeyed.

James let the way into the keep, Tarass trailing behind them all.

Thaw jumped out at him and gave a bark and a snarl, showing his puppy teeth as he jumped back and forth as if waiting for a command from Snow to attack.

"That pup is useless," he said and made the mistake of shaking a pointed finger at Thaw.

Thaw didn't hesitate, he jumped and lunged at Tarass's finger, his sharp puppy teeth catching the skin and tearing it.

"Oh my Lord, Thaw what have you done?" Eleanor cried, seeing blood pour from Tarass's finger.

Tarass grabbed the pup by the scruff of his neck, ignoring his wound.

"Please don't hurt him," Eleanor cried out.

James and Slatter stepped out of the keep just as Snow's hand shot out and connected with Tarass's chest, then ran down along his arm to grab Thaw from his grasp.

"Snow!" James yelled, his face turning pale, fearful for his sister.

"Thaw was protecting me and himself from this fool," Snow said.

"Snow!" James reprimanded again. "Apologize to Lord Tarass."

"An apology will not suffice," Tarass said with a threatening calm.

"Please let me see to your wound," Willow said, having rushed up the steps when Eleanor had cried out, wanting to get Tarass away from her sister. Before he could respond, Willow turned to Eleanor. "You and Snow help Maddie to my mum's solar. I'll tend her there when I finish with Lord Tarass."

"We're not done, Snow," Tarass warned.

Snow's chin went up. "I'll be waiting for your apology."

James shook his head and Slatter smiled.

"This way," Willow said, pushing between Tarass and Snow and seeing the tremble in her sister's hands. She showed strength, but fear poked at her as well.

Once in the Great Hall, she called for a servant to bring water, cloths, and her healing basket.

"What happened?" Sterling demanded, getting up from where he sat at a table, a tankard of ale in his hand.

"A minor mishap," Tarass said. "Go with James and Slatter to his solar. I'll join you shortly."

James hurried Sterling from the room, the man clinging to his tankard as he followed James.

Slatter lingered a moment, locking eyes with Tarass.

"I have no wont to hurt your wife, though I can't say the same about her sister," Tarass said.

Slatter grinned. "Not a wise choice of words when my wife is about to tend you." He walked off laughing.

Tarass glared at Willow in warning.

Willow wanted to tell him she had no wont to hurt him either, unless, of course, he harmed Snow. But she didn't think a threat from her would help the situation.

"My sister feared for her pup, she meant no harm," Willow said, hoping he would see reason.

"That is for her to explain when I speak with her later."

Willow was glad he told her of his intentions. She could make sure she was there when he spoke with Snow. For now, she would say no more, giving the incident a chance to rest from his mind. She led him to the table where the servants had left the items she had requested. It didn't take long to clean and examine the wound and see it was a small tear that should heal nicely.

She cleaned it good, the bleeding having stopped and smeared honey over it, then wrapped it. "Keep it free of dirt," she told him, though had noticed how clean his hands and nails were. Most men had grime under their nails and hands that needed a good washing, not so Tarass. His hands were free of both.

"Are you prepared to pay the Slayer his due?"

His question so startled her that she took a step back. How could he know she spoke with the Slayer? He shocked her again when he answered her silent question.

"I make a point to know everything in the surrounding area that may or may not concern me. Do you realize why one summons the Slayer?" He didn't wait for her to answer. "He isn't called on to protect the innocent. He's called on to punish the guilty. The ones who evaded punishment, but deserved it."

"Slatter isn't guilty of anything," she said, defending her husband.

"So you believe, but if the Slayer finds differently your husband will die. Eleanor told you what happened to the man in the abbey."

Willow nodded, wondering how he had known about that, then realizing Eleanor must have told James and James must have told him.

"That man had brutally attacked two sisters, one died, the other survived and was left with horrible scars and a severe limp. He was an important man and he was never made to suffer for his crime. The surviving sister summoned the Slayer and he saw that the man suffered a brutal death for what he had done. The Slayer also was summoned by a grandmother who knew her daughter was killing her children, each bairn having died before they reached one year. No one would believe the grandmother when she told them she had seen it with her own eyes. When the woman gave birth to a fourth child, the husband told his wife that the grandmother would take the child and raise him so the lies about his wife would end. He was found dead a few days later. That's when the grandmother summoned the Slayer, not only fearful for the child's safety but for her own as well. It's said that the Slayer came upon the deranged woman just as she was about to kill the bairn."

"So the Slayer is no demon commanded by the devil."

"Who else would want such wretched, evil souls, but the devil himself," Tarass said.

"My husband is no wretched, evil soul," Willow argued. "I told the Slayer that I wanted the person responsible for all the wicked deeds to suffer. And if this Slayer wants only malevolent souls for the devil, he won't be taking my husband's soul."

Tarass stood and went to walk away, then stopped and looked at Willow. "You must love your husband very much to pay the Slayer's price."

"He has yet to set a price with me."

"He has only one price… your soul."

Willow' stomach clenched. "You were willing to give yours."

Tarass chuckled. "I can't give what I don't have."

Willow watched him walk away and shivered. The Slayer was in for a battle if he thought she'd relinquish her soul. But just in case, she decided it was best if she saw this settled before the Slayer did.

***

Slatter kept his back to the wall, watching, as James, Tarass, and Sterling talked. He couldn't believe how much Sterling resembled him. It was as if they were twins or brothers. There were some subtle differences, but not enough to take notice unless one was looking. He even walked with that same air of assurance that Slatter did.

"He struck me and I expect him to be punished for it," Sterling continued to argue.

"You looked ready to strike his wife," James said.

Sterling's face pinched tight. "I will not tolerate disrespect from any woman."

"Willow isn't any woman, she's my sister and I will not see her disrespected in her own home," James warned.

Slatter listened as words were exchanged as if the three men would decide his fate. In past situations he would have paid them no heed, his fate his own to decide since he found his way out of any difficulty he had ever gotten into. Now, since Willow, it was more complicated. He didn't want to leave her, didn't intend to leave her, he loved her far too much. He wanted a life with her, a life far different from the one he'd been living.

So he continued to listen to see what he could learn about Sterling and try to make sense of why a nobleman resembled him and why the man wanted to destroy him.

***

Once Willow got to her mum's solar, she sent Eleanor on an errand that would take time, but made sure Snow remained with her. She wouldn't take the chance of Tarass confronting her sister alone.

Willow handed Maddie a tankard of hot cider and a piece of bread sweetened with honey and tears gathered in her eyes as she took both and ate and drank with haste.

"He doesn't feed you?" Willow asked.

"Barely," Maddie said and gratefully accepted another piece of bread from Willow.

"Tell me what happened, Slatter wants to know," Willow urged.

"I think Beck was in cahoots with Lord Sterling, but double-crossed him, something Beck was known for. Beck wasn't surprised when he arrived the one day. What Beck didn't expect was the warriors that poured out of the woods and descended on us. It was over before it got started. Unfortunately, not for Beck. Lord Sterling tortured him. It was during that torture that he revealed that you and Slatter weren't truly wed."

"Then it's true, we aren't wed?" Willow asked, not ready for the answer.

"I can't say for sure. Beck barely was able to turn his head, but he did and looked at me and told me to make sure I told Slatter that he won, he got him good." She wiped a tear away. "Slatter. You tell Slatter that I got him good." He repeated it several times and I got the feeling it was a message for Slatter. That's why I didn't repeat what he said in front of everyone."

"I'll make sure I tell Slatter what Beck said," Willow assured her. "Where is your husband?"

"Sterling is camped on the outskirts of Lord Tarass's keep. Kevin and the few others that survived are being held there in a pen… like animals." A tear slipped from her eye. "Kevin suffered a beating by Sterling and I worry that he will die from his injuries. Sterling wears two faces. When he first arrived he was pleasant and smiling as he spoke with Beck, then it was like he became a different man, an evil man who took pleasure in hurting others."

"We'll do our best to free you and the others," Snow said to her sister's surprise.

Willow did agree with her, though. Her husband wouldn't let Maddie and Kevin suffer or the others. He would do something, but how did she keep him from suffering the same fate?

Once Willow finished tending Maddie's wounds, which there were more than could be seen, and made sure she was well fed, the women returned with her reluctantly to the Great Hall. Willow wished Maddie didn't have to be made to go with Sterling, but she also knew Maddie, fearful as she was, wanted to return to her husband and try to keep him from further harm.

"Eleanor," Willow said when they entered the Great Hall and she saw it empty. "Take Maddie and go have the cook put together a small sack of food that can be hidden beneath her shift. And tell her to make certain it has no strong scents so no one can smell it on her, and hurry."

"Bless you, Willow. I knew you were a good woman when I first laid eyes on you and I knew you were the perfect woman for Slatter. It is good fate brought you two together."

Eleanor and Maddie rushed off at the sound of Sterling's bellowing voice.

"I will not suffer delays in seeing Slatter hung." Sterling strode into the Great Hall followed by James, Slatter, and Tarass.

Willow didn't like that Slatter walked between her brother and Lord Tarass as if a prisoner.

"And I will not see an innocent man hung," James said more firmly than she had ever heard him speak.

Willow wondered then if it was perhaps more for Slatter's protection that James kept him between him and Tarass.

"And you, Lord Tarass," Sterling said, looking to him. "Do you not want to see the man hung who killed your warrior?"

Tarass turned a slow smile on Sterling. "Make no mistake, Sterling, I will see the man who killed Rhodes suffer… suffer greatly."

"If this matter isn't settled soon, I will deal with it myself," Sterling warned.

"That would be very unwise," Tarass threatened.

"I don't fear the likes of you," Sterling said with bravado and a look of distaste on his face, "a half-barbarian."

Tarass approached the man, not a sign of anger or scorn to be seen, nothing at all. He stopped in front of him. "That is a mistake you're going to regret."

"I think not, though I do regret seeking your help with this matter. I assumed you being a titled man would assist another titled man without question. I should have realized a half-barbarian would never understand the decorum of nobles."

Tarass stepped closer to the man. "When this is finished I'm going to show you the decorum of a barbarian to those who insult them." Tarass's hand shot up in Sterling's face when he went to speak. "Not another word or you'll lose your ignorant tongue. My men will escort you to your campsite and there is where you will remain until I say otherwise." Sterling went to speak again and Tarass was quick to warn. "I enjoy tongue prepared raw."

Sterling paled.

Tarass pointed to the door. "My warriors wait to carry out my orders. Don't keep them waiting."

"Where is Maddie?" Sterling called out, stretching his neck up to look past Tarass.

"I am here," Maddie said and stepped out of the shadows.

"Hurry your steps, I am done here," Sterling commanded as if he had made the decision to take his leave.

Tarass turned as the man walked off and called out. "Snow, I will speak with you now."

Thaw started yapping madly.

Snow scooped him up and handed him to Eleanor. "Please keep him safe."

"I will," Eleanor promised.

Thaw didn't like that Snow walked off without him and he refused to stop barking and struggling to free himself from Eleanor.

Willow took her sister's arm and walked with her to Tarass.

"I will speak with Snow alone," Tarass ordered.

"Is that really necessary?" James asked, worry deepening the lines around his eyes.

That was when Thaw broke free from Eleanor's grasp and ran with the force of an arrow shot from a bow toward Snow. But it wasn't Snow he was after, it was Tarass.

The pup launched himself at him, and all hell broke loose.

Chapter Twenty-four

"No!" Willow screamed when she saw Tarass raise his hand to swat the pup away.

Snow's hand shot out seeing a small gray blur sail through the air just as Tarass's arm went up to swat at the pup. The strength of his arm connecting with hers sent her tumbling. Tarass hurried his arms around her, the momentum of his quick action sending them tumbling together to the floor.

Slatter moved with such speed that he caught Thaw in mid-air, the pup continuing to snarl and snap and try to break free and get to Snow.

Tarass was quick to get himself and Snow to their feet, holding her arm until she was steady, though she yanked it away from him and he had to grab it again, since she had yet to remain steady.

"You and that pup are a threat to you both and to everyone else," he accused.

"It is you who are the threat," she argued.

Tarass stepped close to her, his face nearly plastered against hers. "Apologize."

"Never!"

"Snow, do as Lord Tarass commands," James chastised fearful for her.

"How can I apologize when I don't mean it?" she asked, squinting her eyes at Tarass, wishing she could see more than just a shadowy, gray face in front of her.

"I don't care if you don't mean it, say it," Tarass demanded.

Snow realized then that he didn't care how she felt, he only cared that she obeyed him.

"Snow," Willow said softly, hoping to calm her sister and make her see reason.

It was Thaw's continuous snarls that made Snow stop and think. She would do anything to keep Thaw safe.

"I apologize," she said with a huff.

"Remember that and keep that snarling, useless pup out of my sight," he ordered and turned and walked out of the Great Hall.

Willow went to Snow and so did Thaw as soon as Slatter placed him on the ground.

Snow scooped Thaw up and hugged him to her, his small, pink tongue lavishing her face with licks. "Good pup, Thaw, good pup."

"He's going to be your constant protector," Slatter said, coming up behind his wife who reached out and rested a hand on Snow's arm.

"You need to be careful with Lord Tarass. He is a man who cares little for anything," Willow warned.

"Willow is right," James said, his arm going around Eleanor as she stepped close to him. "It is best you remain out of sight when he is here, and Thaw as well."

"I'm so sorry, Snow," Eleanor said. "I couldn't hold Thaw. He was frantic to reach you."

"That's all right, Eleanor. I should have had you take him to my bedchamber. And you're right, James, it is better if Thaw and I avoid Lord Tarass completely from now on. Besides, I simply can't tolerate the brute. How goes things with you and this Lord Sterling?" Snow asked, having heard enough about Lord Tarass.

"I don't know what to make of him and I don't know how we could resemble each other so much," Slatter said. "I am pleased, though, that I finally have an answer as to who has been causing me such strife."

"You honestly believe Lord Sterling, a nobleman, is the man responsible for the things you have been accused of?" James asked with a doubtful shake of his head. "Why would he possibly do such a thing?"

Willow was quick to respond to that. "He said it himself... he enjoys evil pleasures. And what better way not to be made to suffer for them or disgrace your family title, then pose as someone else."

"That certainly is possible, but how to prove it might not be possible," James said.

"What if we don't have to prove it?" Eleanor said and everyone waited for her to explain. "Lord Tarass called on the Slayer for help. He will know that Lord Sterling is evil and see that he is punished. All we need to do is be patient."

"What if he doesn't know the difference between Slatter and Sterling?" Snow asked.

Eleanor lowered her voice almost afraid to speak. "The devil's cohort knows true evil when he sees it."

"But Lord Tarass has yet to get a response from the man," James said.

"I got a response," Willow said.

"You contacted the Slayer?" James asked, shaking his head in disbelief.

"I did, to protect my husband, but we can't wait for him with Lord Sterling so impatient and so adamant about seeing Slatter made to pay for crimes Sterling committed," Willow said, her own words causing her stomach to roil with worry.

"What other choice is there?" Slatter asked. "What proof is there that points to Sterling being responsible for all that has been said about me? And who would believe me over a nobleman?"

"There is another matter that must be considered," James said reluctantly.

"Our marriage," Slatter said and James nodded.

Willow considered telling her husband what Beck had told Maddie that she believed was a message for Slatter, but since Maddie believed Beck meant it for Slatter alone, she decided to wait until they were alone to tell him.

"I believe it would be wise to send for a cleric and have your vows repeated," James said to the surprise of Willow and Slatter. "And we'll do it as quickly as possible."

"I am grateful, James," Willow said. "My mum was right when she told me and my sisters to trust you, that you were a good man just like our da."

"I gave our da my word that I would look after the three of you and I intend to keep it until the day I die," James said.

Eleanor turned a smile, full of pride, on him.

The group talked for a while longer without coming up with any clear solution to the problem.

Eleanor went off with James, Snow took Thaw for a walk, and Slatter and Willow went to talk with his grandmother.

Slatter stopped on the stairs, his arm going around his wife's waist to turn her and rest her against him. "You sacrifice too much for me, wife, defending me at every turn without pause or doubt. It isn't you who will owe the Slayer, if he helps us, but me."

Willow brushed her lips over his, eager for more, but rested her brow to his instead. "I love you beyond measure, beyond anything I thought possible, and I will see you kept safe so that we may have a long, happy life together."

Slatter captured her lips in a hungry kiss, then nibbled along her neck, eager to hear the soft seductive moans that quickened his own passion. He stopped when his thoughts turned to rushing her to their bedchamber, when other matters needed their immediate attention.

"*Later*," he whispered and she shivered. He kissed her quick. "I never thought I'd find love and never would I expect a woman like you to fall in love with me."

"A woman like me?" she asked, running her hand gently along his cheek.

He turned his head to kiss the palm of her hand. "Aye, a kind, good-hearted, respected, admired, unselfish, loving woman."

She smiled softly. "You forget stubborn and pragmatic."

"There are those as well," he said with a chuckle, "and I love those parts of you just as much as all the others."

"You are a lucky man to have found me," she teased, then her tone turned serious. "And I am a lucky woman to have found you, a man whose good heart far outweighs his faults."

"Keep that thought strong, *mo ghaol*, you may need it someday."

"All I need is you," she whispered and kissed him as if she'd never get a chance to kiss him again.

It left them both breathless and he whispered once again, "*Later*."

They entered the room to find Sara sitting up in bed, looking much improved, though there was a worry in her alert eyes.

"What goes on, Slatter?" his grandmother asked anxiously and stretched her hand out to him. "I heard someone arrived here who resembles you. What is this all about?"

"I wish I knew, *Seanmhair*," he said, taking her hand and sitting on the bed beside her. "You told me that you know little about my father, but I need you to tell me *all* you do know."

His grandmother obliged. "It was at the gathering of several clans that your mum met your da. She came home excited and told me she was in love and going off with a man. She never told me his name and never said anything about marrying him, not even a handfasting. She left and I didn't see her until she returned with you," —she smiled— "a small bairn that walked far too fast for being barely one year. I could hardly keep up with you. When I asked what happened, she told me it was better I didn't know." She shook her head slowly. "I wondered if she had gotten herself with a powerful man and a married one at that, and that she feared him."

"Did she ever mention the Isle of Wakelin to you?"

"It sounds familiar." His grandmother scrunched her brow, searching her memory, her eyes suddenly turning wide. "I do recall it, the memory giving me pause through the years. Though it wasn't your mum who mentioned the Isle of Wakelin, but a traveler who stopped for some water. He mentioned he was headed there. I remember your mum, hurrying over to where you were trying to climb a tree, snatching you up and keeping your face pressed against her chest as she hurried into the cottage. She didn't come out until I told her the man had left. I asked her what was wrong and she told me never to speak of the isle, not ever. After that she made sure to keep you away from any strangers that stopped by. I knew my daughter well and I knew she was not only trying to protect you, but me as well." She sighed. "I was so pleased and relieved when your mum met Lander. He was a good man and I knew he'd make a good da."

"He was a good da and he taught me much," Slatter said, thinking how much he missed the man and his mum as well.

"He taught you to be a good man," his grandmother said.

"Some would argue that, *Seanmhair*," Slatter said with a grin.

"Not in front of me they won't or they'll get a good tongue lashing."

"See, you have two strong women who believe in you and defend you," Willow said, leaning forward in the chair by the bed to poke her husband in the arm.

"I like this woman you wed," his grandmother said with a grin that matched Slatter's.

Slatter turned a teasing smile on his wife. "She's a bit stubborn, but she'll learn." That got him a hard jab in the arm from his wife, and he laughed.

"She must be, since I haven't heard you give an honest laugh in some time," his grandmother said and looked to Willow. "Would you mind if I had a few moments alone with my grandson?"

"Not at all," Willow said and stood and wasn't surprised to see her husband tense with concern. She didn't want to worry him and hurried to say, "I'll wait outside the door for you." And when the concern in his eyes faded to be replaced by a wicked gleam, she knew his tongue was about to either tease or charm.

"Fear not, *mo ghaol*, I won't be long from your side, since I know how much you miss me when parted."

Willow clasped her hands together beneath her chin and sighed dramatically before saying, "Dear husband, I beg you not to leave me long without you, since my heart is in peril every time we are apart and I fear I shall die without your attention."

His grandmother erupted in laughter.

Slatter applauded. "That was quite good, wife."

"You have taught me well, husband," Willow said and turned and sashayed out of the room, raising her hand above her head to wiggle her fingers at him in a farewell wave.

"I really really like her," his grandmother said.

Slatter turned to his grandmother. "I really really love her."

His grandmother squeezed his hand. "Then be honest with her before it's too late."

"It could cause her harm as it did you," he argued.

"We've discussed this. I would have told you by now if the two men were interested in more than *your* whereabouts. The oath has kept the secret hidden for years. No one betrays it."

"I believe that's why this problem with this man who resembles me worries me so much. It could destroy what had taken so long to build."

"You won't let that happen, nor would the others, and I believe your wife would feel the same."

His grandmother understood the troubled look in his eyes. "Think of what your mum and Lander had together. You can have that too. I know you always thought that you had to sacrifice everything. You don't. Talk with Willow. She may surprise you."

"She always does." He shook his head. "First, I have to settle this Sterling problem, then I'll talk with my wife."

"You shouldn't wait too long," his grandmother cautioned.

***

His grandmother's warning kept whispering in his head as he and Willow left the keep to go see how Walcott was doing. It meant a lot to him that his grandmother trusted Willow enough for her to suggest he talk with his wife. She had always been a good judge of people, perhaps that had been why his mum hadn't wanted her own mum to know about Slatter's father. *Seanmhair* would have told her if she thought the man no good. And love can blind. Though, he was learning that love could also see past the nonsense and to the truth. Or was it his wife's pragmatic nature that could do that?

Slatter stood aside while his wife looked over Walcott and watching her expressions made him think Walcott was not doing well. That didn't stop his wife from fighting for him. Another healer would probably think him past helping and let him die, not Willow. She was tenacious, even in the way she had treated his simple wound when a prisoner.

It was as if she fought a foe, an enemy out to defeat her. And she fought as hard if not harder than most warriors.

Once she finished seeing to Walcott and making sure he was settled comfortably, she turned and walked over to Slatter.

"We wait. There is nothing more I can do." She turned her head and looked at Walcott as she spoke. "My mum reminded me time and again that it's often the wound or damage done that you can't see that's the culprit. The wounds look to heal well, but I don't know what goes on inside him and that's what worries me as does his constant sleep."

"We can only hope that death wants nothing to do with his cantankerous nature."

Willow couldn't help but smile.

The door opened and Carna stopped abruptly seeing Willow and Slatter. "Sara sent me to sit with Walcott. She told me that Walcott needed my tending more than she did."

"How does my grandmother know about Walcott?" Slatter asked.

"Word spreads fast through the village and keep. Besides, talking with Sara can be," —she narrowed her eyes searching for a word to explain— "comforting, and you simply discuss everything with her."

Slatter understood perfectly.

"You did well with Sara and I would appreciate your help with Walcott," Willow said. "Let me explain what needs to be done and what you need to watch for."

Slatter stepped outside the cottage while the two women talked. It was another cold day, the sky gray, but there was no hint of snow in the air. He was glad for the cold that nipped at his face, it helped clear his head some. Once it did, it forced him to think on what he feared most about the present situation.

Was he or was he not wed to Willow?

He had known fear in his life, but nothing compared to the sheer fright of Willow not being his wife. The cleric could not get here fast enough for him.

Slatter reached for his wife's hand as soon as she stepped near him and his hand swallowed hers in a possessive grip.

"You know you can't get rid of me, don't you?" she asked, understanding his need to cling to her, since she felt the same. They were one and to part them would cause an agony she didn't believe she could survive.

"I told you once, wife, I can escape anything," he teased with a wink.

She smiled and shook her head. "There's one thing you can't escape."

"And what's that?"

"Love."

Chapter Twenty-five

Slatter snagged his wife around the waist and kissed her as he kicked the door shut behind them. There had been no time to sneak off to their bedchamber. He couldn't get through supper fast enough and now that they were finally in their bedchamber, he didn't want to waste one moment.

He wanted them both naked and in bed.

She was as eager as he was, her hands rushing to free him of his plaid.

He helped her in between stripping her of her garments all while not relinquishing her lips.

They fumbled and stumbled through shedding their garments, getting rid of their boots, and he hurrying them both to the bed to fall down on it.

She felt so good, warm and soft, and a sweet scent drifted off her, not to mention her womanly scent that drove him mad with the wont of her. He caressed her breasts, loving the feel of them plump in his hand, the hard nipples begging to be suckled.

His mouth was just about to close on one when she popped up on her elbows.

"I forgot to tell you what Maddie told me."

"You told me it all earlier." The thought of Maddie, Kevin, and the others being held in a pen like animals sent a spurt of anger through him and dampened his passion a bit. Not wanting his time with his wife disturbed, he pushed it from his mind to revisit later.

"No, not that. Maddie felt Beck was giving her a message to deliver to you and only you—which was why I waited to tell you until we were alone—before Sterling finally ended his misery."

Slatter raised his head, his mouth once again having been about to settle on her nipple. "What message?"

"Maddie said Beck looked directly at her and told her to make sure she told you that he won, that he got you. He got you good. He kept repeating, 'Slatter. You tell Slatter, I got him good.'"

Slatter rolled away from his wife to lie flat on his back, glancing up at the ceiling. "Damn."

Willow turned on her side, leaning on her elbow to rest her head on her hand, and placed her other hand on his chest. "What is it?"

"Beck wasn't in cahoots with Sterling, he only made him believe he was. We had an ongoing skirmish. Who could best the other and I always won, not once did he win. That's why he put me in that pit in the ground. He didn't think I'd be able to escape, but just in case he dropped you down there with me."

"Oh my Lord," Willow said, her eyes turning wide with a revelation. "He knew you wouldn't leave me there. You would have escaped if he hadn't put me in that pit with you."

Slatter lifted his wife's hand off his chest and kissed her palm. "I had planned to escape the next morning."

"You stayed for me?"

"I couldn't leave you with him. Beck would have sold you to God knows who and I couldn't let that happen to you. Though, he got greedy in thinking he beat me and won. So he upped the stakes, so to speak, and told me I could keep you if I could poke you while down in the confined pit. He lost and that didn't set well with him."

"So he faked a marriage between us to win?"

Slatter shook his head. "A fake marriage would have given me a way out. That wouldn't give him a big victory. He not only bested me and won, forcing me to wed when he knew I never had any intentions of doing so while making Sterling believe otherwise. He told me one day that he'd get me good and he was letting me know that in the end that's exactly what he did… except."

"Except what?" she asked anxiously.

Slatter turned, easing his wife onto her back. "Beck never counted on me falling in love with you and wanting to spend the rest of my life *willingly* with you."

Willow smiled. "So you do plan on sticking around?"

"Forever… if you'll have me."

A tinkle of laughter fell from her lips. "I had you as soon as I was lowered into that pit with you."

Slatter shook his head and brought his face close to hers. "Not true, *mo ghaol*. I lost my heart to you the moment you entered my cell to tend my wound and completely ignored my attempts at charming you."

Willow ran her finger slowly over his lips. "It's not charming words I want from your tongue."

"It isn't?" Slatter asked, feigning shock, though his teasing smile said otherwise. "You better show me what it is you want."

"First," she said, tapping his lips with her finger, "promise me you will not sneak off anymore without letting me know where you're going and why." When he held his tongue too long, she understood why. "You won't give me your word because you plan on going and rescuing Maddie, Kevin, and the others."

When again he didn't answer, she pushed him off her, though he moved only a little and she wiggled her way out from under him. She went and snatched her garments up off the floor.

Slatter scurried out of bed. "What are you doing?"

"I'm going with you to rescue them," she said and dropped the shift over her head.

"You damn well are not going with me." He grabbed the sides of her shift and yanked it up, but Willow grabbed his hands stopping him.

"I go with you or you don't go at all," she challenged.

He laughed. "You think you can stop me?"

"I can and I will," she said, her chin jutting up.

He brought his face close to hers. "I think not, wife." And with one hard yank her shift was off her and tossed to the floor.

Willow looked to her shift, ready to snatch it up again.

"Try putting it on again and I'll rip it off you this time," her husband cautioned.

"You wouldn't dare," she challenged.

"I'd dare do anything to keep you safe."

"I would do the same for you, which is why I'll not let you go alone."

Slatter shook his head, turning away for a moment and when he turned back again, he had his wife up in his arms before she could protest and carried her to the bed,

Willow was so shocked finding herself up in his strong arms that she didn't even have time to gasp. And she was even more surprised when he sat on the edge of the bed and placed her in his lap.

"You are a sensible woman and I won't lose you over a foolish choice," he said.

"I am not sensible when it comes to you. I am fearful that I will lose you and I couldn't bear that. I could wait in the woods for you and help you get everyone to safety and tend those who need help."

"It's too dangerous," he argued.

"For you as well."

"I'm skilled at escapes."

"And I'm skilled at healing," she said and pressed her brow to his. "I can't bear thinking of you suffering a wound and me not there to tend you. I need to know that you're safe just as much as you need to know I'm safe." She lifted her head and with a hint of tears in her eyes she met his dark ones. "Please let me do this. Sensible or not, it's the right thing to do. Maddie, Kevin, and the others don't deserve being imprisoned. And who knows what plans Sterling has for them."

"You will do everything I say without question?" he asked, shaking his head. "I have to be a fool to agree to this."

"I promise I will obey your every word," she said with excitement. She had missed the misadventures Sorrell had gotten into since she left. And while visiting her and experiencing them again, then the attack, and being put in the pit with Slatter and all the things that followed, she discovered that she didn't want to be sensible all the time. Sometimes an adventure was called for.

Slatter was still shaking his head. "You will remain where I tell you and if I don't return by a certain time, you will not search for me. You will return home and—"

"Inform James what happened so we can rescue you."

"No! You will admit no knowledge of the rescue attempt."

"Fine, but I will come for you… always."

Slatter still hadn't stopped shaking his head. "I know I'm going to regret this."

Willow took his face in her hands. "Never. Never will there be any regrets between us."

Slatter finally stilled his head. "One regret I'll never have is the day we exchanged vows. I'll always cherish that day because it was what I wanted. I wanted you as my wife then and always. And I want us to take our vows again so all know, without a doubt, that we are husband and wife."

Willow's eyes lit with joy. "We'll have a celebration this time, a feast, and family to share it with."

Slatter felt the same joy and it frightened him. He never thought he'd have a woman to love or want him with the tenacity that Willow did and he feared losing her. So why he had agreed to let her go with him on this rescue mission troubled him. Though, maybe, just maybe it was because it might help her understand when she finally discovered the truth about him.

"When do we go rescue them?" she asked.

"When it's deep into the night and the only sounds heard are the creatures of the night. So until then—" Slatter found himself kissing the blanket instead of his wife, since she had jumped off his lap so quickly.

"Now tell me the plan, every detail, so I know what to expect and what I must do," she said, pacing back and forth in front of him naked.

He sat up and watched as her anxious steps gave way to a seductive sway of her hips and a gentle bounce of her breasts.

"Tell me it all, don't leave anything out, and don't forget alternatives in case anything goes wrong."

"I go get them and bring them back here, though keep them hidden from Sterling," Slatter said, paying more mind to how she enticed with every step she took rather than her words.

Willow stopped, her hand going to rest on her hip.

Damn, but he loved when she struck that pose, especially when naked. It really tempted when she was naked.

"That's your plan?" she asked and her hand went up and she shook one finger at him. "No. No. No. You must have a plan." She returned to pacing. "I believe I know the area they're being held. It's to the west of Tarass's keep, a dense patch of woods not far from it."

Slatter didn't hear a word she was saying. His mind was far too occupied with his wife's seductive movements.

"No doubt Lord Sterling will have guards posted," —she stopped and tapped her cheek with one finger— "though he might think that Tarass's sentinels would be sufficient, another thing to consider... Tarass's sentinels."

"That's it," Slatter said, popping up off the bed and heading straight for his wife with determined strides.

With his tenacious gait, Willow instinctively went to back up, but stopped, smiled, and hurried at her husband.

Slatter caught her up in his arms, swinging her up, and planting her firmly against him. "I had all thoughts to take our time, be playful, enjoy each other for a while... no more. You've got me too worked up for that."

Willow giggled. She loved that she could make him want her without even knowing that she did. It was empowering and fun.

He dropped her on the bed and when she went to turn on her back, he turned her over and pulled her up on her hands and knees. "I'm going to give you a good pounding."

She wiggled her naked bottom back and forth at him. "Promises. Promises."

He slapped her backside playfully. "Careful, wife, or you'll get more than you bargained for."

Or would she? she thought playfully.

She gasped again when his hands grabbed her backside firmly and she gasped again when he entered her with one swift plunge. After that she did nothing but moan and probably far too loudly, but she didn't care. It felt far too good for her to care about anything but the way her husband pounded away as he had promised he would.

"You'll wake the dead with those moans," he cautioned with a laugh, loving that he was bringing her that much pleasure not to mention how much he was enjoying it.

"It's all your doing," she cried out, "and I can't wait much longer."

He felt the same. He was surprised he had lasted for the short time he did, that's how much his passion had flared watching her.

He gripped her backside harder and drove into her in rapid succession and that was it... they both climaxed together. Slatter did his best not to roar the roof off the keep, Willow not so much.

She let out a scream that Slatter was sure would tremble the dead.

And knowing his wife, he didn't stop pounding her until he felt her release again and shudder with a final moan.

He dropped on the bed beside her and she rolled over to lie against him, his arm going around her. They lay in silence, wrapped in the pleasure and satisfaction of the moment.

Willow was always amazed how making love with her husband grew more and more enjoyable. And how she simply could not get enough of him.

"You please me beyond pleasure, husband," she said when her breathing had calmed.

"And I will please you like that for the rest of our days."

"Then life will be far better than I ever imagined."

"Aye, that it will be," he agreed, having never imagined himself that life could be so good. "Now rest. We must leave in a few hours and return before dawn."

"But we must make a plan. We failed to make a plan to catch Sterling and now look at the problem he's caused."

"That was before we knew it was Sterling and we had much going on with Rhodes chasing after us, and my grandmother's attack."

"Even more reason to form a plan," Willow urged.

"I've escaped more difficult places before."

"You, on your own escaped. There are several people needing rescuing, that makes escape more difficult."

"I'll find a way," he said with a yawn and was asleep in no time.

Willow laid there unable to stop thinking. She pictured the area where she was pretty sure the prisoners were being held and the surrounding area. Sterling no doubt would place his camp in front of the penned prisoners and with the keep behind them that left only two areas of escape. One lay open to a field and the other the woods, the preferable way to go.

The dense forest would offer a safer avenue of escape, the thick trees and bushes allowing for good places to hide and making it more difficult for Sterling's warriors to follow. But there was another way, through the small MacFiere village and out to a part of the forest where there was a glen. If the prisoners could make it to the glen, they wouldn't be spotted. Besides no one would expect them to go that way.

She strategized the plan, thought of different possibilities if something unexpected should happen, said silent prayers for a safe and victorious rescue, and only then did sleep come to her.

She woke with a start and didn't need to look to see the spot beside her and the room itself was empty.

He had lied to her and gone and left without her.

Chapter Twenty-six

Slatter waited in the woods. In the end, he couldn't let Willow go with him. He couldn't risk it. He'd go mad with worry that something would happen to her. She always slept heavy after making love and with the pounding he had given her, she would probably sleep until sunrise. So when he had looked upon her, sleeping soundly, safe in bed, ready to wake her to accompany him, he changed his mind.

What he would face when he returned he didn't know, but it didn't matter to him since she was there safely tucked in bed.

A bird shrilled and he returned the call. A few minutes later Devin emerged from the darkness.

"Tell me again why we're rescuing the likes of Beck's crew?" Devin asked.

"From what Maddie said most of Beck's crew are dead, only the innocent ones are left. The people who owed Beck. The ones he wouldn't free until they worked off what they owed or paid him, neither a likely prospect," Slatter said.

"He was a lying, thieving, bas—"

"So are we," Slatter reminded.

"Not the same. We're good lying, thieving bastards," Devin said with a hearty laugh.

"Us bastards better get this done quick, since I purposely lied to my wife and told her she could come with me to help rescue the group when she figured out what I was going to do."

"She has a good head on those sturdy shoulders. She's not one you should be lying to and you know she's going to figure things out. What then?"

"I've pushed it aside for now."

"I wouldn't leave it sitting there for long," Devin said.

"Now's not the time for me to worry about it. We've got a mission to accomplish."

Devin nodded. "Let's get this done."

They got as close to the edge of the woods as they could without being heard to look over Lord Sterling's campsite. It was quiet, snores coming from the sleeping warriors.

Slatter continued to glance around the area. Not a soul stirred and not a sound came from the pen that was cloaked in a heavy darkness.

Devin tapped Slatter's arm and shook his head.

Slatter nodded, and they both retreated back into the woods.

"Something's not right," Devin said.

"I felt the same unease," Slatter agreed.

"A trap," both men whispered.

Slatter felt along the ground with his foot for a small rock. He picked it up and gave it a toss toward the pen, but not to land in it. Several warriors bolted forward, their swords raised, ready to do more than simply capture him.

Devin pointed to a spot in the camp to silently let Slatter know he was going to explore the area.

Slatter nodded and pointed to another area, then pointed to the spot where they stood for them to meet back here. He shook his finger, a sign that meant that neither were to take too long.

With silent steps Slatter made his way along the periphery of the camp. Nothing stirred, not a sound but the crackle of the two campfires. A camp was never that silent at night. There were always warriors who couldn't sleep, or nightmares that had men moaning. Sentinels could be heard walking the perimeter of the camp and exchanging words with other guards. Never, ever was a camp this still.

Sterling expected him. He knew Slatter would try and rescue at least Maddie and Kevin. It was why he had beat them both, to anger Slatter enough to make the effort and get caught in this trap. But why would he think Slatter would care about Maddie and Kevin.

Because while people couldn't see any difference between Slatter and Sterling, there was a difference. Slatter cared about those who suffered, Sterling didn't.

Slatter knew it was time to get out of there and he hurried back to find Devin waiting for him and when he saw how anxious he appeared, he grew concerned.

They retreated further into the woods before speaking and kept their voices to a whisper.

"Did you see anything of Sterling?" Devin asked.

Slatter shook his head and his eyes shot wide. "Willow."

***

Willow rushed on her garments, debating what to do. Did she follow her husband? She shook her head. That would be foolish. She didn't know how long he'd been gone, where he was, or if he had already completed the task. Her only choice was to wait for his return.

She looked to the fire and saw that it had died down considerably which meant her husband had been gone for some time and she had slept for several hours. As she added more logs to the fire to chase the chill that consumed her, more so from worry than anything else, she assumed he should be home soon. He'd want to make it back before sunrise so no one would know he'd been gone. How he intended to explain it to her, she had no idea. Though knowing her husband, he would plead that it was for her safety that he had lied or perhaps he had changed his mind.

She plotted her responses as she paced in front of the roaring fire and when the door creaked open and she saw him standing there, she knew one thing.

He was not her husband.

***

Slatter raced through the woods, weaving and ducking to avoid the tree branches that whipped at him as Devin followed behind him. It didn't matter to him if anyone found out about his absence or that he'd been meeting with Devin and Walcott secretly, both men having searched for him when he hadn't returned when expected and finding him here.

His need for revenge grew as he sped through the woods. Slatter was responsible for what happened to Walcott and because of it he might die, and for what? Watching out to make sure no one would discover Devin and Slatter were meeting? Walcott had suffered protecting them and his grandmother had suffered protecting him. His fury grew. And now his wife was in danger? Fear tore at him and fired his anger. It was time he put an end to this now that he knew who was responsible… Sterling.

He had to get to his wife. Had to reach her before Sterling did. Why hadn't he even considered that it might be a trap? How had he allowed himself to fall for Sterling's trick? He was more intelligent than that, always considering all angles before rushing into anything.

Willow.

She had overpowered his thoughts and all sound reason. He'd been enjoying a life with her that he had only dreamed of and in the process he had let down his guard.

Never again.

His worry was that Sterling would reach the keep before he did and pretend to be him. Would Willow fall for his lies? Would she know the difference? Or would the man crawl into bed with his wife and… he shook his head and picked up his pace.

***

Sterling flung his arms out. "No hug for your husband?"

She couldn't let him know that she knew he wasn't her husband. She raised her chin. "You lied to me."

"I thought it best not to tell you of my plans," he said.

That confirmed what she already knew. He wasn't Slatter, since her husband had admitted he had had no plans, but she truly didn't need a confirmation. She could tell from the sinister look in his dark eyes, his smile that was far from truthful or pleasant, and the arrogant way he held himself, that he thought he could do no wrong.

"You told me you wouldn't keep the truth from me."

"A wife doesn't need to know all." He stretched his hand out to her. "I thought we'd take a morning walk before everyone stirred to life for the day."

"I'm angry with you," she said in a way of an excuse, hoping Slatter would return at any moment.

He snapped his hand as if ordering her to his side. "We'll talk."

"We can talk here," she said, letting her annoyance show.

"I'd rather we take a walk." He grabbed her cloak off the peg.

"After we eat," she said.

"The morning fare will not be available for at least another hour, which gives us plenty of time for a walk through the village."

She went to protest.

"I insist."

She knew than that he planned on abducting her, forcing Slatter to come to him. He had laid a trap for

Slatter and she feared what might be waiting for him. Her husband was going to be furious when he realized his mistake. She only hoped it wouldn't be too late for either of them.

"What if I refuse," she said, glaring at him.

He turned a smile that was more a sneer on her. "I didn't think I could fool you, but the keep begins to wake and if you don't want someone hurt—badly—I suggest you come with me."

What choice did she have? If she screamed and alerted the keep to his presence, how many would die coming to her rescue? James? Eleanor? Carna? Snow? She shivered at the thought. She'd want none to die for her.

"My husband will come for you," she warned.

"My plan exactly." He threw her cloak at her. "Unless of course he's fallen into my other trap and he's brought to me."

The thought of that ran a shiver of fear through her as she swung the cloak around to settle on her shoulders, then she approached him with caution.

"Alert someone and that person dies," Sterling warned.

And it made her wonder if he intended to keep her alive until Slatter reached her or if he planned on greeting her husband with her dead body.

They made it through the keep without an incident, but Willow tensed when they came upon Snow as they walked through the village. She had forgotten that Snow walked with Thaw through the village each morning. It was a quiet time when Snow didn't have to worry about maneuvering through the people that were mere shadows to her.

Thaw started barking as soon as the pup spotted them and wouldn't stop.

Willow's heart slammed in her chest. Of course, the pup would know the difference between Slatter and Sterling.

"It's me and Slatter, and I think Thaw is worried you will stop and talk with us and delay his breakfast," she hurried to say.

"Our morning walk always makes him hungry," Snow said with a smile and scooped the pup up. "I'll see you upon your return."

"See you then," Willow said, knowing her sister understood something was wrong. Thaw always ate before his morning walk.

"You handled that well," Sterling praised. "Continue to do so and I'll make your death swift and painless."

Once they reached the woods, Sterling gave her a shove. "Keep walking."

"My brother will find out what you've done," she warned.

"That fool will believe the tale my warriors will weave and I will emerge the hero, having tried to save you from your evil husband. Unfortunately, you died in my arms, begging forgiveness for being so blind to his wicked ways. Now keep walking, my men will make sure Slatter is brought to me." He laughed. "The same men who left his grandmother for dead when she refused to tell them where he was. Dunn will enjoy telling him how he had stuck her just enough for her to die slowly."

Willow didn't bother to tell him that Slatter's grandmother lived. It was better he didn't know. She recalled what her husband had done to the three men who had intended her harm. She was sure the men who had harmed his grandmother would face a similar fate.

"Of course, I'll have my fun with you in front of your husband before I kill him. If you continue to cooperate, I'll keep Dunn and Tyler off you."

She didn't for one minute believe him and she didn't for one minute doubt that her husband would rescue her or that she would do all she could to help him.

***

Slatter burst into the keep, screaming Willow's name, Devin right on his heels.

Snow jumped up from the table where she sat, Thaw giving a strong bark beside her, then quieting. "Sterling has her."

Slatter rushed over to her as James entered the Great Hall with Eleanor.

"It made it difficult to believe since we couldn't find you," James reprimanded. "And I won't waste time asking where you've been. My sister's safety is my only concern right now. I have men gathering to begin a search for her."

"Sterling pretended he was you and that you and Willow were out for a walk together," Snow explained. "Thaw wouldn't quiet. He barked and barked and I knew something was wrong. When Willow mentioned that Thaw was probably worried his morning meal would be delayed if I stopped and talked with them, I knew something was terribly wrong since she knew I always fed Thaw before our walk."

A servant rushed into the room. "Lord Tarass approaches."

Slatter placed his hand gently on Snow's arm. "Willow gave you no indication of where he was taking her?"

"None," Snow said, shaking her head. "I don't think she knew, since if she did she would have found a way to tell me."

Slatter grabbed James's arm as he went to walk past him. "I'll handle this."

"It's best if Lord Tarass is made aware of the situation," James said.

"That won't matter," Slatter argued.

"Lord Tarass can help us," James said.

"Lord Tarass helps himself," Snow chimed in.

Slatter's eyes glared with fury. "I care not what Tarass wants or thinks. I only care about my wife and bringing her home unharmed. I will deal with this."

James barely got his mouth open to speak when Slatter was gone, already out the door, and the man who had arrived with him, following close behind.

Chapter Twenty-seven

Slatter stormed out the door and down the keep's steps.

Two of Sterling's men hurried forward, both sizeable brutes and no doubt the ones Sterling trusted the most to do his biddings.

Slatter stopped a few steps away from them, his shoulders drawn back, his hands fisted at his sides, and his face twisted with fury. "I've got Sterling," he said.

Lord Tarass spoke. "You admit you abducted Lord Sterling from my land?"

"I do," Slatter said with a glare that dared the man to challenge him.

"We'll see to this and we'll see our lordship safely returned," the one man, a front tooth missing and with strips of cloth weaved through the braids to either side of his face, demanded.

"He's all yours. I care not what you do with him," Tarass said, with a dismissive wave.

The man with the braids grinned, the toothless space glaring like a black hole in his mouth as he grabbed for Slatter.

"Touch me and I'll kill you," Slatter warned, "and that's a promise."

The man stopped and gave a nod to the other man. "You'll follow Tyler and me."

Slatter turned his voice low for only the two men to hear when he stepped closer to them. "You'll take me straight to my wife or I'll kill you slow when the time comes."

Both men startled for a moment than grinned, Tyler, the one who had yet to speak keeping his voice to a whisper when he said, "It's me and Dunn who'll be killing you slow while we enjoy your pretty wife."

Slatter had to stop himself from reaching out and snapping both men's necks. He'd wait until later and see them both dead before the day was done. He didn't look back as he walked off with the two men. Devin would have made himself scarce once outside so that no one would take notice of him. He'd wait and watch and follow and be there when needed.

The two men mounted their horses and Slatter walked in front of them as they made their way out of the village, the rest of Sterling's men following behind them. It wasn't long before the two men directed him into the woods while the other men proceeded in another direction.

He was certain that as soon as they departed the village, James would let Tarass know what was going on. He couldn't help but think that Tarass already knew something was amiss. When he had planned the rescue, his one worry was Tarass's sentinels. His warriors were skilled and one did not get past them easily. Yet he and Devin had managed to do so. Had Tarass set a trap as well?

But for who?

It seemed it was taking forever to reach his wife, when it truly hadn't been that long. But he didn't know

Sterling's plans for Willow and the longer it took to reach her the more harm she could suffer. He prayed that wasn't so, and prayed even harder that he wouldn't be too late to save her.

***

Willow tried to keep a safe distance from Sterling, but he hovered around her like an annoying gnat. The cold stone she sat on chilled her backside and sent a shiver through her now and again. He waited impatiently for Slatter but then so did she. She prayed her husband would arrive soon and this would finally be over.

Sterling stopped suddenly and glared at her, then grinned.

The blow came so fast and so unexpected Willow barely had time to blink. It sent her tumbling off the stone, her head hitting the ground and blood pouring from her lip that she felt already swelling.

"Something to anger him and make him lose control," Sterling snickered.

Willow got to her feet and went to wipe the blood away with the edge of her cloak.

"Don't," Sterling ordered. "It looks much worse with the blood."

Willow remained on her feet and kept a steady eye on Sterling, ready to avoid another blow if necessary. She wondered what her sister Sorrell would have done in this situation. She would have tried to escape him by now or she would have driven him crazy with her endless chatter and curiosity.

That gave Willow a thought.

"How is it that you and Sterling resemble each other?" she asked.

"That's a tale better left for Slatter to hear," he said with a chuckle.

"If I were to take a guess, I would say you both have the same father but different mothers and seeing what an evil man you are leaves me to assume your father is just as evil. Slatter's mum must have realized it and wisely left him."

"She was a whore and her son a bastard. Neither of them meant anything to my father," Sterling snapped, then turned an angry glare on her.

"Perhaps but she outsmarted him, running off, no doubt, to keep her son safe," Willow said a slight snicker to her tone.

His hand shot out, but Willow was prepared and he stumbled forward missing her.

"Willow!"

She turned and ran at the sound of her husband's voice, though she hadn't spotted him, barely missing Sterling's hand that reached out again to grab her.

"Willow!"

Her husband continued to call to her, his voice filling the surrounding woods and she was so excited when she spotted him that she didn't see that Sterling had gotten close. His hand clamped around her neck, jolting her to a stop.

Sterling dragged her to the middle of the clearing where they had been waiting, and she gasped for a breath since his grip was tight.

"Let her go, you've got what you wanted now… *me*," Slatter said, rushing into the clearing. He kept his eyes on his wife, not only seeing the fear in her eyes, but feeling it, and it wasn't only fear for herself that dominated both, but for him.

Sterling shoved Willow away and when she went to run to her husband, she saw one of the two men that flanked her husband had a blade pointed at his back, and she stopped where she was.

"Dunn would only be too glad to stick Slatter as he did his grandmother," Sterling said, his grin smug.

Dunn laughed, poking Slatter with the tip of the blade, not drawing any blood, just enough of a poke to let him know what awaited him. "The old crone failed to give me what I came for so I left her to die a slow death. You'll have a slow death yourself while watching us enjoy your wife."

Willow caught the way her husband's muscles tightened in his face. His anger was near to exploding.

"But first I have a tale to tell you," Sterling said, joyous with his impending victory.

"Don't bother, it's obvious," Slatter said. "You're my half-brother."

"Your mother was my father's whore," Sterling spat annoyed he had spoiled it for him.

"And your father didn't like that I was born the better looking one," Slatter said with a laugh.

"He wanted you dead," Sterling said, spittle flying out of his mouth with each word.

"Of course he did. How would it look if there was a man who resembled his heir walking around? What would people say? And would this man try to claim his title and lands that rightfully belonged to his true son? But my mum understood that the man she thought she loved was an evil man and meant her and her son harm, so she did what any loving mum would do… she ran."

"When did you realize all this?" Sterling asked.

"It became obvious after a while. What other explanation could there be? What I am curious about though is why impersonate me? Why not kill me and be done with it? It must have been your father's edict that once you found me I was to die."

"That was his order, but killing you right away would have been no fun, especially when I could do things in your name that was never permitted me as heir to my father's title. I so enjoyed creating havoc in your name, watching people destroyed by what I did and not suffering a bit of blame or repercussion for it. But, alas, my father grows weary of me not finding you and seeing the matter settled. He threatens to send others after you and I can't have him finding out what I did. So, unfortunately, my fun has come to an end and it's also time for you to come to an end." He shook his head. "I had hoped to trick your wife into bed, but she knows her husband far too well. So, I will give her a quick poke while you lay dying and before I kill her."

"At least let me hold my wife one last time," Slatter said.

Sterling laughed, shaking his head. "I know how sneaky you can be and what a liar you are. Actually, we're not that much different. We think more of ourselves than others."

"You obviously don't know my husband," Willow said.

Sterling laughed again. "I know enough to impersonate him."

Slatter's brow narrowed. "You don't know everything about me."

"Tell me something I don't know," Sterling challenged.

"I'm going to make sure that you know you're dying and there won't be anything you can do about it," Slatter said with such conviction that the two men flanking him took several steps away from him.

"That will have to wait. The shout echoed around them.

Everyone turned shocked eyes on Tarass and his warriors as they poured out of the surrounding woods. All except her husband, he moved with speed and seeing the fear in his eyes as he rushed at her, Willow turned and threw her arm up as Sterling went to stab her in the chest. The blade caught her forearm, slicing it.

Slatter didn't hesitate. He caught his wife with one arm as she stumbled from the blow and he swung with his other arm, his fist catching Sterling in the jaw and sending him tumbling to the ground.

Devin was on top of Sterling after that, tying the man's hands behind his back before he came awake.

Slatter clamped his hand over his wife's wound and he almost cringed when blood started seeping through his fingers.

"You have to wrap it," Willow instructed, pain raced through her but she fought it, needing to keep focused to let her husband know what to do. "Rip the sleeve off before you do, then wrap it tight. Use my cloak." She shook her head, a lightheadedness taking hold and she worried she would faint.

"You need to get her back to the keep," Tarass said, hovering around them.

"You set a trap?" Slatter accused while doing as his wife had directed.

"I had to learn the truth for myself, since I wanted the actual culprit caught and made to suffer for his crimes. Now get your wife to the keep. I'll see that Sterling and his friends are returned to Macardle land for now."

Slatter looked to Devin.

"I'll make sure of it," his friend said with a firm nod.

Willow fought against the faint that hovered around her. She needed to stay awake, keep focused so she could instruct Eleanor how to tend her wound.

"You're going to be fine. I'll have you home soon," her husband said before she was handed to someone while he mounted a horse, then she was up in is arms again.

He was worried for her and she was as well. She didn't know the extent of the wound only that it bled and pained her. If it was a deep cut, it would not heal easily and there was always the chance of losing some of the motion in her arm.

She squeezed her eyes shut tight, forcing herself not to think about it, to think only on what had to be done to heal it.

"You're in pain," her husband said and he sounded as if he suffered along with her. "We'll be home soon."

She would have smiled if she wasn't gritting against the pain. After a few moments, it became too much.

She opened her eyes and said, "Faint."

"What was that?" Slatter asked, not having heard her.

She tried to repeat it, but there wasn't time. She dropped into a dead faint.

Slatter's heart pounded against his chest like a mighty hammer when his wife's body turned lifeless in his arms. "Willow! Willow! Don't you die on me. I can't lose you. I won't lose you. You're my world now, Willow. Do you hear me? You're my whole world."

Willow came awake to the sound of worried voices and she felt herself being rushed up stairs. She was home.

"Wake up, wife, I demand it," Slatter said, after placing her on the bed in their bedchamber.

She opened her eyes to see her husband's face planted in front of hers.

"You'll not leave me," he said in a harsh whisper.

His eyes glistened with unshed tears and her heart ached for the pain she saw there. "Never," she whispered and puckered her lips to kiss him.

Slatter slipped his hand under her head to lift it some while lowering his lips to reach hers.

It was a brief kiss, one that let him know she wasn't going anywhere.

He rested his brow to hers. "You're my life, my world, nothing exists without you beside me."

There was no charm to his voice nor did he wear his usual teasing grin. It was all from his heart and

Willow felt her own heart swell with love for her husband.

She went to lift her arm, wanting to touch his face and grimaced with pain. His loving words and concern made her forget about her wound.

"Your wound," he said as if he had forgotten about it as well.

Once her husband moved away from her, she saw that Snow, Eleanor, and Carna stood waiting, their faces pinched with worry.

"Help me sit up," Willow said, reaching out her uninjured arm to her husband.

Slatter looked ready to argue, then shook his head. "You're the healer." He lifted her gently and got her situated comfortably. "What else can I do?"

"Wait in the Great Hall until summoned," she said and raised her finger when he looked ready to fight her. "I need to focus on my wound and with you present that will be difficult for me to do. So please go and let James know what is going on and wait for Tarass and Devin to return with Sterling and his men."

"You'll let me know—"

"As soon as I know the extent of the wound, so will you," Willow assured him. "And you will let me know about Sterling?"

"You have my word." He gave her a quick kiss and was gone.

"How bad?" Snow asked, stepping forward.

"We're about to find out," Willow said.

***

With nothing to do but wait, Slatter felt lost. He paced the Great Hall in front of the large fireplace, around the tables, went to the door, stopped, giving a second thought to waiting outside for Tarass and Devin to return, but worried he'd miss word from his wife.

He cursed Tarass over and over. He and Devin could have easily handled Sterling and his two brutes and the three would be dead by now and his wife unharmed. But where would that have left him? Would anyone have believed the truth?

He stopped pacing. With Tarass discovering the truth for himself, Slatter was free.

The thought opened so many possibilities, ones he never imagined were possible. He sat at a table near the fireplace and gave thought to the future, something he had never done before.

"My sister has been harmed?" James asked as he burst into the Great Hall. "I led the group that went to make sure Sterling's men did not follow to help him."

"Willow suffered a wound to her arm. She tends it now and will let me know how she fares as soon as she's done. Tarass was aware of Sterling's plan?"

"Not of the plan itself," James said, removing his cloak and joining Slatter at the table. "He told me he didn't trust the man and that he'd had enough lies and wanted the truth. He had his trackers ready to follow you. He received word not long after you departed that you were separated from the troop and went after you while sending me after the troop. They're camped not far from here, waiting for Lord Sterling's return. Did Tarass learn the truth for himself?"

"He did and he returns the culprit here along with the two men who harmed my grandmother," Slatter said, anger in his words.

"Those men can certainly be made to pay for their crimes, but Lord Sterling is another matter," James said, anger in his tone as well.

The door opened then and the men they had been discussing, except for Tyler, entered the room, Lord Tarass and Devin as well as four of Tarass's warriors escorting them.

Sterling held his head high, his jaw swollen and a deep purple bruise spreading. Dunn was also a bit bruised and battered, the fool probably having tried to escape Tarass's men.

"I demand you free me and get this brute away from me," Sterling ordered, trying to yank his arm free of the firm grasp.

"Devin. The name is Devin," he said, sticking his face in front of Sterling's.

Sterling turned away from him and gave a nod to Slatter. "He plotted and planned all this. I did what was necessary to protect myself." He turned to Dunn and cast a quick glance around. "Where is Tyler? He was with us when we entered the village."

"Dunn told me, in exchange for my word that I wouldn't kill him, that it was Tyler who waited for my loyal warrior Rhodes and killed him. Tyler cursed him out so I knew it was no lie. I turned him over to my warriors. He should be near death by now since I ordered them to make sure he suffered some before he died," Tarass said without an ounce of emotion and looked to Slatter. "I'm sure you want revenge for what was done to your grandmother, so I left Dunn for you."

"You gave your word," Dunn said all color draining from his face.

"And I kept it. I will not kill you... Slatter will."

Tarass walked over to the table where Slatter sat, poured himself a tankard of ale, took a good gulp, then looked at Sterling. "You are an idiot. You don't think I watched and listened and learned the truth for myself? You actually think I would believe a fool like you?"

Slatter kept his eyes on Sterling and watched his brow begin to sweat, his skin pale, and his eyes dart frantically around the room, the realization that his lies would no longer serve him finally dawning on him.

Sterling's chin shot up another notch, though with a wince. "I am *Lord* Sterling and you cannot take the word of a common thief and liar against a nobleman."

"Don't you mean your half-brother?" Tarass corrected, raising his tankard as if cheering the fact.

"He's a bastard and holds no title or claim to the Clan MacBlair," Sterling argued. "I demand that you release me. You have no authority to hold me prisoner."

"I agree. Release him," Willow said, entering the room.

Slatter stood ready to go to his wife, but remained where he was when she continued into the room. She looked good, her face not as pale as it had been and there was slight color to her cheeks. She had changed her garments and he could tell by the thickness of the one sleeve that her injured arm was bandaged. That she was up and about and looked good gave him hope that all was well with her.

"A wise woman," Sterling said with a bob of his head.

"Aye, I am a wise woman. By releasing you, I am assuring you will get what you deserve for all you have done," Willow said, coming to a stop not far from him.

Slatter had begun walking over to his wife when he saw that she approached Sterling. He would not take a chance of anything happening to her again. He stood at her side, slipping his arm around her waist and resting his hand on her hip to give it a slight squeeze.

Sterling laughed. "I always get what I deserve."

She smiled. "That is good to know. Then you will welcome the Slayer when he comes for you."

Chapter Twenty-eight

Later that night, Willow lay in her husband's arms, resting her injured arm on his naked chest.

"Are you sure your arm will heal well?" he asked still concerned for her.

"I can never be completely sure how a healing will go, but the wound was not deep, a good thing, and if I keep it freshly wrapped as my mum always believed a wound should be looked after, and give the flesh time to knit back together, it should heal well. Though, I fear a sizeable scar will remain."

"I care not about a scar as long as you remain with me," Slatter said and kissed her brow. "Are you in much pain?"

"I've suffered worse pain."

"When?" he asked not liking the thought.

"When I lost each of my parents. I know there is an end to the pain I suffer from the wound. It will be gone one day and soon forgotten. Not so with the pain of losing someone you love. It lingers and returns when you least expect it to hurt all over again. I can't bear to even think of how horrible the pain would be if I lost you. That was why I reached out to the Slayer. I would do anything to keep from losing you."

"But now you owe him."

"I don't believe he will demand much of me."

"Why would you think that of an evil man?" Slatter asked.

"The Slayer is not an evil man. He's an honorable man. Tarass seems familiar with the Slayer's deeds and told me of a few of them. Those the Slayer killed were bad people. People without hearts... without souls. There was no justice for what was done to the innocent and so those left behind, those who loved the ones who died turned to the Slayer for help. And perhaps he does send those souls to the devil, but the Slayer's soul is a good one and the devil can never touch it." She yawned. "The only thing that I can't figure out is how this Slayer lives as long as he has. And I do hope the Slayer sees to Sterling quickly so all threats of him are gone. Though..."

"Though?" Slatter questioned.

"I worry that your father may come after you when he learns of Sterling's death."

"I'm not worried about that. He won't acknowledge me for fear I will try to claim his title and land."

"You can't do that if you're dead," she argued, fighting another yawn.

"Trust me. He'll want nothing to do with me. Now it's time you slept. You need the rest to make sure that arm heals properly.

"As you say, husband," she said playfully.

"Now that's what I like... an obedient wife." He chuckled when he got a jab in the ribs. "Now I know you definitely are healing well."

"I do love you, husband," Willow said, her eyes drifting closed.

"And I you, wife, with all my heart," Slatter said.

He waited until he was sure Willow was asleep, then carefully left the bed, positioning the pillows so she would feel that she remained wrapped around him. He didn't like leaving her, but he had no choice.

He made his way down to his grandmother's room and entered to find her sitting by the hearth.

"Are you sure you want to do this?" his grandmother asked, walking over to him.

"It has to be me," Slatter said.

"And Dunn," his grandmother all but commanded.

"I've already tasked Owen with the chore and he was pleased to accept and revenge his friend Rhodes, since Dunn no doubt waited nearby while Tyler carried out the task. Besides, you know as well as I do this must be done."

"You will be careful,' his grandmother reminded.

"I will." Slatter kissed his grandmother's cheek. "And you know what to do."

She nodded and watched her grandson leave the room, her heart heavy with worry.

Slatter hurried down the stairs to see it done and as he did a shadow slipped out from the darkness and slowly opened the door and entered the room.

"I'll have the truth now. No more lies, *Seanmhair*."

Seanmhair smiled and nodded. "Join me by the hearth, Willow, and I will tell you the tale of the Slayer."

***

Sterling sat by the campfire, drinking ale, his warriors surrounding him. He hadn't known what Willow had been talking about when she had warned him of the Slayer. He had never heard of him and he didn't worry over one man. He could handle him. Then he had noticed the men whispering and not staying close to him, almost as if he had been struck with a plague or curse and feared it would affect them.

He had finally demanded to know from his warriors what was going on. He was shocked to discover that the Slayer was an assassin who had been around for, who some believed, a hundred or more years. That he helps the unfortunate, the innocent who have no recourse when they suffer unspeakable crimes. Some believe the Slayer is the devil's cohort searching for souls to fill his coffer while others believe him a warrior of God, demanding justice for the innocent.

Then there were the words one heard before the Slayer killed him.

Your time has come.

Sterling had laughed when his warrior had told him that. He wanted to know if the person died how was it known what the Slayer said. The warrior had shivered when he answered.

A whisper echoes over the land when someone dies at the hands of the Slayer.

***

"Tales of the Slayer date back a hundred or more years, or so it's been said. I never thought much of it until I discovered the man my daughter loved, Lander, who was a good da to my grandson, was… the Slayer.

"But he's dead," Willow said confused.

"And therein lies the tale."

***

Sterling didn't believe such a foolish tale, but the more his own warriors avoided him, the more troubled he became. If his warriors believed that strongly in the tale, they wouldn't dare protect him against this hungry demon or avenging angel, whichever the Slayer might be.

If he could get home, the walls of his father's fortress would protect him as would his father.

The night grew late and many of his warriors fell asleep as did he, though he woke, needing to relieve himself badly. He called on two warriors to follow him and not take their eyes off him.

He stood with his back to the two warriors, thinking how he couldn't wait to get home. He didn't know what he would tell his father, but he'd make up some story that served himself well. And maybe even hire this Slayer to take care of Slatter for him.

"Your time has come."

***

"The Slayer was born out of necessity and lives on for the same reason," *Seanmhair* explained. "He helps the helpless, those who can find no justice, those wrongly accused. Lander saw the skills Slatter had for a young lad. How fast he could run. How soundless his steps. And how the forest took to him almost as if he was one of their own. So, he trained him."

"And Slatter became the Slayer when Lander died," Willow said.

Seanmhair shook her head. "There is more to the tale."

***

The harsh whisper had Sterling turning in midstream and staring wide-eyed at his two warriors lying on the ground. His eyes darted around, but saw nothing.

"I'll pay you more than what Willow of the Clan Macardle offered you if you let me live and kill Slatter. He is the evil man not me. She lies to you since she foolishly loves him. I tried to save her but she was already under his spell."

"You lie." The whisper was harsher this time.

"No. No. I tell the truth. I swear I tell the truth. I am an innocent in all this. You must believe me and help me. You bring justice to the innocent. Bring me justice, I beg of you."

"Liar!"

Sterling turned so fast he almost fell, the whisper coming from behind him.

"Liar!"

He turned again. The whisper behind him once more. "No! Please you must believe me. I tell the truth."

"You lie."

He turned again and his eyes nearly popped from his head when he saw who stood in front of him. "Devin?"

"The Slayer, and *your time has come.*"

Sterling went to speak when he felt the blade slice across his throat, and felt the warm blood run down on his chest, heard himself gurgle, and thought about Slatter's words to him.

I'm going to make sure that you know you're dying and there won't be anything you can do about it.

His words had proven true and so had the tale of the Slayer.

***

"There are far too many people in need of help for the Slayer to be only one man. The Slayer is not one man but many, sworn to secrecy, his name whispered only when in the direst of circumstances, for when the Slayer is called… death comes with him."

"Slatter goes to fulfill my request of the Slayer. He will kill Sterling, his half-brother."

Seanmhair placed her hand on Willow's arm. "You asked for the one responsible for everything done to your husband."

Willow gasped and shook her head. "No! No!"

"He accepted and now he must see it done," *Seanmhair* said with a tear in her eye.

"No! Oh God, no!" Willow wept. "He goes to kill his father."

***

"Get out! Get out! You've grown tiresome in bed. You can't even arouse me," Lord Robert of the Clan MacBlair screamed at the young lass, rushing to grab her garments and leave the room. When the door closed, he called out, "Good riddance, you whore."

"Another whore that doesn't please you, Father?"

Robert turned. "You've finally returned. What took you so long? Did you finally get rid of that bastard that I should have gotten rid of when he was growing in that whore's belly?" He shook his head as he reached and slipped on a robe. "That's what happens when a woman pleases you in bed. You lose your senses. And damn if I've yet to find someone as good in bed as her. Well, did you take care of it?"

"I did. The no good liar is dead."

"That's one thing you both have in common. You lie." Robert filled a goblet with ale and took a swig.

"That's something we both must have gotten from you."

"Watch your mouth with me, son. I'm not too old yet to deliver you the beatings I gave you as a lad." He went and sat on the edge of the bed. "Tell me, does he resemble you so much that I wouldn't know the difference if I met him?"

"You tell me, *Father*," Slatter said and walked closer to the man.

"What do yo—" Robert's eyes glared with fury and he went to rush to his feet when he realized what he meant.

Slatter gave him such a hard shove that he fell back on the bed, his goblet flying out of his hand to land behind him on the bed, the ale spilling out and soaking into the tousled bedding.

"Where's my son?" Robert demanded.

"Which one?"

Robert sneered. "My only son."

"He's where he belongs... *in hell*."

Robert shook his fist at Slatter. "I'll have your head for this."

"You're going to die, old man, by the hand of the son you never wanted."

"Sterling was a fool. You seem otherwise. Why not take his place and inherit everything?" He sat up slowly.

"Like Sterling did to me, made everyone think he was me?"

"He needed to sew his wild side before settling down," Robert said.

"You knew what he was doing?" Slatter asked, needing to hear him confirm it.

"Small harm to insignificant people. The fool just didn't know when to stop."

Slatter stepped away from him, having trouble believing this evil man was his father.

Robert eased off the bed, reaching under the mattress as he did.

"My mum was right when I asked about you. She told me you were insignificant to us. I see now what she meant. *Your time has come*, old man."

He snickered and yanked the dagger from under the mattress. "You think I'll let you get near enough to kill me, you fool?"

"I already did." Slatter gave a nod to Robert's chest, blood seeping through his robe.

"That nick takes a while before it ends a life. You have maybe a minute or two more, then you join your son in hell."

Robert grabbed at his chest, blood smearing his hand. "You fool. You could have had everything."

"I already do, and you would have never let me inherit. Not your bastard son. You would have killed me at first chance."

Robert choked on his words. "You are my son. You killed me without thought."

"No, I didn't. I killed you to protect my family. You die leaving no heir. Your name will vanish along with the memory of you and your son."

Robert's breathing turned shallow. "I live on in you."

"Never. My children will know the memory of the man who truly was a father to me. Your name will never leave my lips. You are no more."

Robert fought to speak, but he had no breath left and he tried to raise the dagger in a futile attempt to have it end otherwise and fell back on the bed dead.

Slatter threw a blanket over him and left the room.

"My father doesn't wish to be disturbed until morning," Slatter said to the first servant he saw and left the MacBlair keep without a backward glance or an ounce of regret.

***

Willow stood by the window in the bedchamber watching the snow accumulate against the window, the dark night obscuring everything else from view. It had been over a week since she'd last seen her husband and each day he didn't return home, her worry mounted.

She had told everyone that her husband had an important matter to see to and he'd be home soon. No one questioned her explanation, but she knew many didn't believe her. All except Snow.

"He'll be home soon," Snow would say every day.

And every day that he didn't return, she feared he had died.

She pressed her hand to her stomach. She prayed and prayed that wasn't so since she had something important to tell him.

The door opened slowly and she didn't turn to look since *Seanmhair* had a habit of stopping by at night to see how she was.

"Pining away for me?"

Willow turned, tears rushing from her eyes as she rushed to her husband's open arms.

She threw her arms around his neck and buried her face against his chest sobbing.

Slatter scooped her up and carried her to the bed and sat cradling her in his lap. Her sobs tore at his heart. "All is well. I'm well. Don't cry, *mo ghaol*. I'm home and home is where I'll stay."

She couldn't stop sobbing as she spoke. "I... thought... I...lost you. My fault."

"No. No, not your fault, *mo ghaol*. It had to be done." His grandmother would have explained everything to her so she wouldn't think he had left her and would never return. He knew if he had explained it all, his wife would have either insisted on going with him or have followed him and he hadn't wanted that. "It's over, finished. We're free. No more past to haunt me."

Her sobs eased. "You're never to go away like that again. You can never go anywhere without me."

She wanted to know that he would be the Slayer no more. That it was done and over and that was fine with him. He'd served as the Slayer for enough years. Now he wanted something else. He wanted a good life with his wife.

He kissed her wet cheeks. "I have no problem with that, wife, though," he said with a twinkle in his dark eyes. "You do owe the Slayer."

She couldn't keep a small smile from surfacing. "And what is it he wants from me?"

He brushed his lips across hers and whispered, "Your love always and forever."

"You already have that, though there is something I can give you." She took his hand and placed it on her stomach.

He looked at her oddly then his eyes turned wide. "Truly?"

"Aye," she said.

He pressed his hand protectively over her stomach. "I don't think I could be any happier than at this moment."

Willow grinned. "I think I can make you happier."

Slatter chuckled and lifted her as he stood. "Let's see you try."

They went down together on the bed and made each other both very very happy.

Chapter Twenty-nine

Two weeks later

Chaos reigned in the village. Slatter's people had arrived and what was left of Beck's people had arrived two days ago, having been given a choice of remaining with Tarass's clan or residing with Slatter. They had all chosen to stay with Slatter.

Gray skies and cold weather promised a winter storm. They had to get everyone settled fast. They didn't need any interruptions, which was why Willow got annoyed when Tarass arrived with a troop of his warriors.

Willow sent Eleanor to alert Snow to Tarass's arrival, but Snow was a distance away, Thaw busy playing with some children so she didn't think there'd be a problem. At least she hoped not.

James came forward to greet Tarass.

"I want to talk with Slatter and Willow. I have a proposal for them," he said after dismounting.

James waved Slatter and Willow over.

Tarass didn't give James a chance to explain. "In appreciation for seeing Rhodes killer caught and the other information you provided me with, I'd like to offer you and Willow a keep of your own where you can start your own clan with your people. Of course, I'd expect you to pledge your allegiance to me like the old laird had."

"Where is this keep?" Slatter asked, knowing his wife would not want to be far from her sister.

"The McHenry keep—"

"A short ride from here," Willow said, turning to her husband with a smile. "It's a small keep, but the fields are fertile and the woods that surround it teem with healing herbs."

"I brought a troop with me to help move your people there today. I prefer the few people who remain there not be alone through the winter. So what say you?"

"It's up to my wife," Slatter said.

Willow looked ready to say, *aye,* when she caught sight of her sister.

"Go talk with her," Slatter said when he saw his wife's smile fade.

Tarass shook his head. "It's your decision not hers."

Slatter laughed. "I can't wait until you wed."

"My wife will obey me," Tarass said as if there was no other option.

Slatter laughed harder. "We'll see about that."

Tarass turned to James. "A moment with Slatter."

James nodded and walked off.

"This offer is because of what you gave me," Tarass said.

"I didn't give you anything. I simply alerted you to the fact that MacBlair land was ripe for someone to claim it."

"Are you sure you don't want it?"

"I made it clear when I told you about it that I wanted nothing to do with it," Slatter confirmed.

"I left Owen there to oversee the transition and establish a firm footing on the isle."

"I'm glad, since I'm sure you'll treat the people well," Slatter said and cast a glance at his wife, hoping all was going well with her.

***

"How wonderful for you," Snow said with excitement and hugged Willow. "And you won't be far from me at all."

"But I won't be here with you," Willow said, feeling less excited about the prospect of her own home.

"Nonsense, Eleanor is here and is of great help and I can visit and stay for days on end if you'll have me."

"That would be wonderful," Willow said, not having thought about that.

"You need to live your life with your husband just as Sorrell has. I have Thaw and we're very happy together."

Thaw gave a bark, agreeing.

Snow hugged her sister tight, a tear running down her cheek. "I will miss you terribly, but I want this for you. You deserve it. You deserve to be happy. Sorrell will be happy for you and be happy to learn that, though you exchanged vows again, you have delayed the celebration until she can be here."

"She probably got that message by now and hopefully it's helped calm her since the message Ruddock sent after his men returned home made it clear he was having a difficult time keeping her from riding off on her own to return here." Willow giggled. "I wonder if he had to tie her up."

Snow laughed. "She would have escaped. I think she was wise enough to listen to her husband this time."

They both laughed at that.

Willow wished with all her heart that her sister's sight would return and she could fall in love like she and Sorrell had done and start a life of her own.

"Go, I will be fine," Snow insisted.

"Come with us and help us," Willow said.

"No, I will only be in the way. I will come when you are settled and I can learn to navigate the keep. Besides, you and Slatter deserve some time alone. Now go, you have much to do. I can feel a winter storm brewing and you need to get settled before it hits full force." She gave her sister a little shove. "Go and tell that pigheaded man that you accept."

"I heard that," Tarass said as he approached with Slatter.

Thaw started yapping as soon as Tarass got close to Snow. She didn't wait, she scooped him up.

"I'll go start getting your things together, Willow," Snow said and turned to leave.

"Apologize for calling me pigheaded," Tarass demanded.

Snow turned. "Since it doesn't matter if I mean it, I apologize." Snow went to turn and stopped. "And I apologize for the next name I call you and the one after that, since I'm bound to insult you again."

Slatter laughed and got a jab in the ribs from his wife.

"She's an impossibly stubborn woman," Tarass said.

"Thank you for the compliment," Snow called out and kept walking.

Tarass shook his head as he walked off. "There isn't a man alive who would wed her."

Willow felt a sting to her heart.

"Don't listen to him," Slatter said. "Snow has a lot to offer the right man and she'll meet him someday."

"I want to believe that."

Slatter took his wife in his arms. "Then do. Believe she will one day find a man who loves her and who she loves as much as we love each other."

"That would be a miracle," Willow said.

"No, that would be fate, just like what happened to you and me. And your sister is right. It's time we go start our life together."

"There is much to do," Willow said excited again. "Your grandmother is fit to go with us, but Walcott will need to remain here for a while yet. He improves day by day, a miracle for sure. and Carna takes good care of him."

"I've noticed that he doesn't complain around her. I even caught him smiling the other day, another miracle," Slatter said with a chuckle.

Willow took hold of her husband's hand and tugged him along. "Come, there's much to do to get *our* clan settled before the snow starts falling.

It wasn't until hours later that Slatter, his wife tucked in front of him on his horse, sat at the top of a slight rise to look upon the small keep and village where they would build a future together.

A teasing smile played at the corners of Slatter's mouth. "We've come a long way from that whole in the ground we shared."

"It's a memory I'll never forget and will always cherish since it brought us together," Willow said her own smile growing.

"Extremely close together," Slatter said playfully.

Willow's smile faded. "Beck may not have been a good man, but I'm grateful he forced us to wed. Otherwise, we may have never seen each other again."

Slatter's smile vanished as well. "Married or not, I wasn't about to let you get away. You were mine from when I first saw you and mine you'll stay for always."

Slatter kissed her as they rode through the light falling snow to their new home.

About Donna Fletcher

It was her love of reading and daydreaming that started USA Today bestselling author Donna Fletcher's writing career. Besides gobbling up books, her mom generously bought for her, she spent a good portion of her time lost in daydreams that took her on grand adventures. She met heroes and villains, and heroines that, while usually in danger, always found the strength and courage to prevail. She traveled all over the world and through time in her dreams. Some places and times fascinated her more than others and she would rush to the library (no Internet at that time) and read all she could about that particular period and place. After a while, she simply could not ignore all the adventures swirling around in her head, she had no choice but to bring them more vividly to life, and so she started writing.

Donna continues to daydream, characters popping in and out of her head wherever she goes and filling her with tales that keep her writing schedule on overload. You can learn more about her on her website.

Donna enjoys living on the beautiful Jersey shore surrounded by family and friends and a cat who thinks she's a princess, but what cat doesn't, and a dog who bows to the princess's demands.

Titles by Donna Fletcher

Macardle Sisters of Courage Trilogy
Highlander of My Heart
Desired by a Highlander

Macinnes Sisters Trilogy
The Highlander's Stolen Heart
Highlander's Rebellious Love
Highlander The Dark Dragon

Highland Warriors Trilogy
To Love A Highlander
Embraced By A Highlander
Highlander The Demon Lord

Pict King Series
The King's Executioner
The King's Warrior
The King & His Queen

Cree & Dawn Series
Highlander Unchained/Forbidden Highlander
Highlander's Captive
My Highlander A Cree & Dawn Novel

Find more titles and subscribe to her newsletter at
www.donnafletcher.com

Made in the USA
Middletown, DE
14 August 2019